DEVIL IN PINSTRIPES

CU00607225

Ravi Subramanian

/

Rupa & Co

Copyright © Ravi Subramanian 2010

First Published 2010
Fourth Impression 2010

Published by
Rupa Publications India Pvt. Ltd.
7/16, Ansari Road, Daryaganj
New Delhi 110 002

Sales Centres:
Allahabad Bengaluru Chandigarh Chennai
Hyderabad Jaipur Kathmandu
Kolkata Mumbai

All rights reserved.
No part of this publication may be reproduced, stored in
a retrieval system, or transmitted, in any form or by any
means, electronic, mechanical, photocopying, recording or
otherwise, without the prior permission of the publishers.

The author asserts the moral right to be identified
as the author of this work.

Typeset by
Mindways Design
1410 Chiranjiv Tower
43 Nehru Place
New Delhi 110 019

Printed in India by
Nutech Photolithographers
B-240, Okhla Industrial Area, Phase-I,
New Delhi 110 020, India

Dedicated to
"All the Gods of banking, who despite all provocation, resist the
temptation to turn into Devils in Pinstripes"

Mumbai
20 December 2007
Pali Hill, Bandra

The sound of soft droplets of water skipping on the floor and a dim ray of light battling to emerge through the tiny crack between the door and the marble flooring were the only signs of activity in an otherwise dark room. Thick peach-coloured curtains drawn to cover every inch of the single four feet by four feet window valiantly defended the large bedroom from letting the morning sun have a peep into it.

On one side of the room was a bed – too small to be called a double bed and too large to be a single cot. It was custom designed to fit into the room. On the other side, at an arm's length from the bed, was a small table, on which lay an antiquated Intel 486 computer. To the right of the table was a wooden cupboard – the ones made of cheap particle board. One of the doors of the cupboard doubled up as a full length mirror. A shoe rack added to the muddle in an already overcrowded room. As if the clutter created by the disorganised furniture was not enough, there seemed to be more pairs of footwear lying around the shoe rack than inside, akin to the dustbins on the streets of Chennai, which usually had more garbage strewn all around them than within. A large poster of Sachin Tendulkar adorned the wall. Around it were a few small newspaper cuttings, all singing praises about 'Sachin – The Master!'. It sure did appear to be the room of a die-hard Tendulkar fan.

A couple of trousers, a tattered pair of denims and few jazzy coloured tees hung from a cane wood clothes' stand clumsily placed in one corner of the room. A few books lay strewn on the small bedside table. They hadn't been touched for weeks now – confirmed by the fine layer of dust which had settled itself on the covers. A Chinese-made digital clock sat dangerously on the tip of the bedside table. The hands indicated 7.12 a.m. It seemed to be working. Only the colour on the snooze button appeared to have worn off faster than the other buttons.

'Enter at your own risk' were the words splashed on a large poster strategically stuck on the wall that was bang opposite the main door. It was the first thing anyone entering the room would notice. The messy room could easily be identified with a typical, brash teenager's room, where the only way to get rid of junk was to pile on more junk on top of the existing lot, effectively making it disappear from the line of sight.

One could be forgiven for assuming such was the case, had one not sighted a neat looking folder lying next to the computer screen. It was a blue coloured file. Lying on its right, face up, was a brown envelope which had the words 'New York International Bank', printed in bold, on the bottom left corner.

He walked out of the bathroom, fresh from a shower. A few droplets of water drained off him onto the floor, forming a small puddle. Humming a Bachchan hit, he seemed to be in high spirits. After furiously wiping his hands on the towel that he had loosely wrapped around his waist, he carefully picked the envelope and held it up. Stuck on the envelope was a white label which had the name, 'AMIT SHARMA'—his name—written in capitals. His glance floated from the centre of the envelope to the top. Printed there were two very important words. Though in a smaller font, they were about to add enormous meaning to his life. Those were the words he had spent his life waiting for. He had struggled through his college days, waiting to see that very phrase. The two words – 'Appointment Letter' written across the envelope were going to change Amit's life forever, or so he felt that day. At that very instant, the door opened and Chanda walked in.

'Come. Have your breakfast.'

This sudden intrusion brought Amit back from the thoughts he was engrossed in. His thoughts had taken him back in time—almost thirteen years ago. He was about to join New York International Bank. Just out of IIM Bangalore, as fresh as a muffin just out of an oven, a starry-eyed Amit's dream was about to come true. A bollywood-like flashback darted across the screen of his mind – the proud moment when he had walked out of the shower and held up his appointment letter – a letter from New York International Bank. Hadn't he chosen this bank over a career in consultancy with Accenture? Acting against advice from friends, he had made his own independent choice, completely taken in by the flamboyant pitch made by Aditya Bhatnagar during the bank's pre-placement talk. There was not even an iota of doubt in his mind – he was convinced that he was making the right decision. Chanda's entry into the room had interrupted his cherished dream sequence.

Today, on the breakfast table, thirteen years later, he appeared contented. A satisfied look radiated from his face. 'Idiots,' he said to himself as he thought about his batchmates telling him that he was making a mistake. Had he listened to them, he would not be where he was. The stance that he had taken then seemed vindicated today. He was probably the only guy from his batch who had stuck to his first job for thirteen long years. Did he ever feel the need to move from New York International Bank and look for options outside? No way!

'Thank you, God,' he murmured as he lifted his right hand and dug into the dripping aloo paranthas that Chanda had just placed in front of him. Instinctively, he reached out to the butter box for an extra helping. A downward glance brought his growing belly into focus and alongside his hands beat a hasty retreat. He had been putting on a fair amount of weight these days. Hectic travelling schedules and a sedentary lifestyle were the culprits, or so he rationalised. Chanda had been trying to push him to join the local Gold's Gym, but after living for more than a decade with him, she didn't need to be told—Amit would only do something if he wanted to. He was a curious mix of an elephant and a panther. An elephant when something was forced on him—would never move, and a panther when he was convinced about the need to act. If he believed in something, there couldn't be anyone to match his skill and pace in execution.

'It's okay. You don't need to deprive yourself,' said Chanda. She had caught him in the act. Amit just smiled and continued enjoying the *paranthas*. It was rare for them to enjoy a smile together these days.

'Ding-dong,' the ring of the doorbell spoiled an otherwise peaceful breakfast.

'Who could it be? So early in the morning?' asked Chanda. None of the maids came in so early. A mere shrug of the shoulders was the only response that could be elicited from the man who chose to ignore the fact that the door bell actually rang! He was too lazy to get up and open the door himself. 'What's chivalry between man and wife?' he said to himself as Chanda got up to open the door. In any case Amit was too engrossed in his paranthas and *The Economic Times* to even volunteer to get up and respond to the door bell. He could hear Chanda open the door and could sense her talking to someone. Had he stretched his neck backwards, from where he was sitting in the dining room, he could have seen the main door. But, he didn't bother. 'She is smart enough to manage,' he said to himself as he noisily turned a page and moved away from the stock market section. The market had tanked by 346 points the previous day. For three days in a row, the Sensex was down by over 200 points. Today was the fourth day and things didn't seem to be looking up.

'Someone called Rakesh Srivastava. Says he knows you and wants to meet you immediately,' said Chanda as she returned.

'Who?'

'Rakesh Srivastava.'

'Who is he?'

'I don't know. Says he wants to meet you and it's urgent.'

Amit gave a quizzical look. The name did not ring a bell. He did not know anyone by this name. 'Hmmmm...' he sighed. Getting up was unavoidable now. He wiped his hands on the towel that Chanda had left on her chair and walked towards the living room. As he entered, he could see the back of Rakesh Srivastava. The latter would have been close to six feet tall and of a stout build. The denim jeans and a crumpled T-shirt, made Amit realise that Rakesh was not someone from his bank. A rugged leather jacket hung between his folded arms. Muscular from every angle, the veins on his arms seemed to be ready to pop out. His hair was cut really short. From where he was, Amit could only see the contours that lay behind the salt and pepper curly hair.

'Mr Srivastava,' he called out as he held out his hand for a handshake. 'Amit Sharma,' he said as Rakesh turned to face Amit. The formally attired Amit looked overdressed in front of Rakesh. The striped blue shirt, tie and coat indicated that he was ready to leave for work. Having breakfast with the morning newspaper for company, was the last thing he did before he wore his shoes and left for office.

Rakesh Srivastava looked at him straight in the eye. Amit still couldn't place him. How could he? They had never met in the past.

'Amit Sharma,' he introduced himself again. 'You wanted to meet me,' he smiled. It was considered impolite not to smile at a visitor even though the smile was now more of a question than a welcoming gesture.

The smile didn't get reciprocated, neither was the handshake accepted, and that irritated Amit. 'How can I help you?' Amit asked again. 'Do we know each other?' he was beginning to wonder.

Rakesh looked at Amit. A look that was unpleasant and left a thousand questions unanswered. His hand went into his jacket pocket and pulled out something, which he held up for Amit to see. It was an ID card.

'Rakesh Srivastava. Investigation Officer. Crime Branch.' A long pause followed. Amit couldn't understand why he was there. He gave him a blank look.

'Hmm... OKAY,' he shook his head in acknowledgement. 'What can I do for you?'

'You will have to come with me to the police station.' As Rakesh said this, he simultaneously handed him a folded and crumpled piece of paper.

'What's this?' Amit couldn't understand what was going on. The blank look on his face didn't go away but a few folds appeared on his normally wrinkle-free forehead. Without taking his eyes off the stern glare from Rakesh, who didn't volunteer to give any further information, he stretched out his hand, took the piece of paper from Rakesh's hand and opened it.

After giving it a cursory glance, he glared at Rakesh for a fraction of a second and then almost instantaneously, shifted his glare back to the paper. He saw something which he would never have imagined in the wildest of his dreams . . . something which was about to send his fantasy world crashing down. It was a document that was going to have a far-reaching impact on his professional and more importantly, his personal life. His head started spinning; it was as if someone had pulled the rug from under his feet. Beads of sweat broke out on his forehead and meandered their way through the creases formed by the worry lines on his forehead, towards the dam formed by his eyebrows. He looked up at Rakesh Srivastava, with questions in his eyes, concern in his look, and worry in his mind.

Written on that sheet of paper, in black ink—it was evident that someone had hurriedly scribbled on it—were three words: Non-Bailable Arrest Warrant.

February 1994
Bangalore

A nervous twenty something was pacing up and down the corridor, outside lecture room number four, waiting for his turn. Dressed in a two-piece Louis Philippe suit, a Zodiac tie and impeccably polished shoes, he was looking uncharacteristically uncomfortable . . . a bit stiff and uptight as he went about his motions. Every three minutes, his hands would make their way down to the belt, hold them and pull up his ill-fitting trousers. His hands would then squeeze the lower portions of the shirt which would have made their way out of the clasp of the elastic on the trouser, and tuck them in firmly. A cursory walk past the reflective pillar, where he would strain his eyes a bit to see his reflection was next, after which, he would adjust his coat sleeve and tie length. This process would be repeated every few minutes. Clearly, he was not used to wearing formals too often, and this was made even more obvious by the oversized coat which seemed straight off the shelves.

He was going through one of those drills when a stern looking gentleman walked out of the lecture room and announced, 'Amit

Sharma. PGP–II, Roll No. 3'. When he heard his name being announced, Amit rushed towards the lecture room. His heart was pounding. A few fellow humans whispered 'Best of luck' into his ears, but he couldn't hear them. He was too focused on what was going to come. He was finally standing next to the door . . . the door that would lead him to where he wanted to be. He pushed the door, and it creaked open. Taking a deep breath, he walked in.

'Good morning gentlemen,' he greeted the four men seated in the room. He had come across three of them earlier during the day. And now there was this fourth one. The moment he saw him, he felt charged. A feeling of elation took over. Wasn't he the reason why he was there in the room, in front of all of them?

'Good morning Amit,' said one of them, 'Welcome back.' This was the third and final round of interviews for a management trainee's (MT) position at New York International Bank. From an initial lot of 124 aspirants they had short-listed nine candidates and were rumoured to be closing out five MTs from IIM Bangalore.

'Please take your seat.' Amit was waiting for instructions before he sat down on the chair placed on his side of the table, facing the panel. A few pleasantries were exchanged.

'Okay young man, I just have one question to ask of you.' This time, it was the fourth person in the room who had spoken. 'From your responses to the personality test questions, I can make out that you have strong views on almost everything – which is good, but doesn't always work.'

'It has worked for me thus far sir. I take my own time in forming an opinion, but once I form an opinion I have strong views and conviction about them.'

'Good. Then let me ask you your view on the Indian government's response to the Babri Masjid crisis. If you were the prime minister of India during the Babri Masjid crisis, what would you have done?' and then he paused. 'Take your time. Think through before you answer.'

Amit looked at him, admiration filling his eyes. He was a bit overawed by his presence. Aditya Bhatnagar was the reason why he aspired to be a part of New York International Bank (NYIB). Attending Aditya's passionate pitch at the pre-placement talk had inspired him so much, that he had made up his mind the same night. *This was the place he wanted to be. Nowhere else. Any other organisation would be a compromise.*

And here he was! After clearing the group discussion and three rounds of interviews, he was now in front of the final hurdle. The finishing line was in sight. He had to now breast the tape. In front of him was his idol, Aditya Bhatnagar, the new country head of retail banking for NYB. In banking circles, he was discussed as the biggest thing to have ever happened to retail banking.

'Sir,' he began.

'Call me Aditya.'

'Aditya, I am an extremely God-fearing and religious person. However, I believe in religious tolerance too. Humans should not play around with history or try to play God. The unfortunate incidents which took place in the case of Babri Masjid, were not because of religious activism or lack of tolerance. It was an act of a few Hindu fundamentalists and our then Prime Minister P.V. Narasimha Rao just let that be. It happened because of inaction on the part of the government. . . . In life, success is about taking the right decisions and putting in a concerted effort at making it work for you. P.V.N. Rao just failed to take a decision – right or wrong comes much later. I would have taken a decision and converted the monument to an all community prayer home and forcefully executed the same. There would have been some hue and cry about it . . . but public memory is short-lived. The matter would have died down and peace would have reigned.

We are all aware of the rioting that followed. The entire nation was gripped by communal tension. Loss of life, property and more importantly, communal disharmony – all this could have been avoided if one person had acted decisively. If I was him, I would have acted and acted swiftly in the interest of the nation.' He spoke passionately like a man possessed. He looked straight at the panel and not for a moment did he move his gaze away from them. There was a gleam in his eyes. A shine, a shimmer that arises when your eyes are moist . . . moist with tears which well up when you feel passionately about something. It was clear. He was not faking it. Every word of what he spoke came straight from his heart. He went on for another three minutes, outlining in detail the plan for what he stood for. And when he finished, there was silence in the room. The silence lasted for a while, till Aditya stood up, put his hands together and started clapping. Everyone else followed Aditya.

Aditya walked up to him and held out his hand. 'Well said Amit! Well said!'

Amit too held out his hand, a bit nervous. He felt he had overstretched his brief, but it didn't seem so. Aditya looked at others in the room, and then swung his gaze back towards Amit. 'I am sure everybody here agrees that we need young passionate people like you in our team.' All the others nodded in unison.

'Welcome to NYB. I am quite happy to confirm that you have made it to our final list. I look forward to working with you young man,' and he held out his hand once again. Unaware of his own movements, Amit robotically lifted his hand and held it out for Aditya to complete the shake. The others in the room stood up and a chorus of congratulations filled the air. Amit didn't realise till after a few minutes, that he was the only person in the room who was still seated and hurriedly stood up.

A few pleasantries later, he walked out of the room an elated and proud man. He was all set to join NYB as a management trainee and oh boy! Wasn't he proud?

Once out of the room, he did not go back to the hostel. He called Paresh, his roommate and both of them headed to the Meenakshi Sundareshwarar temple, a few kilometres from the IIM Bangalore campus, on the outskirts of the city. He wanted to thank God, for he believed that God had a huge role to play in getting him through to NYB. And what did Aditya end up asking him in the final interview . . . a question on God! It surely was result of a divine intervention.

On the way back, he stopped at the phone booth outside campus and called home. His parents were in Jamshedpur, where his father worked with Tata Steel. Though they belonged to Delhi, Amit's formative years were all spent in Jamshedpur. If there was any place he could call home, it was the steel city – Jamshedpur.

After conveying the exciting news to his parents, he stepped out of the PCO, and looked up at the sky. His right hand instinctively went up to his chest. 'Thanks Dad. For just being there for me.' He traced his steps back to the hostel, stopping en route at the placement office to collect his appointment letter from NYB.

'Hey Amit! Where have you been? We were hunting for you all over the place.' It was Naveen, the placement coordinator for his batch, who called out for him when he was heading back to the hostel. Amit looked at him, a look that conveyed a thousand questions.

'Anderson has short listed you for their final interview. They want to see you in another fifteen minutes. Good that I found you. Just freshen up and rush to Room 4.'

'Can I avoid?'

'Are you kidding?'

'No. I don't want to go to Anderson. I have decided to stick with the NYB offer.'

'Have you seen the package? Anderson is offering 5.5 lakh. NYB's at 3.75 lakh p.a.'

'I know.'

'Then why?'

'You will never understand. Please decline Anderson,' and he walked away without waiting to hear Naveen's response.

'They don't have Aditya Bhatnagar,' he said to himself as he walked back to the hostel. A new life was about to take shape for him.

May 1994
NYB Head Office
Mumbai

The first few days at his new job just came and went. Amit didn't even realise. Time was flying past at rocket speed. The fifteen days of induction were hectic and Amit enjoyed every moment of it. Aditya would address them every evening. Amit looked forward to those inspiring sessions. Aditya was like God to him. For him, 'If God was a banker', he would have been like Aditya. His words were gospel truth. Amit was an enthusiastic participant in all his sessions and tried to make the maximum of his interactions. He worked hard on assignments, volunteered himself for group activities and soon he stood out as a performer par excellence.

Aditya remembered him from the days of the interview. It's natural for anyone to have an affinity towards someone they have hired . . . and Aditya had hired Amit. He had to be special. As far as career was concerned, Amit had a headstart. There was no doubt that if he didn't screw it up, his career would rock. It was the competence he demonstrated which made him even more exceptional.

Finally decision day arrived. Aditya announced the final placements to the team over dinner at the Sunset Lounge, Oberoi Towers – a luxury hotel at the far end of Marine Drive in Mumbai. The view from the lounge was spectacular, but something else was more important. People wanted to know where they were headed to in life and whether they had been given the positions and jobs they wanted. There were about thirty of them in the room . . . eager eyes and restless minds were waiting for their final postings.

Finally the suspense was broken and the placements were announced. Aditya made it very special for all of them. He had got visiting cards ready for the entire lot, with their designations printed on them. He called each one to come upfront, open their box of visiting cards and read out the job and location the person was expected to move to. It was an ecstatic moment for most of them. Receiving the first set of corporate visiting cards is indeed special, as any MBA would know. Amit's name was the second last to be called out. Till then, most of his batchmates had been placed in the auto loans business which was one of the largest businesses for NYB. Not only was it the largest business, NYB was also the market leader in auto loans. This was so close to everyone's heart that they had nurtured it at the cost of other businesses. And to be fair, till date the auto business had delivered larger than life profits for NYB.

Amit walked up to the front, trying to conceal his nervousness. Aditya handed him his box of visiting cards, which he carefully opened. One look at it, and he broke into a smile. A microphone was placed on the podium. He walked up to it, cleared his throat and announced, 'Amit Sharma, Relationship Manager. Bombay Fort Branch.' He took a bow and walked back to his seat.

Bombay Fort Branch, was a very prestigious one. It was in a building where the entire senior management of New York International Bank was based. The CEO, the heads of businesses, the marketing department, etc. . . . all operated out of this building. Not only did they operate out of this building, they also maintained their personal accounts in this branch. It was normal for at least three or four from the bank's senior management team to drop in on any given working day. It was a high visibility branch and held in it the potential to make or break a career. Any screw ups on the bank accounts of senior management could sound the death knell for individual careers. On the contrary individual perceptions could also help shape up various careers. Amit was getting into a steam boiler and he knew it. It provided an excellent opportunity for him to build a relationship with the management team and he was going to exploit it.

What he did not know was that Aditya had handpicked him from the entire team and placed him there. He wanted to keep him under his aegis and for that physical proximity was important. Amit had already been singled out amongst his batch of management trainees. His career was just about to take off and he was already the chosen one.

20 December 2007
Bandra Police Station
Mumbai

The dirty white and blue jeep slowed down in front of the Bandra Police Station on Hill Road. Though it was called Hill Road, there was no hill remotely in sight. The jeep stopped in the middle of a big muddy puddle that had formed right outside the compound. A drain pipe criss-crossing the road had been ruptured again by what the telecom department is best at – incessant digging! The big muddy puddle was proof of their 'hard work'.

Rakesh Srivastav stepped out first, followed by Amit, dressed in a spotless white shirt and a Satya Paul tie. A convict? Did he look like one? He looked more like a corporate honcho who had come in to lodge a complaint. Convicts are not dressed like this. Besides the grim look and a party of policemen around him, he looked pretty much normal.

Just as soon as he stepped out of the jeep, something crashed into the muddy mess created by the gushing water and splaaassshh!

A few kids playing in the nearby area had hit a cricket ball in their direction and as luck would have had it, the ball had made a direct and grand entry into that very puddle, sending dirty muddy water all over Amit. Nature had made her designs on Amit and thus, his impeccably laundered and starched white shirt had turned into an assortment of brown patches.

'Oye!' screamed a constable as he hobbled about to drive the children away.

What have I done to deserve this? He seemed to think as he walked inside the police station with Rakesh leading the way.

'What is this for?' a shocked Amit had asked Rakesh Srivastav, when he was handed over the Non-Bailable Arrest Warrant. The aloo parantha and the dripping butter had been swept out of his mind. From the details mentioned on the warrant, it was not too clear as to what the issue was.

'Mr Sharma, I have been instructed to accompany you back to the police station,' was the statement from Srivastav that helped in no way.

'What happened?' It was Chanda this time. On hearing the word 'police station', she had panicked and rushed into the drawing room.

'Nothing Chanda. You go inside. Let me handle this.'

Chanda didn't pay any heed and instead, looked at Rakesh, questioningly. 'You are . . .?' She knew his name but didn't know what he did or why he was there.

'Rakesh Srivastav, Investigating Officer, Crime Branch.'

'What is the issue, officer?'

'I need Mr Sharma to come with me to the police station. There is a Non-Bailable Arrest Warrant for him.' Words failed Chanda. She just looked at Amit, with shock writ all over her innocent face.

'What have I done?' Amit was getting agitated now. This was no joke or prank. It was serious stuff. He had visited the police station on numerous occasions in the past, but never as the accused. Rakesh Srivastav didn't respond to Chanda or Amit's satisfaction.

Amit and Chanda tried to reason with Rakesh, but their arguments fell on deaf ears. Amit was not even allowed to make a call to the legal advisor of NYB. He had just been carted off in a waiting police jeep and taken to the station.

The spectacle outside his building was embarrassing. As he came out of the elevator, he was shocked at what he saw. In front of him were two jeeps full of policemen. Something had gone awfully wrong. The normally composed Amit was stressed, worried and undoubtedly hassled. He had never encountered anything like this. He was supposed to be the senior vice president at NYB and here he was, being treated like a terrorist!

He was not even allowed to change clothes. One look at him and it was obvious. As he walked into the police station, the clatter of the police boots clearly overshadowed the feeble clap of his hawai chappals. His polished boots were left behind on the shoe rack, as he was hurriedly jostled into the police jeep.

A feeling of nausea took over as he walked into the police station. In the past, whenever he had walked into a police station, it was with a purpose. Stepping out of the place was in his control. Not today though. The entire hall was repulsive. The same pair of hands that held him steadily shoved him onto an empty bench. 'Wait there,' said a stern voice. He didn't recognise the face behind the voice. All looked the same. Two policemen stood guard, to ensure that he didn't run away. Srivastav left them and walked into the adjacent room, leaving him to wonder why all this was being done.

Chanda! What will she do? How will she manage without him? They had old parents living in Jamshedpur. If they get to know how would they react? How will Chanda explain the situation to them? For that, he had to know what was going on.

September 1996
Jamshedpur/Mumbai

In the autumn of 1996, Amit and Chanda solemnised their marriage with a very simple ceremony in Jamshedpur. Both hailed from the same city; their parents worked in Tata Steel (TISCO in those days). The common streak ended there. Their marriage was a perfect example of obedience to the Indian tradition. Like most other Indian marriages in the twentieth century, theirs too was a traditionally arranged marriage. No romance, no courtship. Their parents had met at a colleague's son's wedding and the 'deal' had been struck.

Amit and Chanda were complete opposites. If one was chalk the other was cheese. However, just like all other Indian families where people of different attitudes, opinions, beliefs and judgements stick together and make a life out of nothing, Amit and Chanda were thrown into the quagmire of life.

Chanda was a biotechnologist. She had done her postgraduation in biotechnology and had no interest in corporate boardroom politics. Her aspirations for a doctorate degree were nipped in the bud by her entry into wedlock. Though she had never held Amit accountable for it, somewhere in a dark corner of her heart, she regretted her circumstantial inability to pursue further studies. A career in research was something she had looked forward to and to be successful in that line, a doctoral degree was essential. Not that Amit did not want her to or did not let her study further. It was just that once she got deeply involved in her marital life, she just didn't get the time or the drive to pursue it. After marriage, Chanda moved with Amit to Mumbai.

Chanda's parents had been very impressed with Amit's credentials – an MBA from IIM Bangalore . . . working with NYB . . . decent salary . . . Amit's candidature was a winner from day one. A relationship manager for a son-in-law sounded very happening those days. It upped their prestige quotient by a few leaping notches.

'My son-in-law is a PRO in a foreign bank,' Chanda's mother would show off at social gatherings. Not knowing that there was a world of difference between a PRO (public relations officer) and a relationship manager. Chanda tried correcting her a few times but all her efforts proved to be in vain, an obvious consequence of which was quitting the attempts at correction. She couldn't change her. But one thing was sure – her parents were completely in awe of Amit.

It was no different for Amit's parents. Their pride in their daughter-in-law was very obvious. The first biotechnologist in the family . . . and more importantly, it was an arranged marriage. Till date, the majority of middle-aged men and women (or uncles and aunties) believe that an arranged marriage is the ultimate mark of a respectable family in India. And a 'love marriage' is still capable of being the biggest source of gossip and criticism in the 'society'. Well then, Amit and Chanda's marriage was incapable of providing fodder to the society's gossip mongers. 'My son married the girl of my choice,' Amit's mother would proudly state at family gatherings. And when she would say that, mothers would turn to their sons and daughters and smirk, 'Look at Amit', thus making him one of those dreaded example-setters! Amit and Chanda became a yardstick for their relatives to measure their generation by. And that is why Amit's parents were all the more proud of the marriage and of course their beautiful daughter-in-law – Chanda. Her simple demeanor and humble roots only added, and matched the list of qualities that are supposed to be the trademarks of the ideal Indian bahu. There was just one exception, and that was when she would get irritated on being introduced to others as a microbiologist by her in-laws. 'I am a biotechnologist, not a microbiologist,' she would say. The pride she took in her being a biotechnologist was never hidden.

'If I can be a PRO, you can be a microbiologist,' Amit would say in jest and smile at her.

Chanda and Amit settled into a small two-bedroom tenement in the Bandra area of Mumbai. They were an ideal family – looked good as a couple, were well-mannered and soon won the love and respect of all their neighbours.

As in any foreign bank or an MNC, NYB had a rigorous work culture. Amit would leave in the morning and come back late at night. He would call Chanda at least six times a day and Chanda would do the same. Everyday he would come back home to a delicious dinner which Chanda would have cooked. They had a couple of maids to help her out too. Life was coasting along and beginning to settle down into a routine.

Six months passed.

One day after reaching home and freshening up, a hungry Amit rushed to the dining table. The dinner was laid out and looked sumptuous. Amit hurriedly pulled the chair next to Chanda's. He mumbled a few inanities and the usual complaints about the traffic and roads in Mumbai. Just as he was about to grab a roti, he suddenly realised that Chanda's usual chatter was missing. Something was wrong. Was something wrong with her family in Jamshedpur? Was she not feeling well? A look at Chanda's face made him forget about his hunger.

'What happened Chanda? Are you okay? Your eyes look swollen.'

'No. I am fine. Just feeling tired.'

'Do you want to see a doctor?' He just said that for effect. The way she had responded to his earlier question told him that something was wrong. However, he let that be, hoping that it would resolve by itself. Chanda was an introvert and hence, any further probing wouldn't have helped.

'Aaah. Could be the effect of PMS, he thought.' A quick mental calculation ensued Yes, it's anyway time for those days of the month. Having complete faith in his rationalisation of her behaviour, Amit very conveniently ignored Chandas's mood swing.

However, this soon became a regular feature. The truth was that Chanda was beginning to feel stifled and it was not because Amit had stopped caring for her. In fact, whenever Amit was at home, life revolved around Chanda. The problem started whenever he was not at home. Being an educated biotechnologist, whiling away her time sitting at home was not exactly what she had really aspired for. A doctorate degree, a career, name and fame as a research specialist were some of the dreams that Chanda had cherished and longed for since the day she had enrolled herself into the postgraduate course in biotechnology.

This was also the first time she had stepped out of Jamshedpur. The city of horror and wonder – Mumbai – scared her. Vast, complex and confusing as to defy generalisation, Chanda feared getting lost in this jam-packed and maddening metropolis. Even after staying in the city for a while and trying to get used to its weird ways, things were not getting any simpler. As time went by, it only became worse. In the mornings, Chanda would hate seeing the receding back of Amit. She would dread the long day ahead. This state of mind didn't take too much time in pushing Chanda towards mental depression. Day after day, Amit would be greeted by a tearful Chanda at the doorstep. This was not the woman he had married. Surely this was not PMS. He was concerned and decided to do something himself, and being a relationship manager was useful.

One night when the entire rigour replayed itself, Amit called out to her.

'Chanda . . .'

'Hmm . . .' Chanda had again withdrawn into a shell.

'Come here,' said Amit and gave a couple of pats to the seat next to him, gesturing her to come and sit next to him on the sofa in the drawing room. She was clearing up the table after dinner. Chanda ignored him and continued clearing the table. When she didn't come, Amit switched off the TV, walked up to the table, pulled out a chair and sat on it.

'Bored?' Amit asked her.

She didn't respond. She gave a blank look that pierced right through Amit and rested on the wall behind him. It was as if he was invisible. Amit felt a slight pang of pain in the pit of his stomach. It was as if some sharp instrument had just given a twist to his insides. Loneliness can be dangerous and Amit knew that. Its deadly grips could sometimes push you strongly towards depression – at times too deep to be able to get out of. Chanda seemed to be hurtling towards those depths at a furious pace.

'I met Shankar Raman today.'

'Umm hunn . . .' Again a minimalist response.

'He is the MD of Biotech Scientific Research Institute Limited.'

'Hmm . . .' Though her facial expressions seemed to lighten up on hearing the word 'biotech', it was still not much of a reaction.

'He is a club class customer of ours. He wants to meet you tomorrow. The office is in Bandra.' Club class customers were the crème de la crème of all the customers of NYB. Rich customers who kept all their monies locked up in their bank accounts. These people, by virtue of their relationship size with the bank, demand and also get extremely high levels of service. All of them have a dedicated relationship manager, who is their single point of contact for all transactions at the NYB. Amit was the relationship manager managing

Shankar Raman's account. Over the years he had developed a rapport with the MD of Biotech Scientific Research Institute Limited. Their relationship had transcended the realms of professional association to become a more personal one. Amit had requested his help in finding Chanda a job.

'For what?' asked Chanda.

'His is a biotech company and I spoke to him about a job for you. He wants to meet you to see if something can be worked out.'

Chanda was a bright and intelligent girl and didn't need Amit's recommendation to find herself a job. The problem that she faced in those days was a peculiar one. In 1996, there weren't too many biotechnology companies in India. While it was a sunrise industry in the west, it hadn't really evolved as an industry in India. And whatever limited presence it had in India was in the garden city of Bangalore. Institutes like Biocon and Indian Institute of Science offered great research opportunities, but only in Bangalore. As a biotechnologist, being in Mumbai didn't give many research options to explore.

She did go and meet Shankar Raman the next day.

'What happened?' Amit asked her when he came back from work that night.

'Nothing. It will not work out,' said Chanda without looking at Amit. Her face had no expression. She had a blank look.

'Why? He told me that he will hire you.'

'He is ready to hire me. I refused.' She didn't seem too thrilled about it. Amit ignored her frustration because he knew what she was going through. He just gave her a questioning look. The silence told her that he was waiting for more. 'He wants me to take up a sales job. His research facility is in Pune. I didn't waste time doing my Masters to take up a sales job.'

Amit had expected this. However, he had pushed her to go, hoping against hope that her frustration at home would nudge her to make up her mind to take up a sales job. He was feeling guilty that he had messed up Chanda's potentially successful career. But this option hadn't worked out. Chanda was clear about this in her head. A career in sales wasn't something she wanted.

'Should I ask for a move to Bangalore? NYB has a small branch there. I might get a transfer if I request for it,' he asked her one day, unable to see her continually depressed state. Chanda had even stopped smiling these days and Amit couldn't take it anymore.

Chanda walked up to him, put her arms around and hugged him tightly. While tears welled up in her eyes, she hid her face behind his shoulders and said, 'I am fine Amit. I do not want to screw up your career. Do not worry. One of us has to go ahead. The other person will have to take what comes his or her way. I know that you are the one who can provide for the house. You will get the priority in matters of career. A move to Bangalore in NYB may get me a research job, but will definitely not be as good for you. Aditya may not like this career move at this point either. My frustration is not directed at you. It only comes out in front of you. I am sorry. I don't have anyone to cry in front of.' Despite all her herculean attempts to hide her tears, she couldn't hold them back any longer. Before Amit could take in whatever she had just said Chanda started sobbing violently. Her petite body was shivering while tears gave vent to her sorrow. Amit hugged her tightly and didn't say a word after that. The guilt inside him only deepened when she said, 'Don't force me to join a biotech firm in sales. I cannot do that. I waited all my life for a research job in biotechnology and now if I work in a similar environment in sales, which I know nothing of, my failure, will stare at me every day of my life. I will not be able to take that torture. Won't be able to tolerate it. I will take any job which comes my way in any other industry . . . please . . . please don't push me to do injustice to my education and my aspirations . . .' and she sobbed, sobbed and sobbed. Amit did not know what to do. He just hugged her tightly and tried to console her . . . in vain.

Things changed over the next three months. Chanda gave up her quest for joining a biotechnology firm and joined Standard Chartered

Bank (SCB) in Mumbai as a customer service associate. SCB was looking for postgraduates to fill in for this position and Chanda was a postgraduate. Whether the person was a postgraduate in biotechnology or maths or even the arts, SCB didn't care.

A biotechnologist in a foreign bank as a customer service associate! Life, it is said, is never bereft of surprises, and this was one of those.

Amit accepted this, though he always held himself responsible for Chanda not being able to pursue her dream – a career in biotechnological research.

20 December 2007
Bandra Police Station
Mumbai

Rakesh Srivastav didn't come out of the room for a while. Amit was waiting at the bench along with other convicts. He still couldn't come to terms with the fact that he was sitting alongside murderers and thieves. He was hoping against hope that this was just a nightmare that *should* end soon.

He looked around the room. It was a large hall with about twelve doors leading into different sections of the police station. The walls were painted white, or must have been, many years ago. They had deteriorated into shades of pale yellow interspersed with patches of black – the damp proofing of the walls clearly hadn't worked. As any other government office, large portraits of Indira Gandhi and Jawahar Lal Nehru adorned the walls of this police station too.

To his right, a doctor in a white coat was administering first aid to a man bleeding profusely from a cut on the cheek. It looked as if he had been hit by a sharp object. Seated next to him was a guy, probably in his mid-thirties, who was not at all in his senses. Completely drunk, he had almost collapsed. By the intermittent looks of disgust and annoyance that the injured fellow gave the drunkard, it seemed quite clear that the latter was responsible for the state of the former. The police had brought in both of them.

Seated on the far side of the room, away from him, was a lady inspector. Standing in front of her was a team of women, who seemed to have been picked up from a raid in a brothel. 'What am I doing amidst these folks,' thought Amit as he instinctively reached out for his mobile phone, only to realise that he had left it at home. Rakesh had hurriedly bundled him into a waiting jeep, not allowing him to pick up anything he wanted. He felt like an outlier in the police station – the only decent and honest looking guy.

At that very moment Chanda rushed in. Following her were three others. Amit recognised one of them. He was Rohan Naik, the head of Risk and Security at NYB. But, he did not know the other two. Rohan handled all matters concerning courts, police, security of branches and people at NYB. Chanda too was in her office attire. She was all dressed to leave for work and normally left with Amit. Today, however, things were different – this entire episode had taken both of them by surprise.

He hugged Chanda and looked at Rohan helplessly. Rohan walked up to him and patted him on his shoulder. 'Did they tell you what's going on?'

'No,' Amit shook his head. He was completely at a loss. They had also taken away the warrant copy which was shown to him in the morning.

'Who is the inspector who spoke to you?'

'Rakesh Srivastav.'

'Oh yes, Chanda told me so. Is there anyone else who has spoken to you?'

'No, I have been sitting here since morning doing nothing! Waiting for them to come and talk to me.'

'Where is he now?'

He raised his right hand and pointed towards the half-green and half-brown door at the far end of the room. 'He went inside that room an hour ago.' The shiver in his voice was apparent. The uncertainty was killing.

'Don't worry,' assured Naik. 'We have spoken to Pathak. He was not aware of this. But he said that his office will let the Bandra Police know that they should not harass you in any manner, till we get to the bottom of this.' Pathak, Amit knew, was the Inspector General (IG) of Mumbai Police. He was the seniormost in the Mumbai Police fraternity. If he said something, it obviously carried a lot of weight. Pathak's reassurance to Naik was soothing to Amit's ears and nerves.

Rohan Naik left him and Chanda together and walked towards the room that Amit had pointed towards – the room where Rakesh had disappeared an hour ago. Chanda looked at him and then looked away, staring into the huge wall in front of them. The patches of yellow and black on the wall seemed to tell her the story of their lives. There was a loud silence between the two of them. They hardly spoke these days. Even the police station was no different. They were sitting together on the bench, next to each other. However, neither of them talked. The only thing which indicated that the bond between them was still alive was the fact that Chanda's hand was on his knee . . . a subtle gesture that spoke a million words. It said that no matter what happens, she was with him. Amit's hand rested on top of hers. He needed her. He desperately wanted her support.

1996
Mumbai

Chanda joined SCB as a customer service associate in October 1996. The job kept her busy and kept her away from the monotonous and boring routine of a lonely housewife. It was a high pressure job. Despite the occasional regret of not being able to pursue biotechnology, her first love, she was getting used to it.

Thankfully, the offices of Amit and Chanda were close by. Amit would drive her to work every morning, and pick her up in the evening. Both of them worked late. Hence it wasn't too much of an effort for him to stay back and pick her up. On days that they got unduly late, dinner would be at a roadside shack. Bandra had many of them and it was more than simple to find a convenient and inexpensive joint.

Both of them were at the starting line of their careers and hence, it was important for them to give it their best shot. 'If we don't work hard now, we'll be left struggling later,' Chanda quite agreed with this statement of Amit.

Life went on at a feverish yet exciting pace for the two of them. They enjoyed every moment of togetherness. Mornings were special. They would get up early so that they could have their morning coffee in the luxurious lap of their sea facing balcony. They would enjoy watching the tired waves lash against the shore. It was as if they were looking at Amit and Chanda and saying, 'Thank your stars, you don't need to keep working away through the night like we do.'

Their morning coffee would only be interrupted by the unfailing show of strength and skill by the newspaper boy, who would hurl *The Times of India* and *The Economic Times* from the ground floor with such force and precision that it would land bang to their right every single day. Throwing the newspaper up three floors is not easy, but the Mumbai newspaper boys would manage to do it correctly day after day. After a quick run through the newspaper, the two of them would help each other prepare breakfast. A quick shower later, they would be back in the balcony where breakfast would have been laid out by the one who got ready before the other. Newspapers were banned during breakfast. It was supposed to be their personal time, and both of them adhered to this rule. After a peaceful bite, they would leave for office, never quite sure about whether they would end up having dinner within the quiet walls of their house or amidst the company of tiny nocturnal insects and the noisy chatter of a lively roadside dhaba.

Sometimes, after an exhausting day at work, both would be too tired to talk. Dinner would then be accompanied by a comfortable silent conversation. The silence never disturbed them. It is said that familiarity breeds contempt. In their case, familiarity bred comfort. Chanda would look into her plate of food and feel a smile. She was never the one to blatantly display her feelings, and Amit never failed to understand that. She couldn't help feel lucky for having Amit as her husband. She was sure that he was the man of her dreams. Amit too reciprocated her thoughts.

That night they were driving back home in their Maruti 800.
Amit had bought a new Maruti 800 when Chanda joined SCB. He
didn't want her to travel by train everyday. Mumbai locals can be very
threatening to outsiders if you are not used to it. It was the month
of July and the monsoons had set in. It was about 9.30 at night.

'Shyam had a town-hall* this morning,' Chanda looked at
Amit.

'Hmm . . .' Amit didn't take his eyes off the road. He was a
very careful driver. He knew Shyam. He was the India cards head
of SCB.

'He wants to extend phone banking to twenty-four hours from
the current 9 a.m. to 6 p.m.'

Amit turned and looked at her, and almost immediately went
back to fixing his eyes on the road. It was drizzling and the roads
were slippery. He did not want to take a chance.

'Why?' he asked, as his eyebrows knitted together to form one
straight line.

'Citibank has done that. Apparently your bank is also going to do
it. If we don't do it quickly, we will lose the competitive advantage. It
will soon become a hygiene factor and customers will start expecting
it from everyone.'

'Hmm . . .' Amit didn't volunteer any opinion at this stage.

'So if we don't start a twenty-four-hour phone banking unit, we
will lose customers to other banks,' she continued when Amit did
not say anything.

'When does he want to start this?'

'Next sixty days.'

---

*In foreign bank parlance, a town-hall meeting is an informal gathering
of employees, (a term derived from the traditional town meetings of New
England) where the management addresses the staff on issues which are
relevant. Key messages are passed down the line. The staff is given the
opportunity to voice views and concerns which are then addressed by
the management.

'Would it impact us?'

'That's the problem.'

'What?'

'They want us to start working on shifts.' Currently, Chanda was on regular office hours. She was required to work from 9 a.m. to 6 p.m., though it normally extended to over 8 p.m. Before Amit could give a further thought to this new development, he suddenly realised that it was way too late to go home and cook. They had reached Bandra and the image of a cosy restaurant and deliciously cooked food that doesn't require the remains of your sapped energy levels were enough to nudge Amit into asking a very important question.

'Tavaa?' he looked at Chanda with raised and expectant eyebrows. Tavaa was a popular eating joint on Turner Road in the heart of Bandra. Chanda nodded. Amit turned his car towards Tavaa. He dropped Chanda at the gate and went ahead to park. Chanda went in to place the order so that their rumbling stomachs didn't have to undergo the torturous fifteen-minute-wait! They found a cosy table on the far end of the restaurant, away from the door, and settled down. Being a week day, the restaurant was thinly populated. Their order arrived within ten minutes. By then the discussion had resumed.

'I too will have to be on shifts. Thankfully, they will not put women in night shifts, but they plan to have shifts from 6 a.m. to 10 p.m., where women will have to work. They have still not closed out the modalities. Work is in progress but they will flesh it out over the next thirty to sixty days.'

'What happens if you don't want to do it?'

'Someone asked that question.'

'What did Shyam say?'

'He said that if anyone does not want to be in shifts, they would try and move them to other parts of the bank . . .' and then she paused, ' . . . on a best effort basis.'

'Means you don't have a choice? What should you do?'

'Don't know,' she sounded worried.

'Okay, fine. You relax. Let's take it as it comes. If it becomes too difficult, we'll find something else. Otherwise we'll carry on as it is.'

Amit had put an end to the discussion. He did not quite understand the thoughts going on in her mind. Chanda was more worried about the basics. What will happen to their morning coffee in the balcony if she was on the 6 a.m. shift? What will happen to their dinner time? She hadn't told him that a twenty-four-hour service centre meant that it had to be operational on weekends too. Which in turn meant staggering of weekly offs for all the staff and hence she might not always get an off on a Sunday. Even the day off that she shared with and greatly cherished, was under threat. As Amit said, she decided to cross the bridge when she came to that. It was still sixty days away.

The next week was performance appraisal time for Amit. It was just the middle of the year. The management trainees had completed three years at NYB. After their induction, they had all been put in individual roles and had been given certain deliverables. It was time to take stock and decide if the individual had performed as per the expectations in their new role. In NYB, management trainees were a special lot. They were pampered, taken care of and were managed separately as compared to thousands of other employees. They had yearly meetings with Aditya, something which others would give an arm and a leg for. They had annual reviews with Aditya to take stock of their performance, their career aspirations and how the organisation could help them move towards their mutual goals.

Aditya was a perfectionist to the core. He would prepare in advance for all meetings . . . even if it was a meeting with the lower level and junior management trainees. In preparation for his sessions with the management trainees, Aditya was sitting with the monthly league tables looking at the branch-wise performance of all the branches and that of the individual relationship managers. He went page by page, parametre by parametre trying to look at individual performances.

It did not look logical. Something was really wrong. Something like this had never happened in his career thus far.

Now staring at him were sheets of paper, which said only one very pleasantly surprising thing. Across all parametres, there was only one branch topping the country numbers and within that branch, there was only one individual who was streets ahead of the rest – Bombay Fort Branch and Amit Sharma. While it didn't speak volumes about the rest, Aditya momentarily swelled with pride. Wasn't he the one who had hired Amit?

He stretched his right hand and extended it towards the exquisite Meridian phone on his table and pressed a red button, thereby activating the speakerphone. He dialled an extension number and waited till it was answered from the other end.

'Yes boss?' it was Melinda, his secretary on the line.

'Melinda, can you get Amit Sharma and give him thirty minutes today? Preferably towards the evening.'

'Sure sir!' and Melinda hung up. The meeting was arranged.

At 6.30 the same evening, Amit walked into Aditya's huge plush cabin.

'Good evening young man!' said Aditya as he got up from behind his table and walked towards the sofa kept on the right corner of the room. As Aditya's arm made a sweeping gesture towards the sofa, Amit walked towards the sofa and sat down on the seat, farthest from where Aditya was sitting.

'I don't bite,' said Aditya and he guffawed with pride at his own wise-crack. Amit gave a slightly nervous smile and moved closer. His mind was still busy trying to figure out why he had been called. The performance appraisal discussion was only scheduled for later that week. Above all, Amit was wonderstruck – he couldn't believe that he was sitting on the sofa with the man he so admired! Aditya was the one person he genuinely looked up to. Wasn't he the reason why he had ignored Anderson and joined NYB? It was a dream come true for him to be sharing the same professional space with Aditya.

'Thank you sir,' said Amit, suddenly coming out of the dream-come-true spell and realising that it's about time he showed some manners instead of looking like a child who had just seen Disney Land for the first time!

'I think I have told you this many times in the past . . . and if I recollect, even during your interview . . . my name is Aditya. There are no sirs here.'

'Yes Aditya.' *God! He remembers even this.* Amit was astonished to know that this man remembered even the tiniest of details that would normally have been too insignificant to care for. Amit was surely impressed.

'One year. Long time since your last appraisal.'

'Yes Aditya. It's been one year. A lot has happened.' So was this about his performance appraisal then.

'Good or bad?' asked Aditya in a dare-you-to-answer tone as he casually lifted his legs and placed them on the table in front of the sofa.

'More good than bad Sir . . . errr . . . I mean, Aditya.'

Aditya smiled. 'Did Melinda tell you why I called you here?'

Amit was too shocked to allow words to come out of his nervous mouth. He could feel that 'no' stuck somewhere in the middle of his throat. It was just when Amit really wanted to give himself a rap on his head for acting smart and saying things like 'a lot has happened' that Aditya recognised the blank look on Amit's face and continued. 'I was looking at the branch league tables. Your branch doesn't seem to be doing too well.'

Amit looked a bit confused. *Now where was this coming from? Is this some sort of trick question? If it is then I better keep my smart Alecs to myself and be confident.* 'But Aditya, we are actually topping them. I am sure there is a mistake in the numbers provided to you.'

'Are you saying that my team has given me incorrect numbers?'

'Er . . . no Aditya. I meant that . . .' Amit was at a loss for words. He did not know what to say. Once again, he had opened his mouth and said something which was open to interpretation.

'My friend, if a rookie like you tops the performance charts and takes the branch to the top position in the league tables, what are your other colleagues doing? If I take you out of the equation, your branch performance tanks. Yes or no?'

'I haven't seen it that way sir. We were all very happy to see that the branch is doing well. Maybe we can check and revert.' *Ha! That was a perfect answer. I am sure he is impressed . . . on second thoughts, no, he doesn't look too happy. Okay, let's try to play safe here now.* Amit added, 'The branch manager (BM) would surely know sir.' His level of nervousness had reached greater heights by now. Any rookie would be, when he is in a conversation with the head of retail banking.

'Ha ha. Just kidding. I am sure the BM would have a better idea. I will chat with him separately. I wanted to meet you to let you know, young man, that we are extremely happy with your performance so far. I can see that you have a bright future in this bank.'

'Thank you sir!' He was overawed and relieved.

'I will be personally tracking your performance my friend. I hired you. Remember . . .? If you ever get into a sticky situation, and need help, let me know. I will . . .' The sentence was forced to halt as at that moment, Melinda walked into the room. 'Aditya, call from Martin Stone's office on line one. It's urgent.'

Martin was the worldwide group head of communications. He was based in New York and reported to Tedd Bridge, the CEO of the bank.

'Hold on Amit. I will just come back to you,' said Aditya and he walked up to the phone. He pressed a button and Martin's voice crackled on the speakerphone. Aditya didn't feel the need to be discreet given that Amit was in the room. He was probably showing off in front of the rookie.

'Hi Martin! What's up? What are you doing so early in office?' he screamed into the phone. No matter how educated and trained in etiquettes, when it comes to international calls, something in our Indian vocal cords always prompts us to just scream our throats out! And the accent . . . it changes instantly. Aditya had a distinct American twang and drag when he spoke out to Martin Stone.

'Hi Ady boy. Ain't I glad that I got you?'

'What happened? You don't sound too good.'

'Tedd is steaming Ady. Haven't you seen the front page of the *Wall Street Journal*?'

'No. But what's it about?'

'About you.'

'Me?'

'As in . . . about India.'

'What about India?'

'You haven't seen it? I sent you a scanned copy about ten minutes ago.'

Aditya quickly sat down at his desk. He did not move the line off the speakerphone. In the ensuing melee, he probably forgot that Amit was in the same room. He got busy trying to log into his email account.

'Melinda!' he hollered. He couldn't have used the extension as Martin was on the line. Hence the sudden bellowing.

'Check my mailbox. Take a printout of any email from Martin and bring it in.' He took a five-second-pause which was like the lull before the storm. Just when his expressions seemed calm and composed his facial expressions unexpectedly concocted into an irritated look followed by a sudden and extra loud 'Now!'

Melinda disappeared as swiftly as she had come in.

Meanwhile, Aditya found the much-wanted mail and clicked on it. 'It has just come in Martin. I am trying to open it.' A pause again. 'It's opening. Will the government ever do anything about telecommunications in this country? The bandwidth is so fucking low!' The wait was so frustrating.

The mail was heavy. The image which Martin had sent was large and hence was taking time to open. Aditya waited with bated breath trying to figure out what was going on. Just when he was about to lose his last ounce of patience, the mail finally opened. It opened with such a bang that it hit Aditya extremely hard. He did not know how to react.

'Fucking shit!' he mumbled to himself. It is strange but true – mumbling obscenities act as momentary stress-busters.

In front of him was the image of the front page of that day's edition of the *Wall Street Journal* (WSJ). The front page lead story covered almost half the page and surprisingly, it was on India. The headline screamed in front of him. It read:

'NYB FLEECES POOR PEOPLE IN INDIA TO FILL ITS OWN COFFERS – a story of fraud, abuse of power and disrespect of the legal system.'

Written by Khalid Bilal, a staff correspondent of the *Wall Street Journal*, the article was vitriolic. It was a frontal attack on the India NYB management.

Melinda walked in with the article. With a frown on his face, a look that focussed only on the screen of the laptop and a hand that was suddenly held up, Melinda understood what he meant. It was a clear 'do not disturb' sign. Smart that she was, she quietly walked towards the table where Amit was sitting, gently placed the folder on the table, turned and walked back. From where he was sitting, Amit could read the article very clearly. When he saw the headline, he became curious and began reading through the entire article carefully.

'I am reading it Martin. Hold on,' and Aditya continued reading on his screen. Amit too was midway through the article.

The article was about a bank customer in Delhi, called Naveen Gulati, who had apparently taken a car loan from NYB for buying an

Opel Astra. When the customer didn't pay the instalments on time and regular visits by the bank agents didn't bear any results, the bank handed over the collection to musclemen. These men had forced their way into the residential apartment where Naveen stayed. They waited there for the Opel Astra to be brought in. And when it did come in, they stopped the car, beat up the driver and the occupants, which included a lady, forcibly took possession of the car and drove away in it. According to the WSJ it would qualify as a criminal offence in USA, good enough for the banking license to be revoked.

The story did not end there. As luck would have it, the repossessed Opel Astra turned out to be that of some man called Naveed Bilal and not Naveen Gulati. Both of them lived in the same apartment complex and had a steel grey coloured Opel Astra. And this Naveed, turned out to be the first cousin of Khalid, who was the WSJ staff correspondent.

'What a bastard, this Khalid fellow!' exclaimed Aditya on the phone after finishing reading the entire article.

'You have no right to complain Aditya. It's an India screw up. Tedd is fuming. We are announcing our annual results this afternoon. More than the results, I can bet my ass, this issue is going to dominate the investor meet. Tedd wants to know what you have to say.'

The discussion with Martin was a long and difficult one. Martin clearly communicated to Aditya that Tedd was disgusted with this issue. It only complicated things further that the issue was first reported in the *Wall Street Journal* and hence the India Management had no clue about what was going on. Aditya tried telling Martin that he would investigate and get back. However, Martin had only one point of view – 'Aditya, Tedd needs to see some action quickly. He wants some accountability to be fixed and heads to roll. Nothing short of this would be acceptable to the NYB board. Please do whatever you want to do within the next few hours. We want to kill this issue when it comes up in the investor meeting. Tedd doesn't like being embarrassed. Please remember.' With that, he hung up.

Aditya was clearly taken in by the sequence of events. He did not like being told to do things. Everyone knew that. On his part he would normally make sure that situations are not brought to a head in such a manner that they put him in a spot. He did not like being asked difficult questions. In this case he clearly was under pressure. An unexpected turn of events, not completely his doing, had put him in the limelight. He was wondering what to do when it dawned on him that he had company in that room.

He quickly dialled his secretary's number, 'Melinda, please get me Moses. Ask him to come to my room now.' Moses was the collections head for NYB. He was the one responsible for collecting money from the customers who did not pay back their loans. Quite a thug he looked. Six feet something, muscular and brawny, the story was that he had eight eggs for breakfast, followed by a jug full of apple juice. Nobody had seen him feasting in office though. Probably at breakfast he ate for the full day.

Looking at Amit, he smiled. It was clearly one that was put on. Amit could easily tell. 'Amit, I am so sorry. Something urgent has come up and it needs immediate attention. Can we meet some other time? I will ask Melinda to line up some time with you next week.'

'Sure sir,' Amit couldn't have said anything else. He took the hint and walked out of the room, pitying Naveed Bilal, who had his car taken and bones broken for no fault of his. On his way out, he stopped at Melinda's desk to thank her. It was not necessary, but Amit was just being courteous. From her table he could make out that Aditya was again having an animated conversation with Martin. It was a discussion which was surely going to last long. He turned and walked back to his desk. He had taken a few steps when Aditya walked out of his room and looked at Melinda. 'Melinda, can you ask Prabhat to come in right now, before Moses.' Amit didn't understand the implication but was not naïve enough not to understand that it had everything to do with the call that Aditya received sometime back from New York.

Prabhat, the head of Human Resources (HR), walked in within the next few minutes. He did not have the slightest inkling about why he was in that room. Aditya took some time and briefed him on his conversation with Martin. Moses joined them in another five minutes.

'Go right in. They are waiting for you,' chirped Melinda as he walked in.

'Hi Moses,' said everyone in chorus. Moses did not like the tone of the people present in the room. The drag was obvious. The mood was tense.

'Something wrong?'

'Yes,' said Aditya, coming straight to the point. He shoved the printout of the WSJ article under his nose.

'What's this?'

'What the fuck is this?' said a shocked Moses after quickly glancing through the article.

'That's what I am asking you Moses.'

'I know about this case. This customer's car was wrongly repossessed. We had apologised and returned the car. The agent has been sacked and the agency which did the repossession has been warned. We even sent Naveed Bilal a cake and some flowers to his wife, along with an apology.'

'Well, Mr Moses, clearly, that was not enough. This would not have happened otherwise.' Aditya was furiously waving the copy of the article at him.

Moses was a tough no-nonsense guy. 'Aditya, these things have to be managed. In the collections line, if everything we do starts hitting the press, then all the pages of the daily newspaper would not be enough.' And as an afterthought, he added, 'You seem to have forgotten the days when you were in collections, Aditya.'

Aditya looked at him. Moses had a wry smile on his face. The sarcasm was not lost on Aditya. What Moses was saying was right. What Aditya had done during his earlier days at collections was nothing different from what other collectors do. Mistakes do happen. It was an entirely different issue that ninety percent of the mistakes do not get reported.

'Let me cut to the chase Moses. I got a call from Martin Stone in New York. This has come out in the WSJ, just ahead of our results announcement. This has embarrassed our senior management no end. Unless they have a credible story to tell this afternoon, they will be lynched by the media in today's press briefing on the annual results.'

'So?' Moses was acting difficult.

'You will have to put in your papers.' It was Prabhat who spoke this time around. He had been a silent spectator so far in the entire conversation.

'Says who?' and almost as an afterthought added, 'What if I don't?'

'We will be forced to terminate you. This is a serious lapse. A big lapse in controls and procedures.' Prabhat was getting irritated at this conversation. What the heck? A mistake happens. Hits the media. And not just any ordinary media but, the *Wall Street Journal* in New York! 'Give me a break!' he thought, though he didn't say it out loud.

'And who is this WE?'

'The organisation, and of course Aditya,' said Prabhat.

'Did you ask this man here if he wants to sack me?' and he turned and looked at Aditya, who in turn looked at Prabhat. He was banking on Moses quitting on his own. He didn't bargain for Moses to get difficult. It was all happening so fast that Moses could not have reacted in any other fashion. Survival instincts take over in times of extreme crisis.

'Prabhat, give us five minutes.'

After Prabhat left, he turned towards Moses.

'If I go, you go with me . . . I have enough aces under my sleeve and you very well know that. In my line Aditya, we have to protect

ourselves from "everyone". External scavengers and internal preys. If
something comes upon me, you know what I will do. I have enough
evidence on various matters to nail you and the organisation.' Moses
had never spoken like this with anyone in the organisation, but today
was different. He was battling for survival.

'Relax Moses,' said Aditya. He had to make a decision quickly
and tactfully. It was a tricky situation. He walked up to the phone
and dialled a number. After a few minutes, he kept the receiver
down, looked at Moses and smiled. A few seconds later, his fingers
worked on the phone and dialled another number. While he was
speaking, Moses had walked up to the printer and had picked up a
piece of paper. When Aditya was into his second conversation, Moses
picked up a pen from Aditya's table and began writing something
on the paper.

After Aditya put the phone down, he walked up to the door and
called in Prabhat. When the latter walked in, he looked at Moses,
who extended one hand towards him. In the hand was a piece of
paper.

Prabhat took that paper from him and glanced at it. He began
reading it.

To
The HR Manager
NYB

Dear Sir,
I herewith submit my resignation from...........

.... Sd/
G. Moses

He did not read beyond the first line. It was not necessary. How
the hell did Aditya manage it? It had taken Aditya all of fifteen
minutes to get this done.

Aditya called Martin Stone, minutes after the meeting to tell him that in response to the issue highlighted on the front page article in the WSJ, the head of collections in India had been fired.

Moses' resignation from the organisation was announced the next morning. It was so sudden and unexpected that it took everyone by surprise. His last working day was Friday, which was only three days away. When the mail hit his inbox, Amit knew why this had happened. 'This is corporate life,' he said to himself. 'You pay for someone else's sins.' He forwarded the mail to Chanda in SCB. The subject of the mail was 'It sucks'.

The week after, Moses joined Great Western International Bank as country head of collections. No one knew what transpired behind the scenes. Amit knew that the head of retail banking, at Great Western International Bank, Kaushal Pandey, was a close friend of Aditya Bhatnagar. He was an ex-NYBanker and owed his career to Aditya. Aditya had demanded his pound of flesh from him, and Kaushal had willingly obliged.

20 December 2007
Bandra Police Station
Mumbai

The wait at the station was becoming unduly long. Naik too seemed to have disappeared eons ago. Looked like he had forgotten that there were souls waiting for him on the bench. The two men who had come in with him, also disappeared into the room, that seemed like a black hole. People only went in. No one came out.

Amit was getting more and more fidgety. He had a family to provide for. A reputation to protect. Not many knew that he was now struggling to deliver on either of the two. Family life was hurtling towards disaster and his reputation was now rolling downhill at a feverish pitch. He was clearly at his wit's end.

The reason for this arrest had not been mentioned to him yet. Though the Non-Bailable Arrest Warrant mentioned that it was being issued in response to an FIR filed with the police, the case details were missing. He couldn't figure out what the problem was. Had he known, he could have acted and taken preventive steps. But unluckily that was not to be.

Chanda was also getting worried. She had been married to him for long, and had been through many ups and downs. Recently there had been more downs than ups, but she still held on to their relationship by the last string of the thread. However, she had clearly not bargained for this. What had he done to deserve this? Had Amit done something which would deal a death knell to their relationship? She couldn't say.

Both of them were so lost in their thoughts that they completely missed Naik, who had walked out of the black hole room and had come right in front of them.

A hand on his shoulder made Amit look up.

'Naik, what is the problem?' he asked in a pleading voice. He had never been so helpless. Always in control, this situation was quite alien to him. He shifted his glance to Chanda who was also looking at Naik.

The look on his face was not a confidence-building one. 'We will wait outside,' the two lawyers in black coats told Naik as they stepped outside.

'It's not looking good Amit,' Naik's words belied his expression. It gave no encouragement to either Amit or Chanda.

'We have a situation, and we have no clue how to deal with it. We need to get the legal guys involved.'

'But you mentioned that you had taped up Pathak.'

'Yes we had, but when I called him now, he claimed that he was unaware that this was the case. It is out of his jurisdiction.'

'What does he mean? He owes it to us. We have taken care of him so many times in the past.'

'I don't think so Amit. The case is such. Even he can't do much.'

'Why is it such a big deal? Who can help?'

'No one.' This answer left Amit looking at him with his mouth wide open. He was shocked. His eyes were wide open and he was looking alternately at Chanda and Naik as if imploring them to do something.

'Naik,' he said finally. 'Will someone honestly tell me what the fucking issue is?'

1997– Early 2001
Mumbai

The next three years for Amit were normal. Being sighted quickly as a high potential resource by the senior management helped him. Aditya pulled him up from a relationship manager and made him the manager of a small branch in Mumbai. He was now the youngest branch manager at NYB.

Chanda on the other hand, was going through a torrid time. The shifts and the daily rosters were taking a toll on her. She was finding it difficult to manage. One day she would leave home at 5.30 a.m. to be at work by 6 a.m. and the next day she would leave at 2 p.m. only to come back at 11 p.m. The lack of predictability around work hours made it very difficult for her. She also had to take her weekly offs on days other than weekends and that led to her spending less and less time with Amit.

On days that they would be together, she would pour her heart out to Amit. Working in the banking industry was her decision. She was not the kinds who would give it all up at the first signs of stress. A fair chance is all that she wanted to give to SCB. However, no one could prevent her from being a touch worried that it was eating into her family time and the shifts were not making it any easier.

And then it happened. The big day that Chanda was waiting for finally happened. On 26 October 1999, three years into her job, she got her first promotion. She moved from being a phone banking executive to a supervisor in the tele-banking team. She had a team of her own and was now the boss of twenty-two people. Boy! Was she thrilled? The change in the money was not significant; however, the promotion meant a lot to her. More than a professional move forward . . . there was an even bigger motivation. She was off shifts. A supervisory role meant the return of some stability in their lives.

'Gosh, now I will have to see you on weekends. I was beginning to enjoy my Saturdays without you.' Amit teased her when he heard that the supervisory role meant getting off shifts. But heart of hearts he too was thrilled. Their life could get back on track now.

The late 90s extending into 2001, was the period when a consolidation happened in the Indian banking industry. A number of foreign banks entered the Indian market and quite a few exited the scene as well.

ABN Amro Bank bought over Bank of America's retail business, Standard Chartered bought over ANZ Grindlays Bank, and BNP Paribas decided to exit the retail banking space. There were many such examples. It was a time of turmoil and consolidation in the banking industry. Turmoil for some and opportunity for the others.

Amit was at that stage in his career when opportunities were aplenty. Being a fast achiever, he had built a reputation in the industry too. He was quite happy working with New York International Bank, so happy that the thought of a career shift didn't occur to him at all. While people thought it was time to encash the equity that he had built up for himself in the banking industry, Amit's thoughts were far from theirs. He considered himself to be a career NY Banker – someone who had spent his working life with NYB and wanted to spend the remainder of his career with NYB . . . or so he felt till this opportunity came his way.

One day in early 2001, as Amit was driving to meet a client, he received a call on his mobile. It was a number he didn't relate to. However, he picked it up on instinct. It could have been a customer in need.

'Hi, am I speaking to Amit Sharma?'

'Yes. Who is this?'

'Hi Amit, this is Sharmila Ganguly from Spenta Consultants. I am calling from Delhi. Is it a good time to talk to you?'

'Hmm,' Amit was just wondering why they had called him. He hadn't heard of them.

'Amit, let me introduce ourselves. We are a leading recruitment consultancy firm in India and we specialise in the banking and financial services space. I had picked up your reference from our network quite some time back. There is an interesting position that has come up, which I thought I would run past you and see if you would be interested.'

If Amit ever looked back at his life, this could be counted as one call that changed his life. After this call, his personal and professional life would never be the same again. It was one such moment, the gravity of which one doesn't realise till such time that it's long over and gone.

Though he was not interested, he still had a distance to drive. He had some time at hand. Something in the woman's tone told Amit that he needed to explore more. 'No harm in talking,' he thought. He continued.

'I am listening, Sharmila. Go ahead.'

'Amit, are you aware of GE Countrywide?'

'Yes.' Who isn't, he thought to himself. General Electric had a finance company in India called GE Countrywide. They ran a very successful finance business in India and offered auto loans, personal loans and consumer durable loans in the country.

'They are planning to enter the mortgage business in this country. They have identified this as a business which holds enormous potential in the years to come. You have experience in mortgages right? Home loans? You know what I am talking about?'

'Yes. As a branch manager, I provide home loans to my clients. It forms a sizable portion of my branch performance ranking tables.'

'Oh, great. Now they are looking for someone to lead the project team for the launch of the mortgage business for them. This person could eventually become the business manager for mortgages.'

'OKAY.'

'Would something like this interest you?'

It sounded exciting. GE was a good name – a brand which was big or even bigger than NYB, and could be a good opportunity to fast-track his career. On the flip side, he had no reason to look outside NYB. However, if an opportunity had come knocking at his door, why say no? The only thing stopping him from looking outside thus far was his relationship with the iconic Aditya Bhatnagar, his own boss, Raj Mathur and a few other seniors at the bank. At his level, there weren't too may people who could boast of such big names in the industry as godfathers. They would take care of him if ever he needed any help. The comfort of their presence was overbearing. However, of late there had been rumours of Aditya moving overseas and Raj quitting the bank. Either he could chart his own course or follow them wherever they went. It might not be a bad idea to at least have a 'Plan B', i.e. to try and chart his own course.

'Sounds interesting . . .' A possible business manager's job. At this age, if he was able to swing it, it would be a great career move.

'Where will this job be based?' he continued, suddenly remembering that he had to keep his wife's career in mind too. Her job with SCB was Mumbai based. He didn't want to uproot her again. Hadn't he done that once?

'Delhi or Mumbai depending on the person they hire,' Sharmila added.

'Can I recommend something, Amit?' said Sharmila after a small pause. She continued without waiting for his response. 'Why don't you send me your CV? I will discuss the same with GE and come back to you.'

'Sure.'

The email ids were exchanged and the phone ended with Amit promising to send his CV that night.

'Why do you want to shift?' Chanda asked him when she saw him updating his CV that night.

'It will take me ages to become a business manager here.'

'How does that make a difference? Aren't you happy here?'

'Chanda, it will fast forward my career by a minimum of three years. And GE is not a bad company to work for.'

'But do you think you will be able to manage it if you get it? It's one thing getting something before time, it's completely different being able to manage it without the requisite experience. If you are not ready for it and still decide to take it up, you might be risking your career. Have you considered that you might screw it up big time and muck up the reputation that you have built up over the years? GE will find someone else to do the job, but you will not be able to find an alternate livelihood.'

'You doubt your husband's skills and ability, sweetheart.'

When Amit said this, Chanda couldn't argue with him. She let it be. That night Amit sent his CV to Sharmila Ganguly at Spenta Consultants. For the first time since he got out of campus, he had sent his CV to a recruitment consultant.

A few days later, Aditya ran into Amit in the banking hall. By then, Amit had moved up to be the branch manager of the Fort branch in Mumbai. A branch in which he had started his career as a relationship manager. Aditya had some free time on hand and had come down. A personal cheque was also to be deposited. Amit was in the hall seeing off a client when he bumped into Aditya. They spoke for a few minutes, with the branch performance dominating the discussion.

'How's Chanda?'

'She's fine Aditya. Chugging along at SCB. She has recently been promoted to the next level. She manages the phone banking set up for the entire western region for all products now.'

'Bastard, you didn't tell me. Looks like SCB loves her. She became a supervisor only two years back right?'

'Yes Aditya.' *He remembers this . . . wow! What a guy!* Amit couldn't help being impressed.

'The least you can do is buy me a drink in celebration.'

'Sure Aditya. Anytime.'

'That's like avoiding.'

'No Aditya. Anytime at your convenience.'

'How about tonight?'

'Tonight?'

'Why? Not possible? See I told you, you are a miserly bastard.'

'No no, Aditya, not at all. It's a deal. Tonight it is then!'

'Done.'

'Sure Aditya. You and Natasha, at Indigo Deli in Colaba. I will let Chanda know.'

'Okay. See ya!' Saying that, Aditya disappeared.

That night the four of them – Aditya, Natasha, Amit and Chanda met at Indigo Deli in Colaba. This was the special thing about Aditya. The guy had his shortcomings, but in terms of motivating people and inspiring them, there was no one like him. It's hard to imagine a country head going for a night out with a branch manager to celebrate his wife's success. Aditya was one of kind.

Natasha was looking ravishing in a pink dress. Over the years, she had transformed into a person with an elegant sense for aesthetics and believed in simplicity. The pink flowing dress was complemented by diamond studs and a solitary chain that she wore around her delicate and sensuous neck. She looked attractive. Despite the two children and so many years of marriage, the age didn't show.

Amit had booked a table for four and had specifically requested that they be given some privacy. The Deli owners had given them some room on the first floor where they only had three tables. Amit didn't want to be noticed by colleagues who might just drop in. He was concerned that his dinner with Aditya might become the topic of gossip and loose talk over the next few days if someone sees him there. They ordered some drinks – whisky for Aditya and Vodka for Amit. Natasha settled for some wine. Chanda was a teetotaller and ordered fresh lime soda for herself.

A few rounds of drinks later, Aditya looked at Chanda and asked, 'Why do you work for SCB?' He gave a purposeful pause after that. Almost as an afterthought he added, 'and not for NYB?'

Chanda didn't know what to say. She looked at Amit and then back at Aditya. Aditya had stumped her and left her perplexed.

'Aditya, I don't know.' Chanda stammered. 'SCB was the first job I got and . . . and . . . the fact is also that no one has asked me this earlier.'

'If there was an opportunity, would you?'

Chanda looked at Amit. He was smiling. It was Aditya's style. Invariably, he would put people in a spot by asking completely unexpected questions. Completely unpredictable. That was Aditya.

'Ya, surely. If there is a good opportunity. But why do you ask?'

'Why would you work for NYB?'

'It's a good organisation. Good people . . .' She was still thinking about politically correct things to say.

'If you think so, then why don't you tell this to this husband of yours. Tell him that GE does not deserve him. He will be better served working with NYB.'

When Amit heard this, he was shocked. The smile disappeared from his face in a jiffy. How the hell did Aditya know about GE? The only people, apart from his wife and himself, were the consultant and HR at GE.

'Ady . . . Aditya, I do . . . don't understand. Where did you hear this from? Not true at all.'

'Son, I am paid to keep a watch on all of you. That's my job. You folks are my key resources. If I can't keep a watch on you, then I am not doing my job. What say?' and then he turned his attention to Chanda. 'So what do you want to do?'

Chanda was equally stumped. She didn't expect Aditya to know about GE. If she sounded nervous, it would be a give away. She decided to play on.

'Aditya, I want to get into a product role. As a phone banking supervisor for the western region, I have had exposure to all products and have a reasonably good understanding of what consumers expect. I would definitely consider moving, if I get some kind of a product role. Possible?'

'If not, I will create one madam!' said Aditya in a drawling voice. 'We need people like you to take this organisation to the next level. Not people like your husband who doesn't realise what this organisation can do for him.' Amit didn't react. Whatever he said or did could be held against him. Aditya didn't raise this discussion again, and the dinner went off peacefully.

The dinner ended soon thereafter and both couples went their own ways. Aditya's car zipped through the near empty streets on Colaba enroute their Bandra Pali Hill residence. Natasha looked at Aditya. It was one of those few dinners where Aditya had not had too much to drink.

'Why did you ask Chanda to join you?'

'You will never understand this, Natasha. Amit is one of our key guys. He has just moved to head the largest branch in Mumbai for us. Below him I do not have the bandwidth to replace him. What do I do? I know he is interviewing with GE. If he goes, I know the business will suffer. I need some time to identify a replacement and put him there. If I give his wife a job with us, it raises his stakes here. He will think twice before quitting. Even if he leaves sixty-ninety days down the line, I really don't care. By that time I would have built adequate back up in the system. Giving his wife a job is only to hold him back. It will prick his conscience hard if he quits within days of us giving his wife a bigger job.'

'Aren't you mean, Aditya? The poor fellow thinks that you are helping him.'

'He is a good guy to have. Has a good future at NYB. I am only helping him. And in the process, helping myself. You won't understand Natasha. Leave this to me.'

That night, Chanda and Amit had a prolonged discussion on whether or not Chanda should be joining the bank. Whether it made sense or not? What are the positives of both of them working in the same bank? Oblivious of Aditya's self-centric intent, they trusted him completely. They were willing to place themselves in the hands of someone for whom they were just a means to achieve a number, a target, a goal. Anything else just didn't matter.

'What happens to the GE offer then?' asked Chanda.

'If Aditya gives you a good offer at NYB, I will drop GE.'

'What about the business manager role?'

'It's fine. I will wait for it. I realised today. It's better to work with someone who has your interest at heart, rather than a business manager designation with an organisation where you know no one.'

'I agree.'

And that was the end of their discussion. GE was dumped. Aditya had protected his turf.

2001
NYB Financial Services
Mumbai

New York International Bank carried all its lending business through an independent financial services arm – a company called NYB Financial Services (NFS). The latter was a large company with a network of over a hundred branches across the country. It was a subsidiary of NYB and was managed and run like an independent company, with a completely different management. It had its own CEO, its own board of directors, its own processes and its own set of resources. The only linkage the NFS management team in India had with the NYB management team was Aditya. Given that NFS was owned by NYB, Aditya had strategic oversight on the company. However, the day-to-day operations of the company were run completely independent of NYB.

The company had its head office in the busy Goregaon area of Mumbai. Spread over five floors, the impressive office had over four hundred people working in it.

10 a.m. in the morning. Gowri Shankar walked into the reception area of NFS. The guard stood up as if he was pricked from behind and gave him an energetic salute. He ignored the guard and briskly walked up to his second floor office. A smirk on his face, a swagger in his walk. This was clearly his fiefdom. He was the undisputed king there, and it was pretty evident.

He walked into his cabin, placed the laptop on the table, connected it to the LAN and powered it on. Just when he was about to start working, there was a knock on the cabin door. It was the pantry boy. The guard had informed the pantry about Gowri sir's arrival and the tea had been instantaneously dispatched.

'Aaja! Aaja!' Gowri looked at the pantry guy and waved him in. 'Thodi der kardi aaj,' said Gowri, implying that the tea had come in a bit late. The pantry boy looked up nervously, mumbled something and left the tea on Gowri's table before disappearing quickly. This was Gowri's style. Put the opposition under pressure, even if there is no need to. The tea had come within 120 seconds of him entering his room, despite which he had to comment on the delay.

He picked up his tea and walked across the adjacent cabins to the cabin of Manish Kakkar, the credit director of NFS. Manish was a close friend and confidante of Gowri. After fifteen minutes of gossip, which centred around condemnation of NYB, and glorification of NFS, Gowri headed back to his room, en route checking if there were others who subscribed to his view about NYB.

There was a background to this. Twelve months ago, NYB in India had made a strategic acquisition. In a coup of sorts they had acquired a Non-Banking Finance Company (NBFC) which they later christened as NYB Financial Services.

Gowri, Manish and others were a part of the acquired finance company. It was normal for employees of the acquired company to be apprehensive about the acquirers, who are normally looked upon as predators. Gowri and Manish amongst others carried a grudge against NYB for having acquired what they felt was 'their' company.

This was despite the fact that unlike other normal acquisitions, NYB had been very sensitive towards the employees of the NBFC. They had tried to ensure that people in NFS did not feel threatened or overawed by the presence of a number of people from NYB and had deputed very few people from the bank. This included the managing director to run the company. It was important to have the senior-most person at NFS as someone from NYB, since it aided the cultural integration of the two organisations. However, as far as day-to-day running of the show was concerned, NYB had largely left it to the local management of NFS.

Irrespective, the likes of Gowri were unhappy. They were used to running the organisation like a mom and pop show, like their own fiefdom. Suddenly a large organisation was forced onto them, and they had to follow laid out policies and procedures of NYB which had, to a large extent, curtailed their free run. This was not acceptable to them. Rules often come with fixed accountabilities and that was not something they liked.

As a consequence, Aditya's strategic oversight of the organisation was a sham. There was no reporting relationship between NFS and NYB on paper. The country statutory regulations required that the two organisations operate independently and NFS used this excuse to prevent any kind of interference from NYB. Such was the state of the politics between NFS and NYB that on the face the employees were very cordial to one another, but behind the scenes, it was a completely different story. Hari, the managing director of NFS, who was sent by NYB to oversee the integration, was too weak to take on the NFS coterie and soon, he too fell in line. Rather than take on the militant staff in NFS, he too joined them in the crusade against NYB.

Gowri was in one of those defiant, anti-NYB moods, when he got a call on his internal line. It was the receptionist.

'Yes Neelam?'

'There's a lady waiting to see you at the reception.'

'Does she have an appointment?' The call came to him because his secretary had not come in by then. In the normal course she would have left a printout of his schedule for the day on his table.

'Yes Gowri. She says she has an appointment and that it was lined up last evening.'

'What's her name?' A silent pause at this end, '. . . OKAY. She will have to wait for some time. Send her after about ten minutes.'

'Sure Gowri,' and the receptionist hung up. Gowri got busy with his emails.

'Knock knock!' his concentration was disturbed by someone at his cabin door. Through the glass, he could see a pretty young girl standing there holding a brown leather file in her hand. He looked up and nodded, asking her to come in. The girl was nervous and did not understand Gowri's nod. This made him get up, walk to the door and open it for her. 'I asked you to come in.'

'Thank you sir,' she said sheepishly.

Gowri, held the door open till the lady had crossed him and then stretched his neck, looked outside in the direction of his secretary, who had not come in by then. He looked towards Manish's secretary, who was normally quite punctual and shouted, 'Do chai bolna'. A second later, he looked at the lady seated in his room and asked her, 'Will you have some tea?' The demure thing didn't have a choice and just nodded her head.

Gowri came back and settled in his executive swivel chair.

'Aditya had called me yesterday. Spoke to me about you. He obviously thinks very highly about you.'

'He is just being kind sir.'

'I know. I know . . . he is very kind,' he said cheekily.

After about thirty minutes of sarcastic conversation, he finally asked her, 'So young lady, what kind of job would you like to do?'

'Anything which is challenging and gives me an opportunity to learn new skills.'

'Even a secretary's job is challenging.' When he saw that the comment was not appreciated, he softened. 'Just kidding. Give me five minutes. Just wait outside my room, I will call you in.'

When the girl had stepped outside, he picked up the phone and dialled a number. 'Come to my room. We have to hire someone.'

'Now?'

'Yes, now. Please come quickly Sunil. I have lots of other stuff to catch up on.'

He kept down the phone and dialled another number, '*Kakke yaar, yahaan aana*'. Kakke was what Manish Kakkar was called in NFS.

Kakke and Sunil (the head of HR) were in Gowri's room in five minutes.

'*Yaar, yeh bank walon ne toh is company ko dharamshala samajh rakha hai,*' NYB was referred to as 'The bank' in NFS circles. Gowri was implying that the people from NYB were under the impression that NFS was like a free guesthouse, where they could park anyone they wanted to. He was irritated that the NYBankers had sent someone to him to hire and he did not have a choice.

'Sunil, please hire her and give her a job.' After a pause he added, 'Any job, else that bastard Aditya will be after my life.'

After another short bitching session about the bank, Sunil came out of the room. He looked around the office and called out loudly. 'Chanda! Is Chanda here?'

Chanda was sitting on a single-seater sofa on the other side of the hall. Hearing her name being called out, she stood up and started walking towards Sunil. 'Yes sir, I am Chanda.'

'Great. Chanda, come with me.' Chanda quietly followed him to his office.

By the end of the day, Chanda was hired by NYB Financial Services as a product executive in the personal loans department and had to report to Gowri. A forty percent hike in salary demonstrated how low her salary in the previous organisation was.

That night, Amit called up Aditya to thank him for his help in getting Chanda a job with NYB Financial Services.

'What's your plan?' Aditya asked him.

'Plan?'

'About GE . . . are you planning to join them? I believe they have made you an offer.'

'Aditya . . . I . . .'

'Listen buddy. Don't bullshit me. I know you have got an offer from GE. If you are going I need to know.'

And without waiting for him to respond, he added, 'Give me three to six months. You are important to me. Let me manage your career. I will take care of you.'

'Aditya, it's a business manager's role.' Finally, Amit accepted that he was in discussions with GE.

'I will give you a business manager's job in six to twelve months. Trust me. In this growth phase we need good people like you. And what's twelve months in a lifetime?'

Natasha was in the room when Aditya was talking to Amit. She just shook her head and walked out of the room. She knew that Aditya was conning one more guy.

That night, Aditya had sealed two deals. He had managed to keep Amit from leaving NYB, thereby protected his own business numbers, and he had also bought Amit's loyalty for life. The exit barriers for Amit had been raised.

2001/2002
NYB Financial Services, Mumbai

Gowri was the undisputed king of NFS. Going from strength to strength in the company, he had become a power centre which even NYB couldn't ignore.

In fact, he had played his cards brilliantly. In 1999-2000 when NYB acquired the NBFC, there was a general feeling of insecurity in the company. They had just been acquired and people feared for their jobs, and their careers. Like all takeovers, this one too was accompanied by the fear that the bank would come in and make their jobs redundant, by bringing in their own people, who in turn would bring in their own teams.

In such a volatile situation, Gowri was the most outspoken. He was the politician who emerged as the rallying point for the NBFC team. The only one in the NFS senior management who was quite vociferous in his dislike for the bank and for the people from the bank. These emotions came naturally to him because he was a part of the NBFC from the day it had been formed. Though it was rumoured that his dislike for the bank also stemmed from the fact that at some point in time, he had been interviewed by NYB but his application had been turned down. This was more than enough for him to be caustic towards NYB and NYBankers. Though he would never accept it, he secretly harnessed dreams of working in a multinational bank like NYB.

Gowri's influence ran deep. There were around eight hundred people working in over hundred branches of the NBFC, many of them handpicked by Gowri. All of them who were involved in the business of giving out loans to the lower strata of society, loosely referred to as the subprime loans, and owed their allegiance to Gowri.

The business model of the NBFC was simple and straightforward. They had set up branches in residential areas, dominated by the lower middle class segments. Customers would be encouraged to just walk into the branch to avail loans. From cash loans and loans for buying consumer durables or two wheelers to mortgage loans for buying houses and cash loans against the collateral of property, the company offered every variety.

Loan approving officers (also known as credit officers) would be seated in these branches. They would meet the customer, understand his needs and based on his affordability, approve or decline a loan. The entire branch was managed by a branch manager.

In a branch, the buck stopped at the branch manager, who was responsible for sales, i.e. responsible for meeting branch targets for loan disbursals. He was accountable for approving loans and in case of a customer default, reaching out to the customer and collecting money from him was also his responsibility.

The branch manager reported to a regional manager, who eventually reported to a branch network head, who in turn was answerable to Gowri. The branch managers by vitue of this chain of command took instructions from no one but Gowri. Such was Gowri's control over the organisation.

Gowri's influence ran deep. The master politician, had his own network of informants and did not believe in relying only on his hierarchical control chain for information. The man had his methods. He had the knack to reach way down into the organisation, at times even down to the last level in the command chain. The network of informal 'informants' would feed back information about all the little but important details of whatever was going on in the company. Anything happening without his knowledge or consent would reach him in a matter of minutes. To him, loyalty and alignment mattered the most. He would dole out favours to anyone who was aligned to him – both visibly and in thought process. This also meant better increments, higher bonuses and even quicker promotions for those who towed his line.

Why wouldn't guys at the grass root fall for such benefits? Gowri exploited this weakness in the system and the people. Such was his influence that everything including HR, credit and even financial control was under his sphere of control.

With that kind of power, it was but natural for anyone to resist the advances of an MNC bank. NYB taking charge would mean that all the adhocism in the running of the company would have to go. It could no longer be run as a small time mom and pop show. Everything would have to be accounted for and the central focus of power which rested with him till now was under a big time threat. The free run had to end. The company had to be now run in a manner which was explainable to compliance, human resources teams of NYB and everything was subject to an audit as per NYB policies, which were a lot more stringent as compared to NFS.

While Gowri's control was not something which could be called a compromise of integrity, it was surely not a transparent exercise of power either.

Chanda joined NFS in this background. She had no idea what she was getting into. She joined them in August of 2001 as a product executive in their personal loans department.

The first few days for Chanda were eventless.

'Go read this and come,' Gowri had said after giving her some product and process manuals to read. The stuff was enough to keep her busy for the next three days. She took those documents and just when she was ready to scoot to the safe realms of the desk allotted to her, Gowri called her back. 'And Chanda, if you want to clarify any doubts about anything, just walk up to Sangeeta. Chanda remembered her. She was introduced to her some time back by HR as the head of the branch network for western India.

As Chanda left Gowri's cabin, she smiled at his secretary, who didn't bother to respond. Though that was not what she expected, she just shrugged her shoulders and walked towards her cubicle. The secretary immediately dialled a number and picked up the phone, taking it off the speaker phone.

'She's left,' she whispered into the phone, and hung up.

Within seconds, Sangeeta was up outside Gowri's room. As usual, the colours of her clothes were similar to Gowri's. As soon as she entered the area outside Gowri's Cabin, walking awkwardly in her two-inch long spikes . . . err . . . stilettos, she took off her NFS ID card from around her neck and simultaneously pulled out the ID card which had the name of the old company (the name of the company prior to being acquired by NYB and prior to it being rechristened NFS) and hung it around the shoulder. Using the old ID cards was prohibited. Everyone was formally told to use the new ID card, with the NFS branding and logo. Sangeeta too used the new ID card at all times, unless she was with Gowri. She knew that Gowri was very emotional about it. In fact, Gowri had hung his old ID card along with a copy of his old visiting card on the soft board next to his table.

Gowri's secretary saw it and smiled. Sangeeta winked at her, 'Gowri will like it this way . . . thanks for calling me after that bitch left.' And she made her way into Gowri's room.

'Gowri, why have you hired a product manager?' This was basically a very loud echo of her insecurity.

'What do I do? These bankers want to come everywhere. Our company is a dharamshala. Aditya called up and asked me to hire her. Her husband is one of Aditya's *pappus*.'

'You should have refused to hire her.'

'Don't worry. We will keep her here for some time. She will feel so frustrated that she will quit on her own. For how long can she stand up to us? Ha ha!' and then both started guffawing. The plotting game had already begun. Chanda had no clue what she was up against.

'I can see you are still using the old ID card.' Sangeeta's efforts bore fruit when Gowri asked her this question.

'Ya Gowri. Don't all of us miss our old company? These NYBankers have come in and screwed our company. One day you should start a company and all of us will join you. Together we will create a new company . . . ' she paused for effect and then added in a dramatically serious tone, 'under your leadership, Gowri.'

Gowri's chest swelled a few inches. 'Yes, of course. We must. We must. We can't continue to serve these bastards for long,' and the bitching continued.

Having an overwhelming personality like Gowri, had its own share of effects. It naturally led to a number of clones rising up in the organisation. Sangeeta was the best example. She aped him in every manner. She was a female Gowri and she was also one of Gowri's closest confidantes.

'How was your day?' Amit asked Chanda, that night as he walked in and dumped the keys of his Ford Ikon on the side rack. Last year, he had sold his Maruti 800 and bought this sexy black Ford Ikon. Doesn't your vehicle have to keep pace with your career's progression?

'You first settle down. Take your laptop off your shoulder. I will tell you.'

'Okay, I am waiting,' and he walked off to change into his track pants and the oldest most comfortable T-shirt he ever owned. It's funny but true – you just can't get rid of some T-shirts even if they cross all limits of social embarrassment if displayed in public! They are just so damn comfortable! Ten minutes later, he joined his wife in the kitchen, where she was stirring up some fresh veggies for dinner.

'Was just about OKAY,' said Chanda as if speaking to the frying pan.'

'Why?'

'No. It's just that I thought the place was too cold. Maybe after years at SCB, joining this place was quite a change. Probably I am reading too much into it.'

They settled down for dinner and the discussions moved away from NFS to other routine stuff. 'Let's go out for coffee,' Amit proposed, to which Chanda readily agreed.

'What time do you have to leave tomorrow?' asked Amit as Chanda was locking the door.

'Have to be there by 9 a.m. That's what the letter says.'

They got into the car and made their way to the latest Barista – a new coffee bar that had opened up close to their house in Bandra.

'Arre, I forgot to tell you. Vikram might be moving.' Vikram Oberoi was the head of branch banking and Amit's boss. He too was very close to Aditya and in fact, both Aditya and Vikram had played a role in retaining Amit when he had expressed a desire to move to GE.

'Where to?'

'Don't know?'

'He is the one who along with Aditya prevented you from moving to GE.'

'I know.'

'And what about the promise to make you a business manager?'

'Don't know. I will ask him when I see him. Anyway it was Aditya's commitment, not Vikram's.'

'Ya, but again, he too played a part in retaining you.'

And the discussion moved on. They returned quite late at night and quickly got into bed. They had to leave early the next day.

Chanda was in office bang on time. She was the first to get in. Only the cleaners were shuffling about doing their daily routine of cleaning desks and watering the ornamental plants.

Manish Kakkar was the next to come in. He normally came in early. When he saw Chanda at her desk, he walked up to her and wished her. In a sense, it was Chanda's first week in office and Manish wanted to welcome her into NFS. By nature, Manish was a nice guy. So taken in by Gowri was he that he preferred to live in his shadows rather than take him head on. From his perspective, conflicts were avoidable. Hence, he tended to be seen as a guy who was very much in Gowri's control.

A few souls walked in next. The office started filling in only by around 9.45 a.m. And then, the king walked in. Gowri came in around 10 everyday. As he walked towards his office, he saw Chanda, with her head buried in reading the manuals. His secretary was around. The tea came within two minutes. Everything was going on as per the norm. And then, he did something which he normally wouldn't do. He opened his cabin door, and told his secretary, 'Call Chanda.'

The secretary did as was asked and Chanda was at his door step in the next two minutes.

Gowri didn't speak but just gestured with his two fingers without looking up when he heard a knock on his cabin door.

Chanda walked in. Gowri didn't look up. He again gestured with his two fingers asking her to sit down. His eyes focused on the laptop screen. After about five minutes he looked up at Chanda. 'Hi.'

'Good morning sir.'

'Morning.' No smile on his face yet.

'Have you finished reading the manuals I gave you?'

'Not yet, sir. I have read through one of them. There are two more to go through.'

'When I was your age sweetheart, I would stay up all night to read whatever I had to.' Five hundred pages of manuals in one day was a next to impossible task and he expected her to have read the entire set? It was not fair. He was trying to be tough on her. Chanda was taken aback by this. She did not expect this on the first day.

'If you haven't read it, we cannot have a meaningful discussion. Have you had an opportunity to sit with Sangeeta to understand the process flows?'

'No sir.'

'Young lady, this is not a bank. Definitely not NYB. Here, if I tell you to do something, I expect it to be done.'

'Sure sir. I will do it today,' said Chanda as she got up to leave. She was nearly in tears.

'Sit down. I am not through yet.'

'What does your husband do at NYB?'

'He is the branch manager of Mumbai Fort Branch – the largest branch for NYB in the country.' Gowri had consciously avoided asking her about her family when she had met him for an interview earlier.

'Happy with his job?' Having put her on the defensive, Gowri was generally trying to strike up a conversation.

'Ya, he is. But . . .'

'But what?'

'He has been worried over the last couple of days.'

'Why?'

'Vikram is moving.'

'Who Vikram? Vikram Oberoi?' Chanda just nodded in response.

'Why? Where?'

'Apparently, he is moving to ING Vysya as the retail head.'

'So he is moving out of the bank?' After a brief period of silence, 'That's interesting.'

'Who is taking his job?'

'Don't know. That's why he is worried. Wondering who would come in his place?'

Gowri leaned back in his chair, his head extended and resting on the top end of the chair. He stretched back, even as his hands moved up and his palms engulfed his face. He seemed to be thinking about something. After a few seconds of silence, he got back to his normal posture and looked at Chanda. Clearly, he was thinking of something else, 'Is this public knowledge? I haven't heard of this earlier.'

'No. Vikram mentioned this to Amit as he is very close to him. He plans to formally tell everyone else the next Monday.' Monday was four days away.

'Okay. Thanks. Read these manuals and let's chat again tomorrow. Don't kill yourself. If you can't finish it today, it's fine. We are not in any tearing hurry are we?' and he smiled at her, probably for the first time, as he waved her away from his room. Chanda couldn't help being surprised at this sudden change of heart.

Gowri's fingers couldn't wait for her to leave the room, before they picked up the telephone and dialled a number. After a short ring, it was picked up. 'Kakke, thoda aana mere kamre mein.' It was Manish Kakkar at the other end. He was dying to share the news with someone else. Manish Kakkar's room was two cabins away, but Gowri always called him to his room, rather than walking across. It kind of set the protocol right for other employees. They would infer on seeing Kakkar in Gowri's room that he was probably the junior of the two guys – though this was far from the truth. He was just the less complicated and more amenable of the two.

'Yaar, bade kaam ki cheez hai yeh!'

'Kaun?'

'Chanda! She is damn useful man.'

Seeing a blank look on Kakkar's face, he continued, 'She knows everything that is going on in the bank. Well connected. Good that we hired her. She can now give us inside information.'

'Why? What did she tell you that got you so excited?' Kakkar was too smart and quick to realise what would have happened.

'Apparently, Vikram Oberoi is quitting.' Gowri was excited. Kakkar didn't know Vikram and hence couldn't understand why Gowri was jumping around at this piece of information.

'So?' He was wondering how it impacted Gowri.

'Idiot! Vikram Oberoi is the head of branch banking at NYB. His job is up for grabs.' The look on Kakkar's face didn't change. 'Why can't they give me that job?'

'Aaah . . . but they will not give it to you.' The dismissive tone in Kakkar's voice was evident.

'And why would that be?'

'You are too junior. They would be looking at someone who understands that business.'

'No harm in trying, my friend.'

Gowri was extremely ambitious, wanting to quickly rise to heights unseen of and unheard of in one's career. He could go to any extent to ensure that his aspirations fructified. Today, in Chanda, he found someone who could give him the fodder needed for his competitiveness. She could give him information of what was going on in the bank, and based on that, he could position himself accordingly.

'But I thought you hated NYB. You could not stand NYBankers. What has changed now?' Kakkar couldn't resist a swipe at Gowri.

'Arre yaar, they need people like you and me to go there and help them change into an organisation that we want them to be. The problem is that today they are not like us. We can help them become like what we were before they acquired us. What say?'

The public façade that Gowri put up was one that portrayed him as someone who hated the bank. People from the bank were not welcome into NFS. And if someone did come in, Gowri would make life miserable for them. He was GOD in NFS and he wanted to remain that way. However, heart of hearts, he harnessed dreams of working in a larger business in a larger organisation. The bank provided him with that platform. A move to the bank as a business manager could do wonders for his career and he knew that. However, this public pretence and animosity towards NYB employees was necessary to keep his status intact in the finance company.

The tit-bit that Chanda had inadvertently dropped in front of Gowri, had given her an unexpected break. It had shattered the outcaste image that had been given to her, thanks to her linkage with the bank.

'Why the hell did you tell him about Vikram's move?' Amit was furious when he heard about this at dinner.

'Don't know. It just came out. And after that I couldn't retract.' And then she added. 'Do you think Vikram will get upset?'

'No. But as long as your boss doesn't tell everyone that he heard it from you, it should not be an issue.'

'But you know what? After he heard this, he softened up towards me. He was very nice to me after I told him this.' Chanda had noticed his changed approach.

'He is not an idiot you see,' said Amit as he got up to wash his hands. Chanda didn't understand. Amit, however, could see through. He had heard enough stories about Gowri. They were a part of NYB folklore now. Chanda hadn't heard much of him as she had come from outside. She was just about to become one of the characters in folklore.

2002
NYB FS, Mumbai.
The relationship changes

The coming Tuesday was Gowri's son's birthday – time for Gowri's entire team to join together in the celebration. Gowri's wife had organised a birthday party at Khar Gymkhana. Chanda was invited too.

'Knock, knock,' Gowri's morning mail-responding ritual was interrupted by a knock on his cabin door. He looked up and then broke into a big smile. The entire Mumbai sales team was standing at his door. Leading them was a horrifically dressed Sangeeta. Clad in a long skirt, which did precious little to hide her rapidly expanding waistline and an old kurta, she looked straight out of the Cinderella story. Only the part that she would be playing was that of the witch!

'Happy birthday Arjun!' she screamed or rather squeaked in excitement and the entire Mumbai team followed in unison. Chorus of 'Happy Birthday Arjun' echoed in the air. Arjun was Gowri's son.

'What crap?' would have been anyone else's reaction. Not Gowri. He believed in being obsequious and loved whenever someone indulged in any sycophantic behaviour. His smile only got wider as he got up and walked to the door and accepted the huge bouquet of flowers that the team had carried.

Chanda was sitting on the lower floor. It was a reasonably small office and hence tremors from any commotion in one part were clearly felt in her space. She was wondering what was going on and decided to go and check for herself.

On Gowri's second floor office, Sangeeta had organised this show to appeal to Gowri's self-praising tendencies.

'Back to work, team,' she announced the moment the chorus had died down. Almost as if they were waiting for her instruction, the team disappeared.

'Thanks Sangeeta. Come, come. Come on in,' Gowri offered.

'What time are you leaving today Gowri?' and almost as an afterthought added, 'Why did you come? You should have taken an off today. '

'It's work Sango. Has to get done, right?'

'What commitment Gowri! If only my team had half the commitment as you, we could have doubled our business last year itself.'

'I know Sango. But you more than make up for them.'

'I don't know Gowri, what ails this new generation. They are not prepared to work at all. Look at this woman Chanda.'

'What about her?'

'Hardly works Gowri. Two days into her job and all she does is gossip on the phone. Doesn't interact with anyone. Very snooty she is.'

'Hmm . . .' Gowri didn't react.

'Ask her how much of the reading she has finished?'

'Yes I will.' Sango was surprised. This was not the way Gowri normally responded. Such conversations would normally elicit violent reactions from him. Not this time. 'Maybe he is distracted in thinking of Arjun's birthday,' thought Sangeeta.

Another knock on the door disturbed the two of them and they looked up.

'Hi Chanda! Come in,' said Gowri with a big smile.

'I heard all the commotion and decided to check for myself, what the issue was. On the way, these guys told me and I suddenly remembered. I was wondering why they were wishing you. They should be wishing your son, right Gowri?'

'Ha ha! That's Sango for you. She always overdoes these things. What say Sango?'

'Good joke Gowri,' Sango retorted with a constipated smile.

'Chanda, give me a minute. Sango, is there anything else we need to discuss?'

'Nothing major Gowri. Just wanted to speak with you on the payout structure for our direct sales agents (DSAs). I had mentioned this to you last week itself. Standard Chartered Bank has hiked their commission payout and so our DSAs are leaving us to join them. Yesterday alone, I got three calls from our DSAs in Ahmedabad.'

Direct sales agents were agencies engaged by various banks and finance companies for acting as conduits between them and the customers. They help find customers, sell the loan to them and bring them to the finance company. They are normally compensated on the basis of the quantum of business they help the bank or finance company to generate.

'OKAY. We will talk about it later. I will ask my secretary to call you.' He looked at Chanda and added, 'Come, sit Chanda.'

Boom! Boom! This reaction from Gowri shocked Sango. She was normally the centre of attraction. If Sangeeta walked in, Gowri would cut short all other discussions and speak with her. Not the other way around. Today he had cut short his discussion with her to humour someone else. This was unprecedented in the recent past . . . and that too for a NYBanker's wife.

'Okay Gowri.' She felt quite troubled uttering those two words, before she walked off. The glare that she gave Chanda even as she walked away was not lost on her. 'Will you call me before you leave for the party? I haven't brought my car. I will come with you.' Gowri didn't even respond to the last line. Probably he was not even listening to what she was saying.

The discussion between Gowri and Chanda lasted fifteen minutes. Gowri did not take any calls in that period and was all ears. As the last time, this time too, it ended with – 'What's happening at NYB?'

After another five minutes of casual conversation, Chanda got up to leave. Her right hand pushed the glass cabin door, swung it towards the secretary's chair and stopped. She turned back and asked, 'Gowri, what was the payout bit that Sango was referring to?'

'Oh that. Good you reminded me. She wants to increase the DSA payouts. She is facing a challenge in retaining her good sales guys. Actually, why don't you look at it? Review it and come back to me for approval if you think it is worth it.'

'Sure Gowri,' and she walked off.

That afternoon, Sangeeta received a mail from Chanda. A short, curt, three line message.

Dear Sangeeta,

I believe you wish to increase the payouts for the DSAs on account of competition hiking their payouts. Can you please send them to me? Gowri has asked me to review it before it goes to him.

Regards,
Chanda

A CC was marked to Gowri too.

'What the hell?' muttered Sango. 'Bitch!' she cursed under her breath as she completed reading the message. She instinctively picked up the intercom to call Gowri. He had never done anything like this before, especially when it concerned Sango. After a moment's thought, she kept the phone down. *I will ask him, when I meet him. Anyway today is his son's birthday. Why give him stress?*

The birthday party at Khar Gymkhana was at 4.30 p.m. Gowri's wife, Amrita, had organised it with little or no help from Gowri. Though Gowri was a very devoted husband and valued his family, for him, his career was overbearing. It had to get first priority. Even though he was of high moral values and no one could doubt his character, he often compromised on his family at the altar of his career. The intensity of his professional focus could be gauged from the fact that this was the first birthday party of his son that he was attending. He would often make it a point to travel on work on his marriage anniversary just to demonstrate to everyone else that such was his commitment. Amrita often complained; however, she knew that her husband was an honest man. She also knew about her husband's fondness for Sango, but trusted him and was confident that Gowri knew where to draw the line. She knew it and it actually was, only a platonic relationship.

Gowri was about to leave. Sango was at his door, waiting to accompany him to the Gymkhana, which was a thirty-minute drive from office. The phone rang. 'Suzanna, take the call and say that I have stepped out of office.' And he started walking out with Sango. Suzanna was his secretary. Suzanna pressed a button on her instrument and pulled the call from Gowri's line to her extension.

'Oye Gowri. Phone lele.' It was Kakkar, who had stepped out of his room and was now asking Gowri to take the call. 'It's Aditya, I have told him that you are in your cabin.'

Gowri turned to Sango. 'You go ahead Sango. I will finish this and come,' and he walked back to his room. 'Transfer,' he told Suzanna as he walked back.

The call lasted twenty minutes. He was not the kind who would tell Aditya that he had to go to a birthday party and hang up. When the phone was placed back on the cradle, there was no one around him. One look at his watch told him that he was terribly late for the party, and he rushed out, picking his keys on the way. The entire mezzanine floor was empty. Everyone had left for the birthday party. 'The host is late,' he thought as he rushed. And then he suddenly stopped.

'What are you doing here?' he asked the solitary soul there. 'Are you not coming?'

'By the time I could ask someone to take me, everyone had left.' Chanda was very apologetic. 'I did not want to go alone, so I dropped out. I didn't know that you had not left.'

'Come, come. Pack up. You can come with me.' And in two minutes they were out of the building. They picked up Gowri's car from the parking lot and zipped towards Khar Gymkhana.

Fifteen minutes into their drive, Gowri's mobile beeped. Someone was trying to get in touch with him. 'Chanda, can you see who it is?' said Gowri, without taking his eyes off the road. He was driving like a man possessed and didn't want to be distracted.

'Hello?'

'Hello. Who is this? Chanda? What are you doing with Gowri's phone? Oh . . . where are you?' the rapid fire sequence of questions irritated Chanda.

'We are driving. Enroute to the party, Sango.'

'Ask her to tell Amrita that we will be there in ten minutes max,' Gowri prompted, without taking his eyes off the road.

'Gowri wants you to inform Amrita that we will be there in ten minutes.'

'You guys are on your way?' Sango was surprised. 'When did you leave?'

'About ten minutes ago. Why?'

'I was waiting for Gowri in office.'

'Oh. Okay. Anyway, we have left. Why don't you leave and come now. It's getting late,' and she hung up.

'Poor thing. She was waiting for you in office,' she said, looking at Gowri.

'It's fine. She knows the way. She will come,' Gowri was nonchalant. He was in too much of a hurry to really get unduly hassled.

The party was a tame affair for all of them. Imagine the entire corporate descending for an eight-year-old's birthday party. Arjun's birthday party had more of his dad's subordinates than his own friends. Sango landed late and kept glaring at Chanda all along. She couldn't have expressed her irritation to Gowri. Even if she could, she wouldn't have. The mail earlier in the day and now the faux pas pissed off Sango no end.

'Why do you want me to show the new payout structure for DSAs to Chanda?' she asked him the next day as soon as Gowri came to work.

'Kya problem hai? I have to give her some work. Otherwise, we will be giving her a donation, not salary. Is there a problem?' said Gowri grinning from ear to ear. Sango's insecurity was apparent to him, and he wanted to keep her humoured too. There was enormous value in her being aligned to him. That said, he was genuinely fond of her.

Later in the day, a reassured Sango sent the document proposing a change in the DSA commission payout structure to Chanda. NFS was paying their DSAs five percent of the loan value for every loan that they brought in. Sango was now proposing that this be increased by two percent. For every one lakh of loan, she was proposing a payout of 7,000 rupees as against a payout of 5,000 rupees earlier. The logic being offered for the rejig of the payout structure was that competition banks, the likes of SCB, etc., had increased their payout which was impacting the sales channels of NFS. As per the justification note submitted by Sango, her DSAs were leaving and joining competition.

Chanda read the note on her way back home. She knew what had to be done.

Punctual by nature, she was in by 8.45 a.m. the next day. She was the first one in. Getting down to work on her computer, she cleared whatever little backlog that was there by ten, post which she stepped out to the pantry to pick up a cup of coffee. Hardly had she got back to her workstation, when her intercom beeped.

'What the hell is this?'

'Please introduce yourself?' Chanda was peeved at the tone of the person at the other end of the phone.

'I said what the hell is this, Chanda? Who the hell are you to send me such a mail?' Aah, now she knew. It was Sangeeta. As usual she had come in late and on logging into her mailbox had seen Chanda's response to her commission payout increase request.

Earlier in the morning, Chanda had sent out a detailed response to Sangeeta's request for a review of incentive payout:

> Dear Sangeeta,
>
> I have reviewed the proposed commission payout grid for DSAs.I have also spoken to few of the sales managers that I personally know in competition and have the following comments:
>
> 1. Our current payout to DSAs is higher than what competing organisations pay them for loan originations.
> 2. Competitors feel that our DSAs are highly paid and therefore, have apparently stopped poaching our DSAs. They feel that our DSAs are too expensive to deal with.
>
> In view of this, I would like to request you to provide me with the names of the DSAs who have moved to competition and the impact that this has created on business. I will review the payout grid once you provide these details and then revert. Till then, I am putting this request in abeyance.
>
> Gowri, I will revert to you on this once I have more details as requested, from Sangeeta.
>
> Regards,
> Chanda

Sangeeta had seen this note in the morning and was furious. In that agitated state of mind, she called up Chanda.

'Is there something wrong in my mail?' Chanda said innocently. It would be incorrect to say that this call was completely unexpected.

'Nobody has declined any approval requests of mine. Do you understand that?'

'Someone just did sweetheart.' Chanda was not the one to give up. Mentally, she was very strong.

'I don't know why they even hired someone like you, who doesn't even understand the business. Why don't you just go and handle the call centre, bitch?'

This infuriated Chanda but she kept her cool and added, 'Sangeeta, I will respond calmly to your comments. I am not paid to take this shit from you. If you think there is anything wrong in my message, please take it up with Gowri. He asked me to give my views and I have done that. I am hanging up.' And she kept the phone down. 'What the hell! How dare she speak like that?' she muttered to herself. She was shivering with anger. No one had spoken to her in that tone ever. The phone rang again. She picked it up. 'Hi Chanda.' It was the same voice. 'YA?' She was angry and her tone left no stones unturned in making the other person know that.

'Cool down Chanda. I was just getting irritated. Come let's catch up on a cup of coffee.'

'No thanks.'

'I am sorry madam. Smile now. I am coming down.' And Sangeeta hung up. She came down to Chanda's desk and the two of them went out for a cup of coffee.

This was not something Sango would have normally done, but the problem was that everything that Chanda had said in her mail was true. If she would have carried forward the fight to Gowri, it would unnecessarily bring these uncomfortable issues like sales force management, their productivity, their payouts and related issues to the fore and might affect Gowri's perception of her. Hence, she wanted to quickly kill the discussion. For her, Gowri's impression of her was sacred. She couldn't afford to let Chanda's tirade dent that impression.

That was the last either of them heard of the incentive discussion. It, however, had one impact. Sangeeta realised that Chanda was no pushover and she had to be watchful of her.

'Is something wrong?' Mona asked Chanda, one evening, a few weeks later. She was a part of Chanda's team at SCB before she quit and joined NYB. Now she was a sales manager in the western team, reporting to Sangeeta.

'Why?'

'Today in our team meeting, Sangeeta told us not to pass on any information to you directly. Anything that goes to you has to be routed through her. She didn't say why.'

'Follow instructions,' said Chanda, as she walked away from the coffee vending machine towards her desk. She, for once, considered mentioning this to Gowri, but dropped the idea. Gowri's relationship with Sangeeta was too strong for her to compete against. A strong voice echoed in her head – 'Pick your battles'. She had heard Aditya mention that to Amit once.

On the work front, things only improved for her. Gowri started giving her a fair bit of importance. For him, she was the link into the bank. She was the reliable 'informant' who could dish out all the juicy gossip that did the rounds in the bank – something that Gowri craved for all the time. He involved her in sales, product management, marketing, process management and everything in which she could contribute even in the tiniest of ways. In a nutshell, he kept her humoured and happy, though it came at the cost of Sangeeta's peace of mind. But that was the real Gowri. Outside home, human relationships and emotions didn't matter. Everyone was to be used. Be it Chanda or Sangeeta.

Along the way, Vikram Oberoi resigned. His intention to resign had brought along winds of change for Chanda's fortune at NFS. However, he was retained by Aditya and hence, his position did not come up for grabs, laying to rest Gowri's plans to pitch for that job.

Amit kept hassling Aditya for the promised business manager job, which was taking its own sweet time in coming. Whether opportunities didn't exist or whether Aditya didn't swing them for him, he couldn't tell.

In the midst of all this, however, Aditya got promoted to become the CEO of New York International Bank. As compared to being the head of retail banking, where he served for much longer than what anyone thought he would, he now wielded much more power over a wider canvas. There could have been no better news for Amit.

20 December 2007
Bandra Police Station
Mumbai

*N*aik let out a deep sigh as he moved away his hand from Amit's shoulder and sat down on the wooden plank next to him. Amit's eyes followed him in earnest. It was as if they were pleading. Their helplessness was evident. The eyebrows shrunk around them as if they were holding the weight of the entire face and preventing it from falling apart. The folds on his forehead looked like the cracks in the dry lands of remote Thar Desert. Chanda's hand was on his knee. She could feel it shivering in anxiety. Worry was corroding her from within, but she had to keep a facade of courage, else Amit would have broken down. She had never seen him so stressed.

The anxiousness was not because he was sitting in the police station. It was because he did not know why he was there. Naik had not told him about it.

'I am heading back to office. I will get the CEO to speak to the state home minister. We need to get someone at that level involved in this.'

'Why isn't anyone telling me what happened?'

'It's quite murky Amit. It's unfortunate that you have been brought into this. But it is not your doing.'

'What is that damn "IT"?' Amit was screaming now. Blood-shot eyes and veins throbbing around his temples made it evident that he was very close to losing his mental balance. Hours had passed since he came to the police station, and no one had yet told him what the issue was.

'The dead guy is haunting us Amit.'

'Who? . . . The same guy?'

'Even his family is dead. You know that.'

'Oh shit! This is exactly what I was fearing. Now what?'

'His father has filed a case in which he has also named you. This has the blessings of that state's chief minister.'

'Who is Jai Shankar Ram? The warrant mentioned someone by this name as the complainant.'

'He is the father.'

'What are the charges?'

'Abetment to suicide.'

Amit's hand went up and clutched his forehead. 'Oh my God! But what have I done? I don't even know him. I haven't even met him. How can I abet a suicide? Shit man! This is ridiculous! What will happen now? Please do something. Get me out of this.' And he looked at Chanda, sitting next to him. She looked worried sick. 'This could be a bad one,' he told her. It was becoming unmanageable.

'I will try and move a petition today. I don't want to give you unrealistic commitments. Highly unlikely for us to get you out of this place today. We are being drawn into a political quagmire and you know as well as I do that THAT is not good news.'

'What the hell, Naik? I am a senior vice president in the New York International banking group. No one can treat me like this. I can't be held responsible for doing what the organisation expects me to do.' After screaming at the top of his voice, he realised what he had done. Everyone in the large hall was looking at him. Being the centre of attraction and that too in a place of ill-repute wasn't a particularly exciting proposition. Holding his head with both hands as if it would fall off if he won't, a sudden silence followed as he sank back in his seat. His back arched over and his head came to rest between his knees, his palms still clutching his face.

He looked up again. First at Naik, then at Chanda. And then towards his right, where beyond the pillars, and rows of tables with pot bellied constables sitting behind them, he could see numerous semi-rusted rods of steel. Behind those were faces – extremely intimidating, unshaven and rowdy-like. And then he saw a face, which looked like his own – a shrunken face, an inch of beard on it, unwashed with long dirty hair untidily flowing all over his face. He was terror-stricken at the thought of him behind those very bars. Thankfully, he was shaken back to reality. Rakesh Srivastav was standing by his side. Hand on his shoulder. 'Let's go,' he said.

Amit got up from the bench, Chanda too followed. He looked towards Naik. 'I will come back Amit. Have patience. I will find a way out of this.' Amit just looked at him without saying anything.

'I will be back . . . for sure,' whispered Naik or so it sounded to Amit, as the prison door opened and he was shoved in. Thankfully, he got an empty cell. There was no one else there.

He turned around and looked at Chanda as she followed Naik out of the police station. There was no one with him. He was all alone. Why did this happen? Why was God doing this to him?

January 2003
NYB
Mumbai

Aditya had just returned from an international strategy conference where all the countries presented their five-year strategic plan. It was a forum where potential opportunities were discussed and investments identified.

The presentation by the India team had not gone off well. Aditya was pulled up by the board for the slow integration of NFS into mainstream NYB and also the lacklustre pace of growth for the NBFC in India. World over, sub-prime lending was growing big, and everyone was looking at NFS to grow that business in India.

Lack of business push at NFS was the only complaint of the regional management team, which overshadowed the growth of NYB in all other areas. In all the earlier global meets, Aditya had been a star. For him, something like this was nothing short of loss of face. He wanted to get away from the conference and come back to India, and just blast his way through. Fortunately, for people back in India, he couldn't possibly do so.

One morning, soon after, Amit was driving when he got a call from Aditya's office. 'He wants to see you now.' It was Aditya's secretary. And when Aditya sent an instruction, no one argued. Amit, who was going to meet a client, called up his relationship manager and asked her to step in for him. A minute later, Amit's Ford Ikon was ripping its way through Mumbai's crazy traffic and making its way towards the main office of NYB. In forty minutes, he was standing in front of Aditya's cabin. 'Very fowl mood' Melinda said when she looked at Amit. Aditya saw him there and motioned to him to come in.

Clearly, he was in a belligerent mood. His body language was aggressive and he was moving around extremely antagonistically in his room. Definitely not the normal calm and composed Aditya that he knew.

'Do you know what all we have done in the bank in the last three years?'

Amit just nodded.

'Did you know that we have shown the fastest growth in revenue in the entire Asia Pacific region?'

'Yes Aditya,' Amit nodded again.

'Did you know that our cost saving initiatives have been spoken about at group level?'

'Hmmm . . .' with another vigorous nod from Amit.

'Did you know that all our audits have been very good this year?'

'Yes.'

'Yet the fuckers in the regional office say that we have wasted the last three years and they will not give us any fresh investments.'

Amit knew him very well . . . well enough to know that when the boss is in a bad mood, keep your thoughts under control and do not speak. Aditya wanted to let out some steam and that's exactly what he was doing.

'They are saying that we have screwed around with NFS and that we haven't really internalised it the way we should have.'

'Hmm . . .' *What else could he have said?*

'They claim that the growth in NFS is not the same as what they would have wanted. What can I do if those fuckers at NFS don't listen to us. They just do their own thing . . . implement their own strategies and do not look for synergies with the larger bank.'

'I agree Aditya.'

'Your wife works there. Does she say anything about their efficiency and strategy? Doesn't she come and tell you that they run a *"lala ki dukaan"?'*

'No Aditya, she hasn't complained yet.'

'I have told the region, if you want me to deliver in the NBFC, then give me complete control in NFS. Make those fuckers report only to me. I will change the place.'

At that time, NFS was a group entity of New York International Bank; however, it functioned completely independently. The managing director of NFS reported to the regional head of the consumer finance business based in the regional office in Singapore and not to the India CEO of NYB, which was Aditya. The MD though had a dotted reporting to Aditya strictly for administrative reasons.

Aditya, one would say, had indirect control over the company on account of his influence as a senior in the trade, in the industry and in the organisation. But that was it. His say in the running of the day-to-day affairs of the company was restricted to providing strategic oversight.

'And thankfully, now they have agreed to make this change over the next six to twelve months. By the end of this year, NFS will be folded into NYB from a reporting perspective. This has been committed to me.'

Why is he telling me all this? What do I have to do with this? wondered Amit. Aditya went on for another fifteen minutes making caustic comments on the way the financial services NBFC was being run and how he would change it if he took charge of the company and what changes they would have to do starting now.

'I need your help in this.' Amit looked at him, unable to comprehend the meaning of this statement. The look on Amit's face meant 'HOW?'

Aditya understood his question. 'I want you to move into that company.'

'What?' Amit nearly exclaimed. He was surprised. Shocked would be a correct description of his reaction.

Blissfully ignorant of his reaction, Aditya went on, 'You need to be my eyes and ears in that organisation. Once you move there, I will know what goes on there and what needs to be done.'

'But Aditya . . .' Amit began.

'Look Amit, you have worked with me long enough to realise that I value people who stand by me. Have faith in me. I have never let my people down.'

'Aditya . . .'

Again, he was not able to finish his sentence. 'Amit, I will use my influence on the managing director and move you to a position of stature and authority there. If you have to be my man there, you need to move into the senior management team of NFS. I will work out something for you. Your career is my responsibility. Let me manage it for you.'

'Aditya, Chanda works there. How can I work in the same organisation as her? Won't it be an issue with compliance?' Amit couldn't think of anything better.

'That's fine son. I will fix that. As long as the two of you work for different bosses, it should be fine.'

Amit didn't know how to respond. When in doubt, remain silent, was the mantra he had learnt.

Being perceptive was one of Aditya's key strengths. 'You don't seem to be excited about it.'

Amit didn't respond.

'What if I mentioned to you that it will be a business manager's role?' Aditya had expected Amit to be thrilled about it. Amit didn't show any emotion. It hadn't hit him yet. 'They are looking for a mortgage business head. Hari called me yesterday, asking for some help. Chander, their head of mortgage business has quit, and Hari wants to move fast on a replacement.' Thanks to Chanda working there, Amit knew that Hari was the managing director of NFS.

Amit looked at him. There was a glow in his eyes. Was he beginning to get interested? Aditya couldn't say with surety. 'Wasn't that the job you wanted to take in GE?' He nodded.

'Now that's up for grabs in NFS. How does it sound?' Amit's lips began to curl upwards, the traction, pushing his eyebrows up. He was now beginning to smile. His dream was about to be realised. Only the other day, Chanda had asked him about Aditya's outstanding promise of giving him a business to run. Wasn't Aditya an awesome guy to work for?

Seeing him still thinking, Aditya stood up, patted him on the shoulder and said, 'Think about it, my friend. Opportunities like these don't come all the time. Puneet Singhania has been after my life, chasing me for a move too. I can give him the job if you don't take it. Let me know by tomorrow. I have to head to a meeting now. I will wait for your call.' And he walked out of the room, leaving Amit in his cabin thinking about what had just hit him. That was Aditya. Not only had he teased Amit into getting interested, he had also handed him out the threat of others being in the fray if he delayed the decision for too long.

'Wow! That's great. You and me in the same organisation, in the same office! We can go and come back together,' exclaimed Chanda when Amit told her about the conversation.

'But I am not comfortable.'

'With what?' Chanda couldn't fathom the reason for Amit's discomfort.

'With Aditya's intent in sending me there.'

'You are thinking too much. What if he had only told you that he is giving you the mortgage business to run? Wouldn't you have been interested?'

'Yes, but now I know I am being given the job, not because I am good or deserve it, but because Aditya wants me to be his man there in what he sees as the enemy camp.'

'Why do you view it as the enemy camp?'

'My boss views it so. I don't.'

'Yeah. Boss wants you to go and die fighting the enemy. Give me a break Amit. Can't you see this opportunity staring at you in the face?'

Amit didn't respond. He thought for a while and then looked up. 'What does Chander do?'

'He runs it now.'

'Runs what?'

'Mortgages, of course.'

'I know that, you idiot. Aditya told me about it. How is it currently being managed there, in the NFS structure?'

'Currently mortgages are run out of the branch network. In every location, the branch manager is the king. He is responsible for business development. He has a team below him for selling personal loans, two wheeler loans, and even mortgages. All these guys report to the branch manager who manages everything at a location.'

'OKAY . . . and the branch managers?'

'The branch managers report to the regional managers who report in turn to Gowri.'

'What all does he manage . . . your good old Gowri?'

'All activities in the branch come under him. Sales for personal loans, consumer durable loans, auto loans and mortgage loans.'

'Where does that leave Chander?'

'Chander manages it at a country level from a product perspective. Though the sales channels have a reporting relationship with him too, he ends up managing most of the backend. Gowri's link with the branch managers is too strong for him to get into. He doesn't run the business . . . for all practical purposes he just runs the product.'

'Who is accountable for the business financials? For the revenues and the profits?'

'Gowri.'

'Big guy!'

'But wait . . . how are they going to position this to him?' Chanda questioned.

'Who . . . him?'

'Gowri . . .'

'What about positioning?'

'Arre, if they make you the business manager, won't they be taking away a business from him and giving it to you? As I said, Chander is only a product manager. Gowri runs the sales channels, the way he wants.'

'Oh, you mean he will get pissed?'

'Ya, because part of what you are going to do falls in Chander's area and a significant part lies under Gowri. He is bound to get mighty pissed.'

'That's Aditya's problem. If I agree to move, it's for Aditya and Hari to manage. Not me.' Chanda agreed with this logic of Amit and the issue was dropped.

'So, will you be moving to the vacant cabin on the corporate floor?' The fourth cabin from Gowri's room, right next to Kakkar's room was vacant. Chanda knew that.

'If I agree to move, that is.'

'Whenever I come up to see Gowri, I can also come and have coffee with you.' Chanda was getting ambitious.

'And we could go together for lunch . . . God! Are you out of your mind, woman? That would amount to overexposure!'

'OKAY. I will not even look at you in office. Happy?' Chanda feigned anger.

'OKAY baba. I will have lunch with you everyday. Now smile.'

And then the discussion moved to other routine stuff. In essence, Chanda's excitement about Amit moving to NBFC made taking the decision only simpler for Amit.

The next day he walked up to Aditya and said. 'I will take it Aditya.'

'I am glad Amit. You have made the right choice. Do not worry. I am firmly behind you.' And then, as Amit moved out of the room, he broke into a smile. He had managed to plant his devil into the enemy territory. Natasha would have understood his game plan. But Amit didn't realise that he was being made the guinea pig in Aditya's battle to win over NFS and bring it under his control.

In end January 2003, Amit moved to NFS as the mortgage business head.

The Mortgage Business
NYB Financial Services
2003

The mortgage business was a large and strategically important one for NFS in every sense – over twenty percent of the income and twenty-five percent of the profits of NFS came from this business. It could be anything but small and insignificant.

At NFS, mortgage was run in a manner quite divergent from the way it was run in most of the other organisations. There was a reason to it. Only one reason – Gowri.

Gowri controlled the branch network. The one hundred and fifty strong branch network was in his vice-like grip. He ran a tight shop. Nothing escaped his eyes and ears. His people were everywhere – they swamped the place like mosquitoes in a garbage dump. Nothing there could happen without his permission. So much so that even the MD was helpless. He had a choice. Fuck around with Gowri and see the business tanking or keep Gowri happy and reap the benefits. Hari was a contended peace-loving guy and in his own interest, chose the latter of the two options. He was on a three-year stint with NFS and was happy if someone else got him the numbers while he enjoyed his life.

The branch managers were in awe of Gowri. They too wouldn't dare to do anything against Gowri. To be fair, Gowri kept them humoured and even took care of them. His emotional quotient was very high and the connect with his people was strong. Relationships transcended the realms of professionalism and often got into the personal domain. Personal rapport mattered. You don't run a company on relationships, but Gowri did exactly that. However, to Gowri's credit there were no major blow-ups visible to anyone.

The branches controlled everything that happened in the location. All businesses, personal loans, mortgages, two-wheeler loans, consumer loans, auto loans, etc., were run out of the NFS branches. Even though there were individual resources at various locations running these diverse sets of product lines, they all reported to one individual – the branch manager who was in effect the general manager, responsible for delivery of numbers across products. All the products folded into one individual – Gowri. This was not the way it was intended to be. The respective businesses had heads. There was an auto business head, a mortgage business head and thereon . . . all of them on paper accountable for their respective business lines, end to end. However, Gowri, using his large network of people and political acumen had taken charge of everything within his chain of command. The business managers were resigned to doing a lesser important product management job. They were of significantly junior vintage as compared to Gowri and hence unable to challenge and wrest charge from him. Like the MD, they had also come to realise that in case they had to live in the water and survive, it always pays to be friends with the king of the marshland, the crocodile.

The company had been run in this fashion for too long and it is said that over long periods of time, practice becomes a law. Gowri had become a law of his own in NFS. No one could touch him.

'Please enter your name,' the guard pointed towards the register kept outside the NYS office even as Amit showed him his NYB ID card. 'I am a staff member,' he reiterated.

'*Woh sub bank mein chalega. Yahaan nahin.*' This statement took Amit by surprise. 'All these cards don't work here. You can go in only if you are a staff of NFS. Otherwise, you have to enter your name in the register.' The security guard's right hand went up to his large rounded moustache and caressed them in an upward movement which matched the twirl of his lips. He then turned and looked towards the parking lot, at a new batch of employees who were walking in towards the gate.

'Anyway, from tomorrow, I will have a new card.' Amit considered the fact that he had to get himself a new ID card as he was going to be working in the NFS office. He signed the register and walked in.

Amit then took long strides towards the reception area. 'I want to see Mr Hariharan, the managing director,' he said in a crisp voice to the receptionist.

'You will have to wait sir. He is not in yet.'

'I have an appointment at 9 a.m.'

'Sure sir. But you can meet him only if he comes in. I have told his secretary to let me know the moment he comes in.' The tone and manner was curt. Was it because he was new there or was he reading too much into it. He ignored the fact that it could be because the NFS employees hated any NYBanker in their midst.

'If Chanda was around, I would have at least had a cup of coffee with her.' Shrugging off the thought, he settled down on the sofa in the reception.

It was the twenty-eighth of the month and he was about to take on a new role in NFS. He had moved from the secure environs of his company – NYB – to be a part of the acquired company as a management representative of the acquirer . . . not a very pleasant situation to be in. But he was up to the challenge.

Just as he was rummaging through the zillion thoughts that were crowding his mind, a young girl passed by along with a guy who looked like a goon.

'*Kitna mila gaadi ka?*'

'Phour lakh maddum.'

'*Bus?* Only four lakh? But it was a new car. Just about eight–ten months old.'

'It was approved maddum. Imtiaz sir *ke* approvals *hain hamare paas.*'

'OKAY. Deposit the cash. Had you told me, I would have asked my boyfriend to buy it at this price.'

Amit's interest in eavesdropping on their conversation was more to do with the girl's cuteness quotient than any genuine longing to understand and know what they were talking about! He stopped looking in that direction when the girl moved away from the reception and went towards the cash counter. By then the discussion about the car had stopped.

'Amit.' He looked back at the reception desk. The receptionist had caught him looking intently in the direction of the front office girl. Thank God Chanda wasn't here. She was to come in late that day. She was tired after a long day at work. She had returned home only at 2 a.m. the previous night. An audit was approaching and the entire team was busy preparing for the same.

'Hari has come in. He will see you now.'

Amit got up. He hadn't taken the laptop strap off his shoulder and hence the laptop too divorced itself from the couch. He had carried his old laptop with him. NYB was fine with it, since he was moving within the same group. Walking past the reception, up a spiral staircase, he reached the second floor, the feared corporate floor of NFS. Karen, the MD's secretary was waiting for him. She led him past a few rows of smart looking cubicles, occupied by wonderful looking women, into a large and tastefully done up room. What are so many women doing in a finance company? He wondered as they entered Hari's room.

'Hari, Amit's here,' and Karen left the room.

'Hey Amit! How are you young man?' And he held out his hand for Amit to shake. 'I have heard a lot about you.'

'Same here sir,' said Amit, though the only thing he had heard about the MD so far was that he was a spineless fellow.

'I am so glad that Aditya could convince you to come here. Your wife also works here, right? How does it feel, both of you in the same company? You guys can come and go together. That's a big benefit. I am sure it's a great feeling.'

'I hope so sir. Have never been in the same organisation with her so far in my career. It will be a first time of sorts.'

'Well my friend, if you haven't, you have chosen the wrong organisation to work together. There is a fair bit of energy and excitement here.' And he winked at Amit as his secretary walked in and out of his room. He was obviously referring to the good looking women in and around the second floor. Amit thought it was in bad taste, but didn't say much. 'It sure keeps the motivation level high!' Saying this, Hari broke into a loud Bollywood villain-like laughter. Amit managed to force a smile too.

The discussion lasted an hour, wherein the managing director told him about the business, the organisation, the structure, the work culture, and the complexities, and also outlined his expectations on the business.

'You need to work with Gowri on this. He should be coming in any time. Come, let me introduce you to the team around here.' Hari stood up, gave a slight tug to his trousers, wore his *baba-aadam ke zamaane ki* glasses and led him out of his palatial cabin. 'There is no doubt that we need to work together with NYB and there is no better person than you who can help us with it. You come from the bank. Just be careful that you don't give an impression that you have come here to change everything. Remember, you cannot

achieve anything without the support of your colleagues at NFS.'
Amit couldn't make out whether it was an advice or a threat. A
word of caution or an instruction to refrain. The stress and sarcasm
and the choice of words neutralised the positive impact of the entire
interaction. Amit chose not to comment. He didn't like the stress on
'work with Gowri' . . . and that too coming from a NYB old-timer
Amit was wondering what to make of it.

Hari led him out of the room, onto the floor. It was a large
square floor with cabins all around the periphery. The cabins were
large, well-anointed and had their own privacy. From the cabins,
one could see what went on in the entire corporate floor. A large
area in the centre of the floor was covered by rows of workstations.
The junior staff and the assistants of the 'cabin crew' occupied those
workstations.

Hari started from the first cabin and introduced Amit to everyone
around.

'Shabnam Gujral, product manager for auto loans,' said Hari
and looked at Amit. 'He is joining us from the bank to run
mortgages.'

'Oh, welcome Amit! For the records, my designation is Business
Head – Auto Loans. Hari just loves to call it product manager.
Because that's what we all do.' She looked at Hari with a pained
look, 'Don't we?'

'What a stupid response?' was Amit's initial thought. Towards the
end of his conversation with Shabnam, he realised that there was a
story there which he needed to dig and find out more about. She
was a NYBanker frustrated with the going-ons at NFS. After some
pleasantries, he moved on.

'Manish Kakkar.'

'Hi!' Manish stood up the moment he saw them walking towards
him. He took Amit's extended hand and said, 'I manage credit and
collections. Welcome to NFS.' There was something in this person
which told Amit that he could bond well with him.

He looked at the cute looking girl sitting with Manish in his room. 'Hi! I am Jacqueline. I work with Manish and help him with analytics.' Amit felt a certain degree of warmth in the handshake. He moved on.

'You are Chanda's husband, right?' Amit nodded his head. When Jacqueline saw the discussion showing signs of extending, she excused herself and walked out of the room.

'Arre . . . Kakkar . . . sorry for disturbing your date.' Hari winked.

'Come on Hari!' Kakkar started blushing at this comment. He even looked towards the door to see if it was shut. He was worried that someone else outside would hear this conversation.

'Amit, I would like to let you into a secret. This girl Jacqueline, who just left, has the hots for our friend Mr Kakkar here.'

'Oh . . . that's interesting,' said Amit.

'No Amit, don't listen to Hari . . . he is just pulling my leg.'

'Ha ha. Amit, grapevine has it that she even proposed to Manish once. Unfortunately, the sadly married Manish had to turn her down.'

'If it makes you happy Hari . . . here . . . read this.' Manish picked up a small packet lying on his table and passed it on to Hari.

'Oh my God!' exclaimed Hari when he read the contents. 'My condolences,' he added, smiling slyly. Seeing that Amit was confused, he added, 'His heartthrob is getting married,' while passing on Jacqueline's wedding invitation to Amit.

'And if it makes you happy Hari, she has even asked for a transfer to Hyderabad because her fiancé is based there.'

'I am sure she waited for you and then gave up.'

Amit was peacefully listening to this conversation without adding any of his comments to the discussion. After pulling Kakkar's leg for a few more minutes, Hari, along with Amit, moved on.

'Supratik Guha – CFO.'

'Vipul – treasury.' They went from room to room, till they reached Chander's cabin.

'Chander Rastogi – the outgoing head of mortgages.'

'Hi Amit! Welcome to NFS.'

'Thanks Chander! I look forward to learning a lot from you.'

'Sure young man. I can tell you for sure this is an exciting place.' The way in which he said it belied the sentiment that the words conveyed. Amit's dissonance only grew. First, it was Shabnam and now, Chander. The expressions, their speech, and their frustrations made Amit rethink whether he had made the right choice. Anyway, it was too late now.

'For how many more months are you here?'

'Two more months.' Chander had put in his papers and was serving the mandatory three month's notice period. No one knew where he was headed.

'Oh, great. That gives me some time to settle down in the role. I can fall back on you for advice.'

'Amit, I must say you are stepping into large shoes. Our expectations are very high and I am sure you won't let us down. Aditya has a fair bit of confidence in you. That's the reason why we preferred you even though Gowri was pushing for someone from within.'

'Sure sir.' *Oh, so Gowri was pushing for someone within. That's not great news*, he thought, especially if he had to take Hari's suggestion of working with him closely.

There was one more cabin to visit. It was the largest room, among the cabin crew. Not as large as the MD's though. He bid goodbye to Chander with a promise to return soon and followed Hari towards the last room.

Hari stopped outside and looked at the lady sitting outside the room. 'Suzanna, can we go in?' he asked. Amit for a moment was taken aback. A managing director was checking if he could walk into the room of an employee. Any other day, he would have put it down to humility. But Hari didn't do any of this when he met Manish Kakkar, Chander or Shabnam.

'Of course Hari,' Suzanna retorted and Hari smiled. This cut short his thoughts and he followed Hari.

'Hey Gowri!' Hari said as soon as he entered the room.

'Morning Hari.'

'Hi!' He greeted Amit, but didn't say anything else, because he didn't know him. That was only a façade, because the moment Hari and Amit had left Manish Kakkar's cabin, Gowri had called him and taken a detailed information download.

'Hi! Amit Sharma.' Amit introduced himself to Gowri.

'Oh, Amit? Yes, yes . . . I remember. How are you Amit? Chanda often keeps mentioning you. I should have connected when I saw you. Come. Come on in. Grab a seat.'

Amit looked around. It was the most lavish of all the cabins. The table was exquisite and made of teak. It almost looked princely. The wooden coat hanger on the right added style to the room. A large painting by some unknown painter hung right behind Gowri – a scene where the sun was behind the mountains. Orange sky, birds flying in clusters. The only thing he couldn't tell because he wasn't sure, was whether, it was a rising sun or a setting sun. *Only time will tell*, said the interior monologue as he rested his back against the sofa and almost immediately felt the royal touch of leather. This was clearly the most regally anointed room in the entire company . . . maybe even in the entire NYB group in India.

Hari was with them for a while and then left citing the excuse of another appointment to catch up with. There were only the two of them in the room.

'So Amit, I believe you are coming in place of Chander.'

'That's what I am told.' There was something in the tone that he didn't like. So he responded equally arrogantly.

'Oh ya . . . he is going. *Shaayad jaane ke liye kaha hai humne.*' His eyebrows were raised and seemed to convey a mischievous intent.

He was implying that Chander had been asked to leave. Amit knew that such was not the case, else Aditya would have told him.

'Hmmm . . . but why? He seems to be such a nice guy. Experienced hai. *Bahut saal kaam kiya hai.*' He played along.

'I agree. But you know, he doesn't know how to deal with people. *Uske log khush nahin the.* His people were not happy you see. They went and complained about him. Numbers were also not happening. Someone has to take accountability na. How long can I keep helping him deliver his numbers? And if I am helping him to do his numbers . . . shouldn't I get the credit? No free lunches you see.'

. . . Aaah there lies the problem. Non-delivery of numbers. Hopefully that would not be a problem with him. But wasn't the channel controlled by Gowri? If numbers didn't happen shouldn't Gowri also take the blame? Or was it that Gowri manipulated the channels to underperform and transferred the blame of underperformance to Chander . . . hmm. Interesting times ahead. Get set for the battle. All this while, Gowri continued speaking.

'You don't worry. I will help you out with the numbers. As long as I am there, you can relax.'

Amit didn't like this statement of Gowri. This is precisely what he didn't want to do. He would rather take control of his sales channels which were under Gowri and his branch managers and deliver on his numbers himself. He couldn't rely on Gowri to meet his targets. That would be committing professional hara kiri. Something which Chander and even Shabnam did.

After a few moments of disputed pleasantries—disputed because Amit was not too sure if they were pleasantries at all—he came out of the meeting, feeling a bit weird. Was the guy trying to help or was he trying to act funny with him. He couldn't tell. By then Chanda had come in and was waiting for Gowri to be through with the meeting.

'How are you, stranger?' she said when she looked at Amit. 'How's the first day going?'

'So far so good,' he retorted.

'Let's do lunch together,' she said to Amit even as she walked into Gowri's cabin.

'Interesting guy,' he could hear Gowri say to Chanda as the door shut behind them. He walked over to Chander's room to begin the takeover process from him.

'Hey, come on friend,' Chander welcomed him into the room. 'Welcome to the frying pan!'

Amit just smiled. There was something about this guy which made him very comfortable.

'Tell me, did they sell you this job or did you ask for this?'

'They . . . as in?'

'They . . . the bank, Aditya.'

'Oh ya . . . actually Aditya asked me to move in here.'

'I should have guessed. Come let's start . . .'

Amit was a bit confused at this remark but he didn't probe. This was only their first meeting and he couldn't be seen gossiping within minutes of meeting Chander.

Lunch, for Amit and Chanda, was at Mahesh Lunch Home. The restaurant was extremely cramped. The food though was fabulous. What better place to celebrate their first day at work together?

'How was my boss?'

'He was behaving as if he was mine,' joked Amit.

'Oh, he is arrogant. But good at heart.'

'That's not what everyone says.'

'No, no. I have seen him change. He is quite curt in the beginning. But as he gets to know you, he becomes very friendly. Look at his equation with Manish Kakkar. The story is that he used to hate him. Now he is great pals with Manish.'

'Let's see.' Amit didn't particularly agree, but deferred to her view.

'Where are you going to sit? Have you found a place for yourself?'

'Ya. Hari kind of indicated that I would be sitting in the room to the left of Manish Kakkar.'

'Oh, that's where Brad used to sit.'

'Brad?'

'You wouldn't know him. Bradley Pereira. He was the head of strategy. Has now gone to Dubai. Quit NFS.'

'Ominous seat,' and they both started laughing.

His first day in the new office, and they were already having a romantic lunch. Neither seemed to mind. They weren't sure if they would be able to take these liberties later on.

Back in office, Amit got busy with Chander while Chanda got back to her day job. The last he saw of her was when she was striding with her laptop into Gowri's room along with three others. Towards the end of the day, Manish Kakkar walked into Chander's room. He was an affable, balding, man. He seemed friendly to Amit when he met him in the morning.

'Young man, how has your first day been so far?'

'Good. Quite good. Getting to know things.'

Seeing that Amit's notebook was shut and Chander was packing to leave, he asked Amit, 'Chai?'

Amit nodded.

'*Chal*. Come to my room.'

Amit thanked Chander for his help and followed Manish into his cabin. It was small but nice. Not a patch on Gowri's lavish expanse of a cabin.

Both of them got into the room, and discussed obscurities of life. Manish was a philosophical man and came across as an honest guy. Amit had liked him instantly, when he had met him in the morning. He also liked his values. If a guy could turn down Jacqueline's advances, he had to be of a great moral standing.

Chai came. The office boy left two cups on his table. 'Sugar *mat dalna*,' Amit told him. The office boy looked at Manish apologetically.

'*Doosri leke aa. Phiki laana,*' Manish dismissed the office boy and asked him to get some tea without sugar.

'Aur . . . how's Chanda liking your move?'

'Oh, she is thrilled. At least there is someone to ferry her to work.'

'But you have a problem, my friend.'

Amit responded with a blank look.

'How will you flirt with such good looking women here? It's a pity if Chanda starts interfering with all this.' And they started laughing.

'Slowly . . . slowly . . . careful you fool! Keep it down slowly.' Their interesting conversation was interrupted by a stern voice. It was of a woman and came from outside the room. Amit turned and looked outside the door. Manish didn't need to turn, but he too was looking outside the door. Their view was blocked by an office boy carrying a large box.

Manish got up and walked out of the room. 'Arre Sango. What's happening?'

'Nothing Manish. Just getting my stuff shifted.'

'Where?'

'I am moving here. Into this cabin.' She pointed to the cabin on the left of Manish's room.

'Then . . . padosan . . . you are my *padosan*.'

'Yes Manish. Ain't I blessed to be your neighbour?' laughed Sangeeta.

'When did this happen?'

'This evening, Manish. Gowri called me at around four and asked me to bring in my stuff and move,' and after a pregnant pause added '. . . and I moved.'

'That's great. See you. Let me know in case you need anything. After all, if I don't take care of my padosan, who will?'

'Thanks Manish!' Manish didn't hear her say this because he was already back into the room.

'Who is she?' Amit asked him.

'She is Sangeeta, the branch network head for west. She is rumoured to be moving to head the branch network pan India soon. Gowri's favourite. That's probably the reason why she is moving into this room.'

'Moving into this room? But Hari mentioned to me that I was to move in here.' Amit was surprised.

'Is that so? I am sure there is some confusion. Why don't you clear it out with her? I am sure it can be resolved. Come, let's ask her.' Manish got up.

'No. It's okay Manish. I think I will ask Hari to fix this. We will be unnecessarily embarrassing Sangeeta.' Manish agreed.

Amit got up and walked towards Hari's cabin. Karen was there working on her PC.

'Is Hari in?' Might as well clear the confusion then and there.

'No. He has left. He has a flight to catch. Going to Chennai. Will be back in Mumbai tomorrow evening and in office the day after.'

'Okay, thanks,' and he made his way out. He glanced at Chander's room to see if he was there, but he too had left.

He went down to the Mezz floor where Chanda was waiting. Seeing him, she too packed up and they left.

'Coffee?' asked Amit as they crossed Prabhadevi on their way to Bandra. Chanda nodded.

Amit parked his car in the side lane, bang opposite Siddhi Vinayak Temple and they stepped into the Café Coffee Day outlet for some caffeine and a quick bite.

As they entered the coffee shop, Amit turned, looked behind at the massive temple and bowed his head; his hand rose to his heart and he stood still for a while, as if thanking God for all that he had done for him till date. That done, he walked to the table which Chanda had occupied and made himself comfortable on the quasi steel, quasi plastic chair. Chanda had ordered a cappuccino for herself and a macchiato for him.

'Praying to God?'

'Thanking him for having given me the job of chauffeuring you to and from home,' he smiled.

They started talking about work and the life in office, people, about Hari, Manish, Chander and Gowri. Amit had heard about all of them but had met them for the first time today.

'So when are you moving into your cabin?' It was special for them because in NYB, he always had a largish cubicle but never a cabin to himself. The pride in his voice when he had told her about the cabin, earlier in the day while having lunch was enormous. She was giving him an ego boost by asking him about his new cabin.

'There seems to be a small issue. Will iron it out tomorrow.'

'What?'

'Somebody else has moved into that cabin.'

'How? Why? There is nobody else of your seniority.'

'Sangeeta has moved in.'

'What?' Chanda was surprised. 'That bitch. But why? Didn't you tell her that it was committed to you?'

'No point speaking to her. I will speak to Gowri and fix it. Gowri asked her to move in. He obviously did not know that I have been asked to move in. Tomorrow morning, I will tell him and he will get it vacated.'

'That bitch. She always creates problems for everyone.' Chanda hated her.

'But why blame her? Gowri told her today to move and she moved. What could be her . . .'

'Wait a minute. Wait a minute.' Chanda didn't wait for him to complete and interjected abruptly. 'You said Gowri told her today to take that cabin. How do you know?'

'Oh, I overheard Manish speaking to her. She mentioned to him that Gowri told her at around 4 p.m. this evening.'

'What? Are you sure?'

'That's what she said baba. Gowri wouldn't have known. I will tell him tomorrow and it will be sorted.'

'Bullshit!' She was screaming now. The whole coffee shop, though scarcely populated was looking in their direction. She could see through this.

'Bullshit!' this time the volume was lower. 'Gowri knew about it!'

'How could he Chanda? Hari told me in the morning and then he left for Chennai.'

'Because I told him, Amit! I told him! After lunch when I had come up to discuss tomorrow's presentation, he was commenting about you and I casually mentioned to him that now I will have to serve two masters on the corporate floor. One you, who will be in the cabin to the left of Manish Kakkar and one him in the cabin to the right of Kakkar. He laughed when I said this and even asked if you had been told about the move into the cabin. That bastard! I wish I could . . . I could . . .' She couldn't complete the sentence She was too furious and excited.

The sequence of events now panned out in front of Amit – very clearly, and unambiguously. Chanda had mentioned to Gowri about Amit moving into the room on the corporate floor. Gowri was not too happy about it. He looked down upon people seconded from NYB. After Hari had left, he had called Sangeeta and asked her to move into the cabin. This would ensure that Amit does not get a cabin and would have to wait till Chander moves. Post that, Amit would get Chander's room. Till then he would only have to face embarrassment. What a master schemer! He had worked out a brilliant plan to humiliate Amit and establish his supremacy in the organisation. It was very easy for anyone to be flustered when faced with such a situation particularly in a new organisation.

Had Hari questioned him, he would have feigned ignorance on the proposed plan of Amit moving in and that would lend credibility to his plan of asking Sangeeta to move into that vacant cabin. Chanda wouldn't ask him and Amit was too new to get into a direct conflict. He wanted to prove to Amit that he was the boss. And had in effect managed to make that statement. Gowri wanted Amit to know that NFS was his space and anyone from outside was not welcome.

Amit was shaken by this episode. Not because he valued the cabin too much, but it was not only about the cabin. It was the manner in which it was done that irritated him. He had dealt with many complex situations in the bank in his earlier roles, probably even more complex customer issues, but this was different. He had never encountered this sort of petty politics ever in his life. Anyone else in his situation would have made a different call. He did not follow the norm. That was his style in the past and here too he decided that he would follow his instinct.

Back home it was a difficult night for both of them. Chanda was even more agitated because she was the one responsible for the chaos. Had she not mentioned to Gowri, he would not even have known. She had to now start exercising discretion.

2003
NFS – The second day
Mumbai

Amit walked in confidently on the second day. Hari was not expected to be in office. There was an arrogant swagger in his walk as he raced up to the second floor. By now the security guard knew him and did not stop him, as he had done on the first day.

Gowri was in his room, checking his email. Suzanna was in her small cubicle trying to act busy. Amit walked up and stood next to her for a couple of minutes. From the corner of his eyes, he could see that Gowri was looking at him, pretending though that he was busy.

'Suzanna, can you please help me with a cup of coffee?'

'Yes, of course.'

'And please tell the pantry boy not to add any sugar. Sir does not like coffee with sugar. Right Amit?' It was Manish, who had walked in behind Amit. 'Second day in wonderland!' he chimed in and followed it with a song as he walked into his own cabin.

Amit turned and walked towards the cabin on Manish's left, the cabin that was to be his. It was open. He walked in and settled down on the other side of the table – the side where visitors would have normally sat down.

Gowri walked towards Suzanna and murmured something into her ear. Even if it was related to work, it didn't matter. Manish, being the exuberant of the senior management team, walked out of the room into the open area, and looked around. Seeing Amit, he walked towards him again, 'Arre . . . you are sitting here?'

By then Gowri had also come out of his room. A cup of tea in his hand, he walked towards the two of them. '*Kya haal hai Amit?*' and seeing him formally attired, commented 'Arre, no one wears a tie here. All this happens only in your bank . . . at NYB.'

Gowri conveniently stayed clear of discussing the cabin issue with Amit and began gossipping about other mundane stuff. The gossip went on for a few minutes when it veered towards the loan policies of NFS. Amit asked Gowri if he had the document which outlined the loan and credit policies of NFS.

Before Gowri could answer, Manish chipped in, 'Of course we have. Do you want me to send it to you?'

'My email ID is not set up yet. Can you please send it to Suzanna? I will ask her to print it out for me.' He then looked at Gowri and as an afterthought added, 'With your permission.' Gowri nodded in response.

Before Gowri could answer, Manish again butted in, 'Ya, ya. No problem. Anyway she acts busy. She doesn't have a full day's job. But you know what? I don't need to send it to her. She should have it. A few days ago she had circulated those policies to the branch network. Let me ask her to print them out.'

'Ae, Suzanna,' he called out. 'Remember, you sent out the latest C2P2 last week?' Amit was part of the same group and hence he knew that C2P2 was an acronym for Consumer Credit Process and Policy, the inhouse loans bible. Suzanna nodded.

'Will you please print them out for Amit? Also, printout the covering email which I had sent. That's important too.' Suzanna made a face, but she didn't have an excuse for not doing what was asked of her.

For the next twenty minutes, a frowning Suzanna printed reams of paper for Amit. Over two hundred at last count, including the covering mails, which Manish had forwarded to her and she had sent to the entire branch network, at Gowri's behest.

When Amit saw them, he was amused. Below every email, was a signature, an addition which gets attached to an email, every time you send one, provided it is programmed into your email settings. Below every email which she had printed out for him was a signature:

Regards,
Suzanna
Secretary
NYB Financial Services

Mumbai
Phone Number.......
Mobile......

Normally you would find seniors in an organisation attaching their signatures to email IDs. It was not common, and was actually unheard of, for secretaries to add their signature to emails. But NFS was a different animal. A different kind of organisation and the team in which she worked was of a different make.

This entire episode screwed up Suzanna's morning. She was so pissed with this that she walked up to Gowri's room after all this and was closeted with him for over thirty minutes. Their discussion, one could make out, was animated and furiously gesticulative. Though there was no reason for Suzanna to be upset, there was nothing inhumanly wrong in Amit and Manish asking her to printout those manuals.

Half an hour later, she walked out of Gowri's room and went straight to the wash room. She emerged after about ten minutes, looking calm and composed. It was actually Amit's turn to play mind games now.

He walked up to her. 'Chander mentioned to me that you have the entire branch list with telephone and address details of the branches. Can you please printout a copy for me? Chander wants it too. Please send the list to him as well.'

This time Suzanna didn't smile. She just nodded her head. Within five minutes she was at Amit's desk and handed over the printout to him.

'Thanks Suzanna.'

'Sangeeta was mentioning to me that she will be sitting in this room.'

'Oh yes. Where is she?'

'She is in Pune. Travelling.'

'Oh, okay. I just decided to share it with her. You think she will have a problem? She can sit in the proper side. Till I find some space I will occupy the other side, or the side which is less desired. What do you say?'

'You will have to ask her,' she said curtly and walked away.

'I guess everyone in this place has an attitude,' said Amit to himself as she moved away from him. Amit looked at the paper she had brought for him. It was the printout of the mail she had just sent Chander. It had the list of branches of NFS – all of them, with their addresses and phone numbers. As his eyes trailed the top of the mail and went down the first page, it stopped on something very interesting. It said:

Chander
Fyi
Regards

And then the signature. He stopped. A victorious I-know-what-that-means sort of smile slowly crawled across his face. This time the signature was different from the ones he had seen in her mails in the morning. It now read:

Regards,
Suzanna
Secretary to Gowri Shankar
Head – Branch Network
NYB Financial Services.

The difference was the third line – 'Secretary to Gowri Shankar'. Aah! Now it's working. He now knew the reason for the thirty-minute discussion in the morning. He knew the reason for the anxiety, for the chaos. It was him. Hadn't he managed to get under the skin of Gowri and Suzanna? His eyes were glowing with wolfish mischief now. Gowri had asked Suzanna to change her signature to reflect his name. This was just to send out a signal to everyone that she was only his secretary. Till now no one had even remotely questioned his authority. For that matter, even Amit hadn't. But he was the guy from the bank. He had to be shown his place. He had to be told through surrogates that Suzanna was not his secretary. *Ha ha! Gowri Shankar had been roughed up. Wow!* And how easy it was. He hadn't even done anything yet, and had managed to ruffle feathers.

And then he remembered Aditya's statement a few years back. 'Listen Amit,' he had said, 'in life, you should never ever take stress upon yourself. And if you see it coming, ensure that you stress out others. Your stress will automatically disappear.' How true! Yesterday the sly Gowri was scheming, on the very first day in office, to put him through discomfort. Today he had easily turned the table on him. All he did was go and occupy Sangeeta's room when she was not there and ask his secretary repeatedly for help. It was easy.

The remaining part of the day passed peacefully without much of excitement. Chander was very helpful. From his perspective, he was on his way out. The sooner he got Amit to speed up things, the sooner the organisation would relieve him. Manish was not at all affected by his arrival. By nature, he was a cool guy. Gowri was an outlier. He was the one who had an issue with Amit. Though on the face of it, he was sweet to Amit, the latter was under no pretensions. He knew that the façade would crumble one day. And if Gowri had his way, that day would be far closer than his comfort.

2003
The Location Visits
Kolkata, Raipur

The takeover from Chander lasted for about a week. By the end of the first week, Amit got a hang of the dynamics of the business and became quite self-sufficient. Sitting in his room on the claustrophobic powerhouse called Head Office, he had learnt whatever he could. It is normally said that leadership is all about managing people. As one goes up the ranks in any organisation, success is defined more by the way you manage your teams, your people's expectations, the way you motivate them into delivering what you expect, and how you stand by your people and lead from the front. These are things which make you stand out, rather than subject matter expertise. The latter was not too much of an issue though. Amit had handled mortgages in his earlier roles at NYB. It was not rocket science either. Amit though was a great believer of the former. Something he had learnt from Aditya and practised to the core. He wanted to implement the same values and philosophies in NFS as well.

'Where's Amit? Hasn't he come to work?' Gowri queried Chanda one morning, when he found Amit missing in action. 'Hope all is well?'

'Oh ya. He's travelling.'

'What? On vacation? Without you? Ha ha!'

'No, no! No holiday! Would I be here if he was on a holiday? He has gone to Kolkata for a business review. Chander had set it up.'

'Arre, he didn't tell me. I could have requested him to do something for me in Kolkata.' These things made Gowri very insecure and despite best attempts at concealing, it showed.

'You can call him. He is carrying his mobile.'

'No it's okay.' And the discussion ended as abruptly as it had begun.

A few moments later, after Chanda had left, Gowri was at Suzanna's side. 'Can you get me Amit on his mobile?' and he walked back into his room.

'Hi darling!' Seeing a call from office, Amit instinctively assumed it was Chanda. He knew that Chander was on leave that day and it was too early for anyone to call him from office.

'Amit. Suzanna here.'

A brief moment of embarrassed silence later, Amit found his voice to say, 'Oh hi. I thought it was Chanda.'

'Gowri would like to speak with you. Transferring the call.' As usual her voice was icy cold.

'Hi Amit! *Kidhar hai*? Where are you?'

'I'm in Kolkata. Came to meet the team.'

'*Kya hua*? Any stress? *Koi problem*?'

'No. Just getting to know my team better. If I have to take charge from Chander, I need to take over the team as well. Process and policy can be anyway learned in due course. What do you say?'

'Oh ho! *Bata diya hota*. You should have told me.'

'Why?' he said brusquely and then after a pause added 'did you have some work here? Tell me. I'm sure I'll get some free time. I can manage if you want me to do something for you.'

'No, its okay. You come back. We will chat. When are you back?'

'In office the day after. Tomorrow, I am going to Raipur. Will reach Mumbai late tomorrow night.'

The conversation ended there. But Gowri was very bitter after it. He did not like the way the conversation went. He was definitely not used to this. How could someone question the authority of THE king? Nobody visited the branches without a prior discussion with him. Even Chander had followed that rigour. If he knew about and tacitly approved any location visits, before they were to happen, he could stage manage them to ensure that he is in complete control of what goes on during those site visits. His rulebook also assumed that nobody can have the guts to do things without his nod of approval and Amit had just managed to successfully get his goat!

All the product managers informed him before they travelled to any other location. Amit was setting a trend which he didn't like. The self-appointed dictator decided that this had to be fixed before the other product managers also start doing their own thing.

That night, when Amit called up Chanda, he was not surprised at what he heard. 'Gowri was furiously jumping up and down the floor throughout the day. He seemed like a maniac let loose! Something was definitely wrong. I couldn't figure out what the reason was, but he was quite worked up.' Amit kind of knew what had influenced his behaviour and felt gleefully manipulative.

Amit landed in Raipur the next morning. It was a short flight from Kolkata. The landing was rough. Earlier, the take-off was rough and the flight too had been quite bumpy. Ominous signs of an impending rough visit to a remote city. However, on landing there, he was pleasantly surprised to find that Raipur was a quaint city in eastern India – well maintained and clean. It was quite different from what he had expected to see.

Unfortunately, the taxi which was supposed to have picked him up did not arrive. Muttering a few inane abuses under his breath, he finally chose to hire a private cab. After hunting for over thirty minutes, he finally found one and managed to land at the NFS branch.

As he walked into the branch, blank, quizzical, irritated and amused looks greeted him. No one recognised him. It was his first visit. 'I am here to see Ratnesh Jha,' said Amit in a crisp voice to the customer service executive.

'He has not come in today,' said the man with the most mechanical and bored voice on earth. How was he to know who Amit was?

'Why?'

'Don't know sir. I will just check.' And he walked into the branch manager's cabin.

'Sir, Ratnesh hasn't come in? There is someone asking for him? What should I tell him?'

'Yaar, take down his number. We will call him back. Tell him that Ratnesh will come tomorrow. He has got stuck.'

'Hua kya sir? What happened to him?'

'Arre nothing. Some idiot is coming from Mumbai. Uska boss hai. Last night Gowri had called me. He wanted me to ask Ratnesh to stay at home and instead wanted me to meet this guy. That's why he is chilling at home.'

'Okay sir.'

'And listen. Keep this to yourself. Fizul mein naukri jayegi nahin toh.'

The branch manager's room was about fifteen feet from where Amit was standing. He couldn't see Amit; else, he would have realised that he was indeed the guy from Mumbai. An even bigger folly was that he did not shut the door or keep his volume low when talking to the customer service executive. Amit heard every single word that he uttered.

To Amit's maturity, he did not say anything. He did not even let the people in the branch know that he had heard all of it. If he had to battle this, he had to do it smartly. What's the point in proving his superiority to the guys in the locations? He had to battle it out with Gowri.

The reality in NFS was staring him in his face. A hundred and fifty branches of NFS were spread across locations far and wide, but the entire branch network was completely and solely under Gowri's stronghold. At all locations, the branch manager was the senior-most guy. All the product sales guys for car loans, two wheeler loans, and even mortgage loans implicitly or explicitly reported to the branch manager. This was a structure which allowed Gowri unparalleled access to and control on every business which even the business heads couldn't exercise.

The question was to what extent would he be able to wean people away using his personal charisma? They would never listen to him. They would do only what the branch manager told them to do. And the branch manager would listen only to Gowri. They had been conditioned that way. Gowri was the godfather. Irrespective of what he said or did, the organisation structure was flawed and he knew that.

Today's Raipur example was a case in point. The sales person for mortgages in Raipur knew that Amit was coming. Amit was the senior-most person in the mortgages business. However, Ratnesh decided to heed to the branch manager's command. Things seemed to be crystal clear to Amit now. It couldn't get more real than this. He had to do something. Sitting in Mumbai, there was no way he could get control over the sales teams unless he fixed Gowri. The proximity his sales teams had with the branch manager would only ensure that his authority over them gets diluted.

'One battle at a time,' he said to himself and walked into the branch manager's cabin.

'Hi! Amit from Mumbai. I am here to see Ratnesh.'

'Oh sir, good morning.' The BM got up from his chair and gave the most nervous handshake that Amit had ever encountered. He had not expected him to walk in so early. The realisation that Amit might have heard his conversation with his staff had not dawned on him yet.

Amit though was extremely nice and courteous to the branch manager. With an expression that made him look like he could never know what goes on in the dirty corridors of corporate power struggles, he sat down with the branch manager and patiently reviewed the market and its dynamics and NFS' performance in the Raipur market. Never during his three hour discussion with the branch manager did he give any indication of the fact that he knew about the politics that was being played behind his back. After the review, he asked for and met folks from the debt recovery teams, the personal loan sales guys and also the customer service people at the branches. Apart from the branch manager, everyone else was quite happy to see him. The entire machinery through which the power-hungry Gowri operated seemed to be well-oiled. The nuts and bolts were in their places. 'Okay,' thought Amit, '. . . time to loosen up the first screw!'

'When was the last time anyone from Mumbai came here to see you guys?' He realised that no one from the head office had come and met them in ages and tried to needle the branch manager. Hadn't he intentionally chosen one of the smallest markets for a review? He knew that no one would have visited the location in ages.

'Kakkar sir was here about six months back.'

'And Gowri?'

He came for the branch inauguration last year.' And after a pause added, 'We do regular reviews with him.' The branch manager was beginning to get defensive.

'I understand. However, a review over the phone is not as good as a visit. Do not worry, now you will have enough seniors coming in to check on the health of the branch.' His parting remark left the branch manager sheepishly wondering if it was a threat or a compliment!

As he was leaving the branch, his mobile started beeping. It was Manish.

'Hi Manish!'

'Abe Amit, *kahan*? Raipur *mein hai?*'

'Ya Manish. Just finished with the branch.'

'When is your flight?'

'Some time later.'

'Will you do me a favour?'

'Of course, tell me what do you want from here?'

'I don't want anything. I need you to do something for me. It will not take much time.'

'OKAY.'

'How well do you know Raipur?'

'As well as one can get to know a city on his first visit.'

'Okay. Understood. Look, Shanti Nagar is not too far from the branch. If you take an auto rickshaw from the branch, you will be in Shanti Nagar in ten minutes. In the Shanti Nagar main road, look for a big Nathu's restaurant. You cannot miss it . . .' and he gave him continuous instructions for the next three minutes after which he hung up.

'I will call you if I get stuck,' Amit had promised.

He was beginning to get excited. Unwittingly he had got an ace up his sleeve.

It took him a little over ninety minutes to finish the work which Manish had asked him to do. Post that, he headed to the Raipur airport and waited for his flight. From the airport shop, he picked up a copy of If God *was* a *Banker*. Flipping through the pages, he wondered whether the days of God being a banker were over? These days, bankers behave as if they were the Gods . . .

When the boarding announcement was made, he walked through the security check and boarded the waiting Jet Airways flight to Mumbai. He looked at his watch and noted that it was exactly 7.40 p.m. – two and half hours to Mumbai and another forty-five minutes to get home. By 11 p.m. he should be home. That meant another nine hours before he left for office. Any other professional would have been muttering abuses under his breath under such circumstances. However, Amit's mind was a different place altogether. He was wondering how he would pass his time. His excitement guaranteed sleep deprivation. The wait for tomorrow was going to be excruciating . . . and tomorrow was fourteen hours away.

2003
The First Confrontation
NFS – Mumbai

Amit woke up on the first ring of the alarm that he had set on his cell phone. On any normal day, he would have lazily pressed the snooze button and managed to get those extra divine ten minutes of sleep. Today was different. Sleep had all but deserted him. Chanda was wondering what the secret behind his jumpy behaviour was. He did not tell her anything. 'Professional ethics,' he would say at a later date.

He had fixed up a meeting in office at 8.15 a.m. – much earlier than his normal in-time of 9.30 a.m. He walked into the co-room, the room that he shared with Sangeeta, a few seconds after the clock ticked over 8.15 a.m. He was the first to have arrived. A few janitors were cleaning up the tables and getting them ready so that the office got into squeaky clean shape before everyone walked in.

Amit ticked off one of them and asked him to get a cup of coffee. 'Make that two,' Manish had just walked in with a big grin on his face.

'What is it with you that you always come in when I order a cup of coffee?'

'There is an old Hindi saying which states that while you are eating, an enemy walks in; while you are sleeping, your love walks in and while you are drinking, your real friend walks in,' said Manish as he walked into his room and dumped the bag into his seat. 'No alcohol, so we will drink coffee to our friendship,' he smiled.

On any normal day, Manish would have opened his bag, pulled out the laptop, plugged it in, and checked for emails. The Singapore office, which was their regional hub, opened a couple of hours before India. Hence, it was normal for his mail box to be clogged even before anyone in India woke up. Today, he dumped his bag on his table and walked up to Amit. By then the cleaner had come in with coffee for the two of them.

'Look, I too have taken after you. I have started having coffee without sugar.'

'You can do with some weight loss.'

'Ha ha! Come let's go.' And both of them walked into the board room on the same floor. Only the two of them – Amit and Manish.

They were closeted in the room for about thirty-five minutes when there was a knock on the door. It was Sunil Pande, the HR head. He peeped in through the board room door. Seeing the two of them, he pushed the door open. 'Quickly shut the door and come in,' said Manish. Through the small slit in the door, as it shut itself under the recoil of the spring, Amit could make out the silhouette of Suzanna passing by. She glanced in their direction and saw them sitting there. The door banged shut even as Pande took his seat at the far end of the table.

Within minutes, Manish Kakkar's phone started ringing. Amit and Manish were seated right next to each other and from where Amit was, he could see the flashing screen of Manish's mobile. The name repeatedly flashing on the screen was Gowri's. Kakkar glanced at Amit. A smile came on to his lips and he picked up the phone.

'Ya?'

'What's the issue?'

'Nothing.'

'Nothing? Then what are all of you doing in the board room. Sunil told me that Amit had called him last night stating that he wanted to meet him urgently in the morning and now you are with him. Any problem?'

'Arre nothing. We'll talk when you come.'

'Tell me now.'

'Gowri, I will talk to you when you come. I cannot tell you anything now.'

'I will be there in half an hour. See you,' and he hung up. Amit was smiling. From the moment he saw Suzanna staring at the three of them in the conference room, he had been expecting Gowri to call one of them. Gowri was very wary of any meetings happening without his knowledge or presence. He discouraged this shit. And now there seemed to be a serious meeting happening on the corporate floor, right next to his cabin, and that too without him. A nasty grin took over Amit's face. The thought of an insecure Gowri worried about their discussion pleased him no end.

'Gentlemen, please put your phones on silent and let's not get distracted by any calls coming in.' This statement of Amit, put a stop on any chances of Gowri calling Sunil, especially after an unsuccessful attempt at getting information out of Manish Kakkar.

From the moment Manish disconnected his call, Gowri was extremely restless. He didn't like to be kept in the dark about what was going on. Being in control was his style. He got out of home and drove like a maniac to reach office.

He parked his car in a lane opposite the building and walked furiously to his office. When he reached the corporate floor he didn't walk to his room. 'Where are they?' the entire floor could hear his question which was directed at Suzanna. She pointed towards the board room.

Kadaaak! The door flew open as Gowri walked in. 'What's going on folks? Will someone tell me?'

'Arre Gowri. Come, come. Good to see you. How come so early today?' Amit was having some fun.

'Relax buddy!' he was getting irritated. There was a congregation happening in his company and people were secretive about it. It had never happened earlier. This was the first time. He was the one who kept the secrets . . . no one kept secrets from him.

Gowri sat down on the chair in the boardroom, as if saying that he would not go from there unless he was made a party to the discussion that was on.

'OKAY,' began Manish 'Gowri,' we wanted to have this discussion before you came in because we know it's close to your heart.'

'I am listening'

'We have just about concluded our discussion. Vikas needs to go.'

'What?' Gowri was shocked. 'You are kidding.'

'No he is not.' It was Amit who spoke. 'Vikas needs to go.'

'Just because he didn't suck up to you when you went there!'

'We will discuss that offline Gowri. But Vikas needs to put in his papers today. Else . . .'

'Else what?'

'We will have to terminate him,' Manish came in.

'But why?' Gowri looked at Sunil, who had a helpless look on his face. Vikas was one of Gowri's handpicked resources who had so far demonstrated complete allegiance to Gowri. The latter had seen him grow from a sales executive to a branch manager.

Vikas was the star sales manager in Kolkata, when Gowri plucked him out and put him as a branch manager in Raipur. The former owed his career to Gowri, and the latter was his godfather.

'Will anyone tell me why the fuck does he have to go?'

He was losing his patience. Very poor at managing anger. Amit was enjoying this.

'Gowri. I think the guy is on the take. He is making money out of us.'

'What?' and after a pause added 'Says who?'

'Me.' The fact that it was Amit, infuriated him even more. But he controlled his temper and his words and kept looking at Manish.

'Okay, let me tell you the entire story Gowri. You are aware of the car repossession process. In case a car loan customer continuously defaults on his loan instalments, we repossess his car.'

'I am aware,' said Gowri with his jaw tightly clenched. 'I have done this business longer than you have buddy.'

'Normally we avoid repossessing the car, but in case the loan value is large and if after repeated follow-up the customer does not pay, we go and do repossess . . . as a last recourse. To ensure that it does not backfire on us we inform the local police authorities and take necessary precautions, so that no one can accuse us of skirting the law and file a case against us for criminal intimidation.' The last sentence was added as an afterthought when he saw Rekha, the compliance head walking into the room. Amit had sent her a message in the morning asking her to join in.

'Once the car is repossessed, it is in our custody. We park it in our parking yard and follow up with the customer for his instalments. The customer is informed that in case he does not pay up, the car will be sold and our money recovered from the sale proceeds. At this stage, normally, customers pay up. Collecting becomes easy if the resale value of the car is higher than the outstanding loan amount.'

'I know all this. Why are you telling me this crap? Tell me what the problem is!'

'What I am telling you is the genesis of the problem Gowri! Be patient and hear me out. In case the customer does not pay up even after the car is repossessed, we then go ahead and sell the car. In some cases we are able to sell the car for an amount lower than the loan value, in which case we follow up with the customer for the difference or write off the amount in our books. If we are able to sell the car for a value more than the loan outstanding, we return the excess money to the customer. For example, if the customer owes us two lakh and we are able to sell the car for 2,30,000, we take 2 lakh and return the excess 30,000 to our customer.'

'So?' Gowri was getting frustrated now. He knew all this. There was no need to reiterate this. 'As I said earlier, I have done this longer than you have. Tell me what the problem is.'

'DL2CAM 0192, a Delhi registered Toyota Corolla. Loan in the name of Aakash Gulati, a businessman in Delhi. Has business interests in Raipur. Loan for 8 lakh. Stopped paying after five instalments.' It was Manish who began the story.

'When after repeated reminders he did not pay up, we issued a notice to repossess the car. The car was repossessed by our agents in Raipur three months ago. The car is about a year old.'

'What is the relevance?'

'The outstanding on the car loan is Rs 7.65 lakh. Given that he had not paid his instalments for the last six months, I had given a go-ahead to dispose off the car and recover our money. Yesterday morning I got a request from Vikas asking for approval for selling the car at Rs 5.1 lakh – a ridiculous price for a Toyota Corolla which is about a year old.'

'A new one costs Rs 11 lakh. I am sure you would be aware.' Amit butted in and the sarcasm was not lost on Gowri. He was not amused. A dirty stare was all that he could return to Amit. Couldn't say anything else. If looks could kill, Amit would be dead by now.

'I went back to him on email. A year old Toyota Corolla should definitely get a better price. On that mail I asked him for reasons why the car would not sell at anything beyond Rs 5.1 lakh. He replied stating that the car has been involved in an accident in the past and is severely dented. This has impacted the second hand sale price of the car.'

'That seems logical. A dented car, involved in an accident will not get a good price. Commonsense. Isn't it?' Gowri tried to reason.

'Yes it does. But that's not the end of it.' He pulled out three colour printouts from his folder and passed them on to Gowri. 'These are the pics of the pearl white Toyota Corolla which he sent me yesterday morning.'

From the pictures it was clear that the car had been involved in a frontal accident and its bonnet had completely crashed. It would cost a fortune to repair the car, notwithstanding the amounts paid by the insurance firms.

'So where is the problem? The car has had an accident. Hence we cannot get a good price. I can't understand. Am I missing something here?'

'Amit, will you take on from here?'

'Before I begin, let me show you a video.' Amit switched off the lights in the room and turned on the projector. It was connected to his laptop.

'Will you stop this jazz and tell me without fucking around?' said an agitated Gowri.

Amit ignored Gowri's tirade and fiddled with his laptop. 'Let me play this for you.'

The clip came on screen.

The clipping was of a car yard, where a number of used cars were parked. Amit zeroed in on a pearl white Toyota Corolla. It started from the back of the car, then went around the car to the right, back again, then to the left and slowly moved ahead, finally coming to rest at the front of the car. It was a clumsily shot video. Clearly someone had used a mobile phone to shoot the clipping. After pausing for a moment, the video closed in on the bonnet. It was a sparkling car in mint condition. The video then slowly retracted and the angle tilted downward towards the front number plate. The person who was shooting the video purposely went closer to the number plate and stopped right in front of it. The video lingered on the number plate for some time and then the clip ended. The movie stopped and the last clip was in front of their eyes. It showed a clear shot of the number plate of the car.

It had the number DL2CAM 0192.

'This is the car in question, right? DL2CAM 0192?' Amit looked at both Manish and Gowri.

'The problem is that I landed up in the most unexpected of places yesterday. Since I was in Raipur, Manish asked me to visit the yard and do an inspection of the facilities available there and also to do a surprise check on this car. In fact, the visit was scheduled at the last minute because I had some time at hand, and I decided to help Manish.'

'I still don't understand what the issue is,' muttered Gowri.

'Either you are naïve Gowri, or you think we are idiots.' Amit was beginning to get irritated. 'Can't you see the picture which Vikas sent Manish?' Amit pulled it up on the screen. It was a badly damaged Toyota Corolla with its bonnet smashed to smithereens. Amit pulled up the last screen shot of the video again – the image of the bonnet of the car he had shot on his mobile phone. Both the images appeared side by side on the screen.

'Completely different cars!' Manish looked at Gowri and said.

'What does this show?' Gowri asked.

'Now don't be naïve Gowri.' Amit was back to having some fun.

'Enough mate. Let me explain,' Manish chipped in.

'Gowri, clearly Vikas has sent me a picture of a different car. He has used the image of a dented car to get an approval to sell a perfect car in mint condition at a lower price. The car in picture would sell for at least Rs 8 lakh. Vikas has clearly struck a deal with a used car dealer. He would sell the car for 8 lakh. The car dealer would only issue a payment of Rs 5.1 lakh to NFS. That would not raise any eyebrows, because Vikas holds my approval. The balance of Rs 2.9 lakh would be pocketed by the used car dealer and Vikas.

Apart from this there could be no motivation for him to send a wrong photograph. The right car is parked in the yard, but the photo is of a different car.'

'I suspected it. That's why I asked Amit to go and do the check without anyone getting wind of it. Unfortunately, the mortgages guy was not in office and Amit had time on his hand. Hence he was able to identify this bastardisation of the process.'

'Look Gowri, Vikas has made a cool profit of Rs 2.9 lakh which he would either pocket in full or share with the others in the chain. This is the way this racket operates.'

'And God only knows how many people up the chain get their cuts in this,' added Amit, much to Gowri's irritation.

'What do we do now?'

'We will have to ask Vikas to go. He has been found lying for suspected financial gain. Something which is not tolerated in our organisation. I am sure you would agree.'

Gowri didn't say anything.

'Would you want to speak with him and give him the option of resigning?' Manish asked Gowri. 'He has a choice. Either resign or face the ignominy of a termination.'

'Why should we even give him the option of resigning? He should be terminated.' Amit was very vocal about his thoughts.

'I will speak with him,' Gowri said and got up and headed towards the room, not leaving any scope for Amit's protest to be discussed. He stopped at the door, turned towards the two of them, 'What are we doing about Raman Bhaskar? The collections guy in Raipur? Why aren't we discussing him? He should also be sacked.'

'Ideally, we should have. But Gowri, Raman Bhaskar is on leave. He has been unwell for over fifteen days now. I will investigate his involvement when he comes back.'

'It's OKAY. He is a good guy. Maybe we should just move him out of collections and spare him with a warning,' said Gowri.

'But GOWRI . . .' Manish argued.

'Let's chat about it offline,' cut in Gowri and the matter ended there.

By the evening, Vikas had sent in his resignation. With Gowri's help, the unrepentant Vikas even found a job for himself. While Gowri had not tolerated unethical behaviour in the past, this was the first time he had helped someone who had committed a fraud to get away lightly. This probably had a lot to do with Amit being involved in the investigations.

Deed done, Gowri was furious. Vikas was his guy. How the fuck could Manish have used Amit, a novice, someone who had come into their organisation yesterday, to work against Gowri's guy? He should have at least mentioned this to him. Was his authority waning? He was extremely fidgety and felt let down.

'If only you had mentioned this to me, I would myself have terminated the guy,' he said to Manish later that evening. 'Why did you have to ask Amit to do this? You know these bank guys. Now word will spread all around the bank that such things happen in NFS.'

'It just happened that Amit was in Raipur and I casually asked him to find out. Anyway, good that we identified this fraud,' said Manish as he packed his bags.

The drama over, towards late evening, just before he left for home, Amit picked up the phone. He had held himself back all through the day. Now, he had to let go. He dialled a number and someone picked up. 'Hello?'

'In life friend, just remember one thing. If you fuck around with others, others will fuck around with you. You fucked with me and now you are paying the price for that.'

'Nonsense. Who is this?'

'Had you not asked Ratnesh to take an off yesterday when I was in Raipur, he would have kept me occupied throughout the day. I wouldn't have had any time to investigate this Toyota case. Now see the result. You screw with me, I screw you back . . . and I am known to screw badly my friend . . . and even Gowri cannot save you from me.' Saying this, he hung up leaving Vikas holding the phone in his hands and the call disconnected tone in his ears. He had clearly taken a *panga* with the wrong guy. Hadn't he done this at Gowri's insistence? Gowri should have protected him. He was now left facing the consequence of following instructions.

Amit did this with a purpose. He knew that sooner or later, the news of the resignation (or sacking, as people would get to know later) would spread like wildfire. It was hence important to capitalise on this to make his position stronger in the organisation. If people knew that one of Gowri's favourite was sacked at Amit's insistence, they would hesitate to take him on. Hence, it was important from his perspective that Vikas knew why he came after him. He knew that in the chaos that would follow, it would become a Gowri v/s Amit kind of battle, and in this background noise, all the reality about Vikas's misdeeds would get camouflaged. He didn't want that to happen.

October 2003
Chanda's Woes
NFS-Mumbai

Things were happening too fast at NFS. It had only been a few weeks since Amit had come in. Sangeeta moved in and out of her cabin on the corporate floor. She was extremely uncomfortable with Amit sharing her cabin forcibly. She wouldn't get the required privacy. Even when she was on calls with her family, Amit would not move out of the room. Realisation that he was doing it on purpose didn't take too much time to dawn on her. He was going all out to irritate her and successfully too. The comfort that she had in her old small cubicle was gone. She went and cribbed to Gowri, but to no avail. What could he have done? Wasn't he the one who created it?

Life was galloping rapidly. Never a dull moment for any of them.

'Did you know that Ratnesh is moving as branch manager for a branch in Kolkata?' Chanda called him on the intercom one day.

'How can he? He is in my business.'

'I don't know. An announcement on his move has come out.'
'Send it to me.'

Within seconds a pop-up appeared on Amit's screen saying that he had an unread mail.

Amit clicked on it and opened the mail. He read the same twice over.

Team,

I am happy to announce the appointment of Ratnesh Jha as Branch Manager, Gariahat Branch, Kolkata with effect from 1 April 2002. Ratnesh joined our team in the mortgages business, about nine months ago and within this short span of time, has built up a great business in Raipur. I am confident that he will do even better in his new role. Ratnesh will report to the Regional Head of East – Somesh Kikani.

Regards,
Gowri

'What the heck?' he thought to himself and called back Chanda. 'What nonsense is this?' he said as soon as Chanda picked up the phone.

'I don't know. Apparently he makes all these decisions here. It is an accepted norm.'

'Who makes these acceptable?'

'Don't know. But that's the way it has been here.'

'OKAY, let me talk to him,' and he kept the phone down. He thought for a while and then turned towards his laptop and started typing a mail.

Dear Gowri,

I just got to know that Ratnesh has been moved from his role with the Mortgages business in Raipur. Ratnesh is a good guy and I am very happy for him. I wish him all the best as he takes

on the new role. However, at this point in time, I would like to
make certain things very clear to you:
1. This is the last move in the Mortgages team which has
    happened without my concurrence.
2. All promotions, salary corrections, increments, etc., in the
    Mortgages team will be done by me.
3. All future moves which concern anyone in Mortgages need
    my prior approval.
Please disengage yourself from people-related issues in my business.
I thank you for your support so far. I will call upon you for help
and support in case a need were to arise.

Regards,
Amit

Within the next five seconds there was a pop-up on his screen,
which read 'one new message'. He clicked on it. It was from Gowri.
He had replied on his earlier message.

Dude,
We need to talk.
Gowri

Amit was quite worked up. He didn't like such a casual retort to
his serious mail. He was pissed. He was in no mood to let this up.

Gowri,

I have nothing further to discuss. If you disagree, I would rather
get HR and Hari involved. Please let me know.

Regards,
Amit

Amit had started to bark and niggle. Within forty-five seconds
Gowri barged into the room. 'What is your problem dude?'
'As in?'

'Why can't you mind your own business and be happy with it?'
'That's precisely my question?'
'Look dude, enough of fun OKAY. I run the branches the way I want to. Nobody has asked me any questions in the past. I don't . . .'
Trrng Trrng . . . Amit's phone rang. It was from Chanda. He decided to pick it up.
'Hi!'
'Was speaking to Anamika. She is moving to Delhi. They are moving Kirpal in her place as a branch manager to Ludhiana.' Anamika was the branch manager for NFS in Ludhiana and Kirpal was the mortgage sales guy in Ambala. The latter was in Amit's chain of command.
'What?' Amit shook his head in disgust and walked out of the room to avoid any sensitive conversations in front of Gowri.
Gowri remained in Amit's shared room. He was furious at the response he got from Amit. He had to close this issue today. Amit was talking on the phone and taking his own time. 'I will move from here only when I fix the problem,' said Gowri to himself and sat down on the chair that was on the same side of the table where Amit would normally sit.
He looked around the room. There were a few trophies in the room. A few pictures, almost all of them of Sangeeta. She had not cleared all her stuff from the room. Many of them had Gowri in them. His gaze continued to roam and then skipped to the other side of the room. In transitioning, they skipped over the screen of Amit's laptop. The screen was open and on the screen was a mail from Gowri. The same mail which announced Ratnesh's move. The mail, he could see, was forwarded from Chanda's ID. How stupid of him for not having realised? There was a mole in the house. Chanda was feeding him information against Gowri. He was now even more furious. Even more pissed at himself. Shouldn't he have seen this coming? He had to now deal with Chanda more than anyone else.

Sangeeta had many a time bitched to him about Chanda, but he had ignored her whines. What upset him was that he should have proactively seen this coming. But somehow Chanda was in his blind spot.

'OKAY, I will call you. He is in my room,' and Amit walked back into the room.

'Yes Gowri? What were you saying?'

'No, it's fine Amit. We will talk later. And he walked out towards his cabin, leaving Amit wondering about the sudden change in mood.

Back in his room, Gowri was in a very pensive mood, when a knock on his door woke him up from his knitted eyebrows and staring into one insignificant spot on his table expression.

'Gowri, I came to give you the MI which you asked for.' It was Chanda who had come up.

'Give it to Suzanna. I will take it from her.'

'Okay. Let me know if you need anything.'

'Hmm . . .' something was wrong. She could sense it. But he was not saying anything. She quietly walked back to her desk.

Gowri buzzed Suzanna and asked her to get Sangeeta to come in.

'Gowri, she is on her market visits, will be in office in about twenty minutes. By the way, Karen called. Hari was asking for the final draft of the presentation to be made to the NYB advisory board tomorrow.'

'What time is my presentation scheduled?'

'9 a.m.'

'Okay, ask my team to be present. All of them need to attend this meeting. All my direct reports (DR). Tell them to wear formals. Ties are compulsory.'

'Okay Gowri.' And she turned to leave.

'Wait.' She stopped. 'Give me a printout of the list of people who will be there. I will tell you who all I want there.'

She stepped out and was back in a minute with a printout of a list of Gowri's DRs and handed it to him. It was a list of the core members of his team. Gowri looked through it. After a minute of intent gazing, he stretched his hand, picked out a sharpened pencil from the pen stand, ran it across a name on the list and handed it back to Suzanna. Suzanna looked at it and then looked at Gowri. She couldn't believe her eyes but then realised that it was time for her to leave. Only one name was stuck off. Chanda Sharma was not to attend the next day's presentation with the advisory board. Gowri had struck her name off.

An hour later, Suzanna sent out a mail to the team instructing them to be a part of the morning meeting with the advisory board . . . to all except Chanda. Chanda got to know about it when she reached office the next day at 9.15 a.m., and found everyone from her team missing. They were all at the presentation which had begun fifteen minutes ago. She tried asking around, but didn't get any answers.

Over the next few days instructions went out to the team, through Sangeeta that interactions with Chanda needed to be kept to the bare minimum and only on a need basis. Gowri was cutting down her access to information, which in a way could be used against him. Her name got dropped off all MISs which were circulated to the branch managers. Amit had earlier asked Gowri to stop all MI related to mortgages from being circulated from his office. Gowri did not heed his advice. He just dropped Chanda from the mailing list. The people down the line were in any case aligned to him. The branch managers owed their careers to Gowri and hence were very careful and circumspect in their dealing with Amit and Chanda. This suited Gowri.

These tactics became a regular practice. As Gowri sat on his king-size chair and languorously crossed his legs, he realised that he had discovered a goldmine. The secret to dealing with Amit was right in front of him – Chanda. She was his trump card. As long as Chanda's career and self-esteem was at stake and under threat, Amit would behave well towards him. The belligerence that Amit displayed had a lot to do with Chanda not being impacted. If he somehow visibly demonstrates to Amit that his attitude towards Gowri would impact Chanda, Amit would be under control. Why didn't he think of it earlier?

Chanda began to feel the heat. She was increasingly being cut off from everything that she used to do in the past. Gowri hired a junior MIS manager to work with Sangeeta and got all the work done through him. A lot of product management stuff which was done by Chanda earlier moved to the marketing team. Gowri did it so very smartly that no one could point a finger at him publicly. He couldn't be seen to be publically antagonistic towards Chanda; else, he would fall flat on his face.

In fact this was Sangeeta's idea which was paying off. That day when Gowri had seen the mail announcing Ratnesh's move on Amit's laptop, he had called Sangeeta in to bitch to her.

'Gowri, if Amit is cantankerous towards you, why should you be tolerant towards Chanda?'

'Hmm . . .' Gowri was still very pensive. He had just seen the mail from Chanda to Amit. Sangeeta was right.

'Gowri, she is not aligned to you. You need to somehow push her on the back foot.'

'That's going to be difficult. We can't be blatant about it. Let's subtly move her out of her core responsibilities. Else they will go running to Aditya.'

'You cannot because you have a stature to protect. I can.'

Gowri's eyes lit up with a wicked glint when Sangeeta said this. 'Oh yes, of course. You can do whatever you want. No one can stop you.'

'And of course, you will protect me if something goes wrong,' confirmed Sangeeta.

'Of course Sango, you know that.'

'I will push her enough to put her on the defensive. We need her here. She is your trump card Gowri. As long as she is affected, Amit could be kept under check. The day she quits and goes, Amit will be a free bird. Let's make use of her Gowri.'

And the deal was done. Mind games with Chanda had begun. If Amit had to be kept in check, then Chanda was to be abused. Maybe Chanda's frustration would make Amit mend his ways and fall in line with Gowri. That was the game plan. Poor Chanda had no clue that hell was going to break loose on her.

December 2003
The Frustration Piles
NFS-Mumbai

The drive back from the Nariman Point office to Bandra was a long one. Today it seemed longer, given the silence which prevailed inside the small confines of the Ford Ikon. Amit was at the wheel and Chanda was sitting next to him. Amit tried to get Chanda's attention, but Chanda refused to be moved. She did not open her mouth to say anything.

The year gone by was a painful one for her. She had taken enough of shit all through the year. She was ignored, treated shabbily, and not given her due in the organisation. Not once did she whine. She was left out of an offsite citing some stupid cost cutting as an excuse. Gowri had said that given the limited number of people they could take on an offsite, guys from the head office should stay back and only the sales guys from the branches should be going. She didn't complain. When she got to know Suzzana was going and she had been left out, it hurt her badly, and yet she didn't grumble.

There were many points in time when she contemplated quitting. Amit also advocated this to her. 'Why are you going through all this? Either you look for a different job or I will,' he had said.

But no, Chanda wouldn't give up. 'Amit, that's what these guys want. They want me to succumb to their idiosyncrasies and quit. And why? Because they think that you will have an access into their camp only till I am there. The day I quit, you will lose all that and will become vulnerable. I don't care about what they think but I will not quit and let them have their way. If you want to quit and go somewhere else, it's your call.' Her fierce competitive streak was surfacing. Independent and focused on her career, the desire to achieve things on her own was getting compromised, and she was not willing for that.

But today she made no such claims. No such talk. She just didn't open her mouth. Despite Amit's best efforts at humouring her, nothing changed. They crossed Worli, passed Prabhadevi, went past the Siddhivinayak temple, past Dadar and reached the inevitable traffic jam in Mahim. Still Chanda didn't respond to his overtures. The traffic was inching ahead very slowly. It gave Amit some time to take his eyes off the road and talk to Chanda. He turned and looked at her. She was sitting motionless, listening to the radio, mumbling nothings.

'Chanda,' he touched her. She did not respond. Didn't even turn and look at him. She was sitting there, seized like a zombie. Amit got worried. 'Chanda! Are you fine?' Chanda finally reacted. She looked straight into his eyes, tense and worked up.

'Only if you let me be Amit. Only if you let me be.' And then she collapsed,' sobbing uncontrollably. Amit tried to hug her, but the signal turned to green and he couldn't. He had to move on from where the car was standing. Traffic was bumper to bumper for over a mile from there and he was in the middle lane. He couldn't stop the car on the side and console her. Helplessness took over. Finally he reached Bandra and turned over into the road leading to the reclamation area and stopped the car. The road was wider and with less traffic, and hence there was no one honking from behind, forcing him to move ahead.

'Chanda. Chanda, what happened? Why are you crying?' He was worried. Though Chanda was prone to shedding a few tears in the past, this was the first time he had seen her weep like this. Her entire body was shaking . . . it was a frustrated helpless cry.

'You are screwing up my career. It's only because of you that I am in this state!' Amit was shocked. She had never spoken to him in this fashion. 'You first killed my biotechnology career even before it took off and now you are bent on dooming my banking career too.'

'What have I done Chanda?' his first reaction was to defend himself. Immediately he realised that he should not have done that.

'What have I done? Who asked you to come to NFS? Had you not come I would have been better off? Much better off.'

'What happened Chanda? Tell me. Why are you behaving like this?'

Chanda just lost it. Her sobbing intensified and she put her head between her knees and sobbed and sobbed and sobbed.

Amit didn't know what to do.

A few hours earlier

Amit had just returned from a trip to Delhi that afternoon. He walked into office and straight to his shared room. Chander had been retained in another role and hence his room did not get allotted to Amit. He continued sharing his room with Sangeeta.

Sangeeta had gone out. As Amit settled down in his den, he glanced at the table in front of him. On the table was a sheet of paper with a grid on it. The grid had names of the people in the branch and their performance ratings. It was the end of the year and therefore appraisal time and performance rating time too. 'Impressive. She is quite organised,' he thought to himself as he casually flipped through the piece of paper. Ideally he should not have looked at it. It's inappropriate to look at someone else's documents without the person knowing about it. But all this protocol was damned in NFS.

'Let's see if she is a tough boss,' he said to himself as he picked up her sheet to see how she had rated her people. He had heard that women made terrible bosses.

What he saw shocked him no end. In that list were names of people from the mortgages business who operated out of the branches, people from the auto loans business, and people from the credit team among many others. *What the hell are these names doing here? Who has rated them? Why was I not told?* He had been working on those ratings himself.

At that very moment Sangeeta walked in. 'Hi Amit,' she tried to be nice.

'What's this Sangeeta?'

'Oh this? These are the performance ratings of people in my team.'

'My team! Won't you guys ever give up?'

'What?'

'Who gave you the authority to decide the performance ratings of these guys?'

'I think you should ask Gowri that question. I will do what I am told to do.' And she turned and walked away.

A furious Amit charged into Gowri's room. 'Gowri, how many times have I told you to stay away from me and my team?'

Gowri looked at him and did not say anything.

'What's this?'

'How do I know? It is in your hands.' Gowri was cheeky.

'Don't try to be smart Gowri! You have asked Sangeeta to do the performance appraisals of all staff in the branches including those in my vertical.'

'That's the way it has been done so far.'

'I thought we changed it.'

'You wanted it to be changed. I didn't change it. The guys have a reporting into the branch managers as per the approved organisation structure.'

'Only for administrative purposes,' retorted Amit. Since the business model of NFS involved doing business in remote locations, the branch manager had oversight only for administrative purposes and they were still controlled by Amit in his business vertical.

'Year after year, I have been doing this. What's different now?' That was a fact. Every year, Gowri had bulldozed the business managers and used his overbearing personality to brow beat them into agreeing with his rating. Ratings drove increments and decided bonuses for every individual. Over time people realised that it was Gowri who was their '*annadaata*' and not the business managers themselves. That's how he managed to build an aura around himself. He was called the king for nothing.

'Enough! I will speak with HR. Let's see what they say.'

Amit walked across to Sunil, the head of HR. He was furious. Gowri was a guy who was known to be a wheeler dealer. What about HR? HR should have been unbiased in the entire show. They couldn't be seen as taking sides. Something like this would never happen in NYB. But NFS was like a banana republic. Anything could happen here as long as Gowri willed it.

Sunil had no explanation for what had happened. All he said was that it was incorrect on the part of HR to have asked Gowri for the ratings. Someone in HR at the lowest rank had just followed last year's process. The earlier business managers didn't have an issue with this process. The fact that Amit wanted it differently was not communicated down the line in HR.

The head of HR tried to talk Amit into letting it be. 'Why don't you give your inputs to Gowri and let him incorporate the feedback in his ratings?'

'Fuck no! Sunil, I manage my team my way. He cannot decide who gets what in my team. I can bet my ass the guy would have screwed around with the mortgage guys in the performance ratings.'

'I don't think so,' Sunil was vociferous in his defence. 'He is quite fair in his approach.'

'Fair my foot!' Amit was furious. 'Why don't you check?'

Sunil and Amit then got down to checking the ratings of the individuals in the mortgage team. NFS operated on a performance rating scale of one to ten. If an individual was given a performance rating of one, it indicated a stellar performance and a performance rating of ten was indicative of a horrible performance – a performance which meant the person was no longer required in the organisation. They did some analysis of the ratings given by Gowri for the personal loan guys in the branch network and compared them with the mortgage guys.

It took them approximately thirty minutes to come up with the analysis on an excel spreadsheet.

Ratings	Branch personal loans	Mortgages
1–2	26 %	8 %
3–5	65 %	52 %
6 and above	9 %	40 %

The numbers were staring at them.

'Do I need to say anything more Sunil? Ninety-one percent of the personal loans guys have got a rating better than five and only sixty percent of the people in mortgages have got a performance rating higher than five. Even in the top performer's bracket, twenty-six percent of personal loans are top performers while only eight percent of the staff in mortgages are rated as top performers. Is this the right way to do things? No wonder you have glamorised personal loans, Mr Gowri Shankar's product, in this organisation. Everyone wants to get out of mortgages and move to personal loans. To the branch business. Isn't it time to set it right? You have the responsibility, Sunil, to ensure that such shit doesn't happen.' And then he paused. Sunil didn't say anything. 'Please correct this. I will send you my ratings by this evening.' And he walked away. He stopped outside his cabin and stretched his neck to look back into the room and added, 'Sunil, if I complain about this, you could lose your job.'

This worried Sunil. He had never looked at the performance ratings in this manner. This could seriously land him in trouble if Amit went ahead and executed his threat.

'Let me fix this for you,' he said.

'You better!' muttered Amit as he walked away.

Within the next fifteen minutes, Sunil was in Gowri's room. They were closeted for over thirty minutes. Sangeeta was called in a couple of times. Amit could imagine what was going on.

Within moments of Sunil exiting the room, Amit got a mail from Sangeeta who was sitting three feet away from him.

Dear Amit,

Please find enclosed the ratings which have been recommended by the branch managers for the Mortgages team. Please go through them and provide your team's ratings directly to HR by today EOD.

Regards,
Sangeeta

The mail was marked to Sunil and Gowri. Amit saw the mail and smiled. This could have been done earlier. Why did they have to get into a confrontation?

Oblivious to all this, Chanda was going about doing her work as usual. She had just come out of a training session on personal loan products for new joinees. This part of her job was something she liked. Training came naturally to her. It helped her escape the stress, the tension, and the worry of her strained relationship with her boss. When she was inside the room with all the new joinees, she would go into a different world. A world of make believe . . . a world where everything was hunky-dory. Where people tried to be nice and build harmonious relationships with each other. It took her away from the compulsions of reality.

After the training, she walked to her desk. Someone from the branches had sent her an approval request for the payment to be made to a sales agent. It was nearing 7.30 p.m. In the normal course, she would have logged off and left for home. She tried calling Amit on his extension. No one picked up. Maybe he had gone to the loo. She decided to wait.

'If I have to wait, might as well finish the pending work. Less work for tomorrow,' she thought and opened her email. A few sales agency payment requests were responded to. Some approved and a few rejected. A job had to be done with diligence irrespective of motivation levels, and she was not the ones who would allow her state of mind to impact her work. Amit had also taught her to lay down ground rules and processes for everything at work so that they don't need to revisit requests again and again. 'If someone sends you an approval request, he must know with a reasonable degree of certainty if it will go through or not.' She smiled to herself when she thought of that. After sending out the approvals, she normally printed a copy of every approval given and filed them separately. She did the same today and walked towards the printer on her floor. Its toner had run out and hence it couldn't print. She then decided to spool it to Suzanna's printer on the corporate floor, which was just a floor above hers. 'I will anyway have to go to that floor to check on Amit,' she thought as she fired the prints.

She collected her bags, logged off her system and walked up. 'I will collect the printouts and file them tomorrow,' she said to herself as she climbed the stairs.

Amit was there talking to Manish Kakkar who was also ready to leave. When he saw her, Amit reacted, 'Chalen . . . let's go?'

'I am waiting,' she said as she walked up to the printer. She picked up her lot of printouts and stood at the door waiting for Amit to come.

'Amit . . . Amit . . . are you there?' It was Karen who came running out of the MD's cabin to speak with Amit.

'Karen? You haven't gone home? It's well past your bed time,' Amit smiled at her.

'I am just leaving baba. Your boss wants you for a minute.'

Amit looked at Chanda and she smiled partly in desperation, partly in irritation. She walked to the nearest sofa and plunked herself. Looking around, she saw that all the cabins were empty, except Amit's and Manish's. Everyone had left for the day. The clock above the board room door was pushing 8.30 p.m. She was hoping Amit would come out fast. Casually, she ruffled through the papers that she was carrying, the ones she picked up from the printer. There were six sheets in all that she had printed and she started counting them in her mind as she went through them. Two sheets of payment computations, one blank sheet from somewhere unknown – probably a problem in the page setup, an email to Suzanna, an order for a print . . . wait a sec. Email to Suzanna? She didn't print it. Probably picked by mistake. She needed to put it back. It was not hers. She got up and removed the email from the lot of papers she was carrying. As she was taking it back to the printer she saw her name in the email and her curiosity was aroused. After all, she too was human. A quick glance told her that there was nobody on the floor who was observing her. Except for Manish, there was nobody there. Period. Amit and Karen were the only others and they were in Hari's room. Satisfying herself that she would not be caught infringing into someone else's space, she started reading the mail. After she read the mail, she glanced up, looked round the room, quietly folded the mail, put it into her bag and went and sat down on the sofa. The smile had been wiped off from her face.

Quietly, she waited for Amit to come back. Fifteen minutes later they were driving on Marine Drive, on their way back to Bandra. Initially Amit thought that she was upset about his making her wait for him. However, after a few miles of driving, he realised that was not the case.

And now Amit was sitting in Bandra reclamation, with a howling Chanda, wondering what was wrong.

He put his arm around Chanda and pulled her up. 'Will you please tell me what is wrong? If you keep howling like this without telling me what happened, I can't do anything.'

She had regained composure by then. Dipping her hand into the bag she fished out a neatly folded piece of paper and passed it on to him.

Amit took it from her and opened it. It was dark outside. He switched on the car lights and strained himself to read it. It was an email sent to Suzanna—from Gowri.

It read:

Suzanna,

Please make these changes in the master file that you have with you.

Gowri

Below that was a chain of messages. 'Read from the bottom,' she said. And Amit went to the last mail in the chain of messages. It was from Sunil to Gowri.

Gowri,

In light of today's discussion with Amit, I would request you to forward the mortgage performance rating recommendations to him. I have asked him to send us the final ratings of mortgage resources. He will be considering the inputs provided by the branch managers before arriving at the final rating.

Regards,
Sunil

On top of that was another mail sent by Sunil to Gowri.

Gowri,

Further to my earlier mail, you may have to relook at the ratings of the people in the personal loans business at the branches. If I move out the ratings of the mortgage personnel, they look skewed. You have too many people who are rated 1, 2 and 3. We need to change that. You may need to look at forceranking your guys and not have more than 40% of your employees rated 1–3. I would be grateful, if you could look at this change and revert by the end of today.

Sunil

This was followed by an exchange of mails between the two of them wherein Gowri marginally changed the ratings of a few people . . . a change that wasn't significant.

And then came the big one. The last mail from Gowri to Sunil, which was forwarded to Suzanna . . . this is how it went:

Sunil,

There is a minor error in the sheet I sent to you earlier. I need to change the rating of Chanda Sharma. Please change it to 6. Her rating was earlier erroneously input as 3. Please let me know in case you have any queries.

Gowri

To which Sunil responded:

Gowri,
Understand. Thanks.
Regards,
Sunil

'Bastards!' screamed Amit. Thankfully the car windows were rolled up. Else the entire reclamation area would have heard this.

'Why scream at them? All this is because of you. A rating of six? I am in the bottom twenty percent of my business in terms of performance. That's what anyone who sees this rating would think.'

'But that's not true.'

'Who knows that Amit? Who knows that? Everyone will think I am a useless shirker, who does not deserve to be in her job. All because this husband of mine cannot manage his relationships at work.'

Amit wanted to react but he did not. He knew that this was an outburst of pent up emotions and wanted her to pour it all out. He could understand what she was going through.

After a long conversation that night, a pointless one at that, they returned home. It was a long and lonely night for both of them. The air of silence between them also seemed to be fighting at that point of time. For the first time in their lives, they slept on the same bed as strangers. Chanda held Amit accountable for most of her problems. She was not willing to see any rationale in Amit's behaviour. Was this the beginning of the end?

20 December 2007
Bandra Police Station
Mumbai

Amit was alone in his cell. It was a small eight feet by ten feet cell, with a solitary ceiling fan for company. He had never been in a jail . . . ever in his life. This was the first time anyone from his family had been jailed. It was shameful. 'What would his parents think of him?' he thought to himself.

Soon, the long dreary hours gave way to the dark and lonely night. It was the second night in his life that he knew he would not be able to sleep. The earlier time, it was a night which changed his life. His thoughts went back to the night when he and Chanda argued at Bandra Reclamation. Reclamation in Bandra is that part of the bay, where during the day you would see young couples trying to forge a relationship. Numerous couples escape from the confines of their small homes and prying neighbours and come to this stretch for a feeling of seclusion. It gave them a sense of public privacy. One would find all of them, lovers trying to cement a relationship, wannabe guys and girls dating each other, stealing that occasional kiss, the first hug, etc. And it was at the same place that he had felt the first strain in their relationship. But today he needed her. He needed her support. The loneliness he felt today was no different from what he had felt that night. The night which started at Bandra Reclamation had not ended yet . . . the longest night of their lives. Their relationship had come apart at the seam after that night. He was struggling to keep the relationship alive. If that was the worst night in his life, this was not far away.

He looked out of the police station. From his cell he had a clear view of the hall and beyond the hall into the road. There was a smell of liquor in the air. Umpteen numbers of drunkards, pimps, murderers and whores all over the place. In his mind he added one more member to the long list of professionals he had just called out – banker. The only thing that differentiated him from the rest of the crowd was his attire, his impeccable pinstripes. If God was a banker, he wouldn't be in jail. That clearly made him a devil . . . a devil in pinstripes.

Life for him had taken an unexpected turn after that night with Chanda . . . a turn from which it would have been very difficult to come back on track. 'It is not the end of the road . . . just a bend,' he had said and consoled himself . . . little did he know that beyond the bend was a steep fall to wilderness, where he ran the risk of losing himself.

A constable came by and asked him if he needed a blanket. Amit just nodded. From the available ones, the constable pulled out a better looking one and gave it to him. Amit looked as if he was from a good family, and that look got him an extra pillow too. That night, he was the most well-mannered convict in that police station. Probably the most well-mannered person ever in that jail. Period.

2004
NFS – Mumbai

Chanda was extremely upset at the ratings given to her. She felt that she had given the organisation a lot more and that she deserved much more respect in return. What upset her even more were the circumstance under which her performance ratings were downgraded. She felt shattered and her dwindling sense of self-respect left her even more reticent. At times she considered confronting HR or Gowri about the entire episode, but she let it be. 'Why demean myself? I know I am better than this. He is just being vindictive.'

As a fallout of this, she almost stopped talking to Amit about work. If at all Amit would try speaking with her, she would avoid it in every way possible. Things were taking an ugly turn. As Amit's frustration mounted, it was becoming difficult for him to manage her behaviour and it increasingly downsized his patience levels too. 'Why doesn't she understand? I cannot hold back and stop pushing Gowri just because she is my wife.'

It was January. Time to celebrate the new year and the fantastic performances of the previous year. As was the norm, Aditya organised a massive party for the entire management team of NYB and NFS. Held at the Imperial Ball Room of Taj Mahal Hotel in Colaba, it was a gigantic affair. Everyone was invited with their spouses. For Chanda it didn't matter, because she in any case got a separate invite as an employee of NFS.

Amit and Chanda landed at the hotel well in time for the party. The party was to begin at 8.30 and they were there by 8.00. Surprisingly, traffic had been quite clear from Bandra. They were among the first ones to arrive. Aditya was already at the hotel overseeing the arrangements for the party. One wouldn't often find a country head overseeing preparations for such a party. Aditya did. The two of them were meeting Aditya after a long time.

'Hey young man, how have you been? And who do we have here? Chanda, you are looking gorgeous. Looks like NFS has been taking care of you.'

Chanda's reaction was very curt. 'If only. Aditya.' She was very direct.

'As in . . . ?'

'Nothing Aditya. It's just too much of work to be done,' Amit hastily interjected. Aditya noticed the glare that he gave Chanda after that. All through the night, Chanda was extremely aloof, and did not mix with people at all. Amit kept chasing her and tried to keep her entertained, but nothing helped.

'If you did not want to go, you should have told me earlier. I would have made up some excuse for us and stayed back!' Amit was upset at Chanda's behaviour and told her so, once they were back in the safe confines of their car. 'You messed up my fun too!'

'You should have gone on your own. Why did you have to drag me there anyways?'

'I thought it would be a good change for you. A change of environment, meeting up all the folks and mingling with them would lighten up your mood. But, no! I was wrong!'

'They are all "your" folks, "your" guys! People who have messed up my life and my career. These are the guys who sent me and then you to NFS. My life changed the day you came there. And I hold no one but you and your Aditya responsible for that. He is a selfish son of a bitch, who sent you to NFS for his gains. Doesn't care a fuck about what happens to us!' Chanda exclaimed almost in tears. It was completely forgotten that it was the same Chanda who had sung praises of Aditya and convinced Amit to take on the NFS assignment even when Amit was quite apprehensive about Aditya's intent.

Seeing Chanda get into another one of her hysterical moods, Amit just kept quiet and didn't say another word. 'How do I get things back in shape?' was the question that was occupying his mind all the time. While he thought about it, he couldn't figure a way to do that. Every passing minute seemed to be adding a mile of distance between Chanda and Amit. His conversations with Chanda were very limited. She had become a recluse. Earlier, she would call him at least ten times a day, either on the intercom or the cell phone. That had stopped. It was now only Amit calling Chanda, never the reverse. He couldn't figure out where he went wrong. The politics between him and Gowri was taking a toll on their family life. The lack of peace of mind at work was impacting their peace at home. The 'Gowri factor' had begun to shape their lives negatively.

The next day was a Sunday and was spent entirely at home. Chanda was all the same – sulky and mum. At various times, Amit offered to take her out for dinner or for a movie, but Chanda was never game. Amit was now a really worried man.

He left home the next day at 7.30 a.m. Routinely on Mondays, he would leave home early, to be prepared for the morning reviews with Hari that began at 9.30 a.m. Chanda would come to office by herself. He was nearing office when his phone rang.

'Hello?'

'Hey Rambo! What's up?'

'Nothing Aditya, driving to work.'

'I know. That's why I thought I will catch you now.'

'Yes sir.'

'Is everything okay?'

'Ya, why?'

'Didn't look so to me.'

'As in . . . ?'

'The party day before yesterday. Both of you didn't look like the Amit and Chanda I knew.'

'No Aditya. Just a bad day.'

'I can understand you being like that, but I have never seen Chanda like that. She looked unhappy with what she was doing. And if I remember correctly, she said it too.'

Amit didn't respond. Just kept quiet.

'Tell me Amit. If you don't tell me, I can't help you.'

After a bit of persuasion, Amit opened up. He told him about his conflict with Gowri. The issues with the structure. How the branch managers were scuttling the growth of his business. How they were stonewalling every initiative of his, and most importantly how his tiff with Gowri was impacting Chanda professionally and also having a detrimental effect on their married life.

'Why didn't you tell me about this earlier?'

'I tried a couple of times, but you were too busy. And these are problems I thought I should and could handle myself.'

'Will Chanda be interested in moving to the bank? I can give her a role in retail banking here. If she moves out of there, at least your personal lives will be back on track.'

'I don't know. If I ask her, she will pounce on me!'

'Anyway, ask her and let me know. If that helps you guys to settle down, I will be happy to do it for you. And you do not worry. You are made for bigger things. At some point in time, I want to throw that Gowri out and give you the entire branch network. You hang in there and keep your chin up. I am expecting one round of restructuring to happen in the next ninety days. A lot of things are happening globally within the organisation and I expect it to get a lot clearer in ninety days from now.'

'Okay Aditya,' and he hung up. For the first time since he joined NFS, he was late for the Monday morning briefing.

During the day he told Chanda about his conversation with Aditya and asked her if she wanted to move to the bank, and indeed he got pounced at . . . as expected. 'I listened to you and came here. Am paying for it. Let me manage my own issues now. Please tell Aditya . . . NO THANKS!' Amit tried to convince her, but after the rating incident, Chanda had stopped seeing rationale. The bone of contention was that given the sensitivity of her being there, Amit should have been more careful and choosy in picking his battles. Her biggest crib was that he went ahead with work and his battle with Gowri, as if she never existed.

Amit went back sore faced to Aditya to communicate Chanda's refusal.

'Don't worry Amit, I will fix it. I will manage Gowri. I need to somehow get him out of that place and give that job to you. I only have to manage some sensitivity at Hari's level.'

Amit was not aware of the sensitivities he was talking about. He tried to think, but couldn't think of what could be the sensitivity Hari would have if Aditya wanted to get rid of Gowri. Life had many if's, but Amit was not prepared for the one coming next.

Mid-2004
The Organisation Change
NFS

The next six months were hell for Amit and Chanda. The chasm between them showed no signs of narrowing. Amit at one point in time considered quitting his job and moving to another company. At least that would put the equations at ease in NFS. Gowri would stop being antagonistic towards Chanda. He would again accept her into his fold. Treat her as one of his own people and work towards ensuring that she was happy in that organisation.

He did start looking out too. It was a painful phase for him personally. The general banking industry in India in 2004 was going through a quasi-recessionary phase. The job market was cold. Senior level positions in general were lacking. GE was the only competition which was hiring. However, because Amit had refused a job with GE, they were not too keen on hiring him again, when he needed to move. Large organisations have large egos. He didn't understand this fact till he experienced it.

Standard Chartered Bank gave him the position of a regional business head for mortgages for western India. Coming down from a national business manager role to a regional head, even if it paid more, was not something he would have wanted to do. Life was really getting frustrating for him.

Because of Chanda's behaviour, he had even gone cold towards Gowri, who in turn started exploiting it. When Gowri turned against Chanda, he had done it with a purpose. He knew that at some point of time, this attitude of his would prevent Amit from rising up and going whole hog against him . . . and this, he knew, would bind Amit's hands. It was only unfortunate that Chanda was caught in the crossfire.

Amit's self-esteem started taking a beating. He was losing his assertive traits. Hadn't he always called a spade a spade? No longer. He tried to buy peace. This had a telling effect on the Sharma family. Neither of them enjoyed working in NFS.

One had an option to move out. Self-esteem and self-pride prevented Chanda from moving to NYB. Amit desperately wanted to move out to protect his self-confidence, but was not getting a job which fitted his stature and experience. For them, hell on earth was NFS.

Gowri, on the contrary, the shrewd manipulator that he was, grew from strength to strength. Amit's weakness got touted as Gowri's strength. He openly started criticising the bank, the people from the bank, and their failed attempts to run NFS. His demi-god status only touched new heights in NFS. Whether Amit's backing off had an impact, nobody could tell, but one thing was for sure – it did not have such a positive impact, as was expected, on the personal relationships between any two of the three of them.

In the midst of all this, Aditya returned from another of those country managers' conference in New York. This was the mid-year conference of country CEOs across the globe, a meet where business level strategies were discussed, debated, decisions made, and investments agreed. India was represented by Aditya and Hari.

Dear all,

I would like to hold a townhall for all senior and mid-level managers in Mumbai, tomorrow at 10 a.m. in the large Board Room No. 2 on the 2nd floor. Please make it convenient to attend. In view of this, all other meetings scheduled for the day stand cancelled.

Sd/- Aditya
20 June 2004

Amit was surprised to see this mail on his blackberry on Sunday night. However, he dismissed this as another one of those numerous meetings to download information after a foreign jaunt. He showed it to Chanda, who as usual didn't respond. Amit left home early next morning. He didn't want to be late for Aditya's meeting.

The board room was full of people when Amit walked in. There would have been sixty of them at last count. Each and every chair was taken. People were even standing all around, speaking in hushed voices. 'What's going on?' he thought to himself. He had absolutely no clue. Sometimes being in a subsidiary group company had its own negatives. One had to make an extra effort to keep in touch with the core organisation. He had over the last year or so, lost contact with NYB . . . ever since he moved to NFS. The buzz around suggested that there was something amiss and he had no clue about what it was.

He joined the crowd. Some smiles were exchanged. A few of them were his old friends. He had worked with them in his past roles at NYB. A couple of them met warmly and they exchanged notes. He tried to fish for information, but nothing was forthcoming. This was probably because no one knew. The room was sounding and even looking like a fish market. At that moment the door opened and in walked Aditya. A hush descended on the room. Aditya walked to the head of the table and took the seat reserved for him. Everyone was looking at him with eager eyes, as if he was going to announce a fifty percent increase in their salaries.

'Is everyone in?' asked Aditya as he looked around. No one responded.

'Shall we begin?' still no response. 'Okay, then I assume we shall.'

'Sorry folks for calling all of you in, at such a short notice.' And he looked around. No response.

'As all of you are aware, Hari and I had been to New York for a global conference and we returned only last night.' And then he looked around. 'Hari? Where are you Hari?'

Unseen by anyone, Hari had sneaked into the room and was standing at the back. Amit turned back and saw him. He was surprised to see the person standing next to him too. It was Gowri, dressed in a pinstriped suit. In the last eighteen months, he had never seen him wear a tie, leave alone a formal jacket. He was standing next to Hari. He remembered Gowri's statement to him the day he joined NYB – 'No one wears a tie here . . . only in your bank do people wear such things.'

'Why don't you come up Hari, so that everyone can see you?' called out Aditya, and Hari walked to the top of the table and took the seat next to Aditya.

'It was announced at the global conference and something which I would like to share with you all, that the organisation structure will undergo a change.'

'Aah . . . so that's the reason,' thought Amit, vividly recollecting his conversation with Aditya wherein he had mentioned to him that the organisation structure would change in about ninety days. Never mind the fact that the discussion was over 180 days ago.

'Till recently you had a product-wise reporting the globe over, i.e. till now NFS which is an NYB-owned consumer finance company reported to the regional consumer finance head in Singapore. Similarly, our insurance company reported to the regional insurance business head in Singapore. This structure prevented us from exploiting synergies between the bank's retail banking business and these subsidiary companies.

'It has now been decided that globally, we will move to a geographical structure. In other words, the country management for the bank will be responsible for all businesses in the country irrespective of whether they are run through the bank or through subsidiary companies. The retail business of NYB, and the MD of NFS and the head of our insurance subsidiary will report to me, the CEO of NYB. We made a half-hearted attempt at this change a year back, but we didn't execute it the way we should have. Now it has been mandated at the highest level. And will be effective immediately.'

'Great,' thought Amit. 'Now Aditya will have greater control on the way NFS was run.'

'There are a few other structural changes which will take effect as a result of this decision.

'My close friend Hari [sic . . . thought Amit . . . when did he become close?], after five years of stellar contribution as the head of NFS, will move on as head of retail banking for Taiwan. The formal announcement will be released soon. Probably by this evening.'

'What the hell?' muttered Amit under his breath. 'What happens to all of us now?' he turned and looked at Gowri, who was cool as a cucumber, and smiling. Amit looked back at Hari and then turned and glanced at Gowri again. The smile was still there. This time he winked at Amit making him conscious.

'Hari's move gives us the opportunity to showcase one of our brightest talents . . . actually the brightest talent the group has seen in the recent past. Friends, I present to you the new managing director of New York International Financial Services Limited, Gowri Shankar!' Amit's jaw dropped. He was shocked. Till now, it was only Chanda who reported to him, and now he too would have to report to him. The entire room went up in applause. 'Gowri, will you please come up to the head of the table,' Hari called out to him.

Gowri walked up to the head of the table with a swagger not seen since the time of Vivian Richards. On the way, as he crossed Amit, who was standing on the side, he bent, face near Amit's ear . . .

'Gotcha!' he said slyly and walked away from him. The entire room was a noisy party after that but the only thing that echoed in Amit's head was 'Gotcha!' This was ridiculous. How could Aditya do this? He should at least have given him a hint of what was coming his way. A regional sales manager job in another bank now seemed better than reporting to Gowri. As if the complications he had in his life were not enough, God had sent him another issue to deal with.

'Friends, Gowri has been with the group for a long time and has almost single handedly led the NFS franchise from where it was a few years back to the great institution that it is today. Please join me in congratulating Gowri.' And the room broke out into a thunderous applause again. 'We will be going from here to NFS to make this announcement,' said Aditya as he disappeared from the room, followed by a serious Hari and a grinning Gowri.

Was he expected to follow them to NFS? Probably he would be better off here. He picked up his phone and dialled Chanda's number. No response. Probably she was in a training programme. There was no one else he could call and speak with. He was wondering what to do. Life had played a cruel prank on him. Even as he was lost in this thought, his phone rang. The screen was blinking. Chanda's name flashed on it.

'Hi.'

'How was the meeting?'

'You will get to know soon.' What else could he say?

'What do you mean?'

'Hari is moving to Taiwan as retail bank head and . . .'

'And what?'

'Gowri is taking over his job.'

'What? Get serious. I am in no mood for a joke.'

'I am not kidding Chanda. They are on their way there to make the announcement. And that bastard is with them.'

'I don't believe this. What is all this crap?'

'I feel like putting in my papers right now.'

'Don't be stupid and impulsive. We need your salary to survive.'

'What else? I can't report to him. It's just not possible. You know the guy is weird. And after all that happened between us . . . never! You know what he tells me while going up to the table? "Gotcha"! Bloody . . . gotcha, my foot.'

'Don't worry Amit. Something will work out. I am sure. God does good things for good people.'

'Yeah. I hope so. I will see you soon.' And he hung up. Chanda was worried. What would happen now? They had all their eggs in one basket. Now they were at the mercy of one guy. And a spiteful one at that.

Aditya and Hari, followed by Gowri, arrived at the NFS office to a tumultuous reception. Word had got around that Gowri was the new MD of NFS and there were a host of people waiting at the reception to welcome the MD designate. It was like an Indian marriage reception. Chanda did not come out. She watched the entire display of psycho fancy from the first floor.

A similar drill happened at NFS – Aditya announced the change at NFS. The new boss was to report to Aditya which was made very clear to everyone. Before he finished his speech, he invited Gowri to come in and say a few words.

'It is a momentous day for me. I have been chosen to head this company,' began Gowri in a clumsy fashion. 'It's a dream come true for me. It is a victory of sorts for all you NFS guys that one amongst you has become the MD and not someone from the bank.'

'Bastard,' murmured Aditya.

'I will ensure . . .' Gowri went on and on with his election speech.

'Beep-beep.' The message tone on his phone diverted Aditya's attention. He lifted his phone to look at the message. He pressed the read button.

'Aditya, I was shocked when you made the announcement today. I feel I have been compromised. I don't think I can continue to work in this environment. I need to meet you sometime tomorrow. I would like to put in my papers when I see you tomorrow . . . Amit.'

Amit's mind was in a state of a suspended centrifuge. The churn could just not be contained. He had debated this thought in his mind and had decided to face the consequences. 'At times in life, you have to stand up for your convictions, though the path may not be the easiest,' his father had once told him.

Aditya saw the message. A smile came on his face. He looked at Gowri who was still basking in his new found glory. The audience was swallowing every word of what he was saying and following it up with one thunderous applause after the other. With the smile still intact on his face, he brought the phone closer and began typing a response. After a few amendments to the message, the final draft was ready. He pressed the 'send' button and got back to Gowri's histrionics.

Amit was on his way back home when the phone beeped. A message had just come in. He picked up the phone to read the message. It was from Aditya. Was expected of Aditya to have responded. He pressed the open button and the message appeared on his screen.

It read: 'Shut up and get to work. Trust is important son. I hired you. Will never let you down. If you think any differently, you would have been better off in GE.'

He read the message again. And then again, and again. There was something about the message that he couldn't comprehend. What was Aditya saying? The only thing he could read there was that he had not been compromised. Aditya had a plan for him. He parked the car to the side of the road. He had reached Mahim, three-fourths of the way to his home. The entire incident replayed in his mind again and again. The point where Gowri walked past him and whispered 'gotcha' in his ears was the worst moment of the morning. It had made him lose his mental balance and that provoked him to send the message to Aditya. And now this message from Aditya. He was confused. Maybe he should just trust Aditya and bide his time. He turned his car and drove towards the NFS main office. 'I will take it as it comes,' he said to himself.

By the time he walked into the office, the commotion had settled down. He strode confidently into the office and went straight to Chanda's mezzanine floor workstation. When she saw him, she came up to him and said, 'I got this weird message from Aditya.'

'Ya. He had sent it to me. Maybe he marked it to you too for your information. It was a response to a mail I had sent to him.' Aditya knowing very well, the turmoil in their minds, had sent the message to both of them.

'What are you going to do?'

'Nothing. I am going to meet my new boss.'

'What? Have you lost it?' by the time she could finish her sentence, he was gone.

On the corporate floor, he walked up to Suzanna, 'Where is Gowri?'

'Inside, with Hari,' and she pointed towards the passage leading to Hari's cabin. Amit walked straight into Hari's cabin. The three of them – Aditya, Hari and Gowri – were in Hari's cabin, discussing something, when Amit walked in. When they saw him, all of them abruptly ended their discussion and looked in his direction.

'Hi Aditya.'

He looked at Hari, 'Hari.'

'And you Gowri, congrats man! Good show, great job. I am sure you will be a worthy successor to Hari. We all are with you man!'

Aditya got up and shook his hand. The smile hadn't disappeared from his face. 'I am sure you will make a great team.'

'Sure Aditya. Competition better watch out for this crack team,' he said jokingly.

After a brief and extremely courteous conversation, Amit walked out of the room. Gowri was left wondering the reason behind this sudden shift in Amit's approach. 'Maybe he's now realised that he cannot fuck around with me.' A brief moment of silence later, he muttered to himself, 'For all that he has done so far . . . it's payback time!'

It had been extremely difficult for Amit to put up a friendly façade in front of the entire team. It hurt his self-esteem, his pride, and his strong sense of self-belief. Reporting to Gowri was not something which he would have ideally liked to do. However, in light of Aditya's message, there was some sense of relief in a corner of his mind. Aditya would normally not have sent out such a message.

Chanda, a bit perplexed at his reaction to the news of Gowri's elevation, came up to the corporate floor to see if everything was okay. From a distance, she saw Amit smiling and talking to a few of their colleagues. She felt relieved. The stress signs on his face had disappeared. The look on his face was a relaxed one. She couldn't possibly guess what had brought about this change. He saw her looking at him and smiled at her. She smiled back. Something felt really good and Chanda realised that this feeling had been missing since a very long time. The romance which had kind of disappeared seemed to be lingering somewhere in the corner of their eyes. She walked back to her desk, a load off her chest. Amit had reacted in a manner which she could never have expected him to.

The discussion between Aditya, Hari and Gowri, ended with a cake cutting ceremony. The team outside, spearheaded by Sangeeta, had ordered a cake for Gowri. It had, 'Gowri, You are a born leader' iced over it. Gowri's chest swelled up a couple of inches when he saw that. He was proud of his achievement and modesty was something he had never heard of.

Even as the cake was being cut, Aditya nudged his way through the excited staff members and stood right behind Amit. Amit didn't know of it till he actually felt someone's breath on his ears. Startled for a moment, he looked back. 'It's me idiot. I am always behind you. Remember that. See me for dinner at 9.30. Out of the Blues, Carter Road, Bandra. If you feel like it, get Chanda along. Else it is fine.'

And then he looked the other way and began to clap again joining the chorus. He left soon after.

'Gowri is calling you.' Suzanna came to Amit soon after Aditya left.

'I will be there in a while,' said Amit while intently gazing at the computer screen.

'He wants to see you now. Says it is urgent,' Suzanna almost immediately came back to bug him.

'Okay. Coming.' Saying this and giving a sigh alongside, Amit got up and walked back with her.

'Come Amit. Take a seat.' Wow! Already behaving like a CEO. 'Maybe he wants to make conciliatory overtures,' thought Amit to himself.

'Thanks!'

'So what do you think?'

'About what Gowri?'

'Do you think you will be able to work with me?' Gowri was fairly direct. He was staring directly into Amit's eyes. His tone and expressions seemed like throwing a challenge rather than asking a question.

'Why not?'

'I thought you didn't want to . . .'

'Says who?'

'So, you are fine with it?'

'Yes, of course. I am a professional guy and if my organisation demands that I work with you, I will.'

'Look Amit, there have been problems in the past. And this has been the issue with you guys from the bank. You think everybody except you bankers are idiots. If you want to work with me, you will have to visibly change that approach. I am a guy who does not like insubordination. If I ask for something, I am not particularly democratic in my approach, and you know that.'

'Ya Gowri,' he said, while in his mind he felt 'once a dog, always a dog'.

'When I had conflicts with you Gowri, you were a peer. Now you are the boss. So things will happen, the way you want them to.' It was very difficult for Amit to say these things with a straight face. He, however, did manage that.

'They better be that way my friend. I will ask Suzanna to fix weekly update meetings with you and Sangeeta. I want her here too, because she will formally take over as network head after me.'

'Sangeeta as network head?'

'Yes, she is the only one who has the credentials. There is no one more qualified than her.'

'Sure. She is a brilliant lady.' Amit was beginning to feel nauseated.

'Thanks. That's what I wanted to talk to you about.'

Amit got up and walked out of the room. 'And by the way,' Gowri called him back, 'Chanda would now report to Sangeeta. I will tell her. Thought I would let you know too.' Amit cringed when he heard this. Chanda's dislike of Sangeeta was legendary and so was the reverse equation. He just nodded and left.

Back in the safe confines of his room, he was pissing mad. He did not like the way Gowri had spoken to him. Almost bordering on condescending. 'What does he think of himself?' Had it not been for Aditya he would have put in his papers. He dialled Chanda. 'I am going home. Will you come now or later?'

Chanda looked at the watch. It was only 4.30 p.m. 'It's fine. You go ahead. I will come by auto rickshaw.'

'Just thought I would let you know that your current boss and my next boss told me that you would be reporting to Sangeeta, the new branch network head.'

'Oh wow! The beginning of my end, is it?' and she let out a chuckle. 'I will wait for it to be announced.'

Amit went back home early. He was very dismayed by the way things had shaped up during the day. In the morning, when he had left for the de-briefing session which Aditya had called for, he did not expect this change to happen. Now it had left him high and dry. His only hope was Aditya. Why did he call him for dinner? He decided to wait and watch. Internally, he had set himself a deadline of forty-five days. He would endure Gowri and his sadomasochistic attitude for the next six weeks. If nothing happens during that phase, he would quit. That was his game plan as he went into the meeting with Aditya.

Three days later, early on a Sunday morning, his phone rang. It was his mother calling from Jamshedpur. 'Amit, what is this?' She sounded worried.

'Why maa, what happened?' he was trying to shake off the last traces of sleep.

'Are you sure you want to do this?'

'Do what?'

'Chanda's mother told me about your move.'

'Yes. I will soon be moving into my new role.'

'We are all concerned beta.'

'Concerned about what maa?'

'It's a very dirty line son. Too much of *maar-dhaad*. The police also gets involved at times.'

'Maa, it all depends on how you manage.'

'Bauji was telling me that the general environment is also bad. Why do you want to get into something like this and that too at this time?'

'Don't worry maa. It's a good job.'

'Don't you think you should also consult bauji? Your father had always advised you on what is good for you.'

'I will speak with him and tell him why I accepted it. I am sure he will be happy. I'll be fine, maa.' Saying this, he hung up.

21 June 2004
The BIG Change
Mumbai

The dinner that night with Aditya was very noisy. Aditya had picked Out of the Blues because it was next door to his place. It suited Amit too, because it was in his neighbourhood too. In a city like Mumbai, distances can become pretty daunting especially if you have to travel during peak hours.

Aditya was dressed casually in a Ted Lapidus jeans and an Armani T-shirt. Had Amit worn the same shirt, it would have looked like a fake, but on Aditya, it looked more expensive than an original. Amit had come straight from office and hadn't changed. He was in the normal office attire, though the tie had come off.

Amit was in fact waiting outside when Aditya came in. The driver stopped the BMW Convertible right outside the gates of the restaurant. Aditya looked out of the sexy machine and seeing Amit, got down, turned to his driver and said, 'I will come back on my own. You can go home.'

As they were walking in, Aditya bent down. He was a couple of inches taller than Amit, and whispered, 'We have company.'

'Where? Who?' Amit was taken in by surprise.

'Eleven 'O clock. Last table.'

Amit immediately turned and looked in that direction. Sitting in that corner, very much like a couple in love, were two of his colleagues – Gowri and Sangeeta.

'Probably they decided to celebrate their success together,' said Aditya as he picked a table in the other end of the room. 'I don't want to disturb them, nor do I want them to disturb us.' The restaurant was dimly lit and it was unlikely that they would be seen from the other end.

After they settled down and ordered their drinks, Aditya began his story. 'Look Amit, what I am going to say is classified information. Extremely confidential. I would want you to keep it just to yourself. If I get to know that the word has gotten out, I know the source. It has to be either you or me. And if it ain't me, God help you.'

'Sir, happy hours will end in five minutes. Do you want to order any more drinks?' A waiter interrupted their conversation.

Aditya looked at him and said, 'Whatever we just ordered, make it two of them and give us our free drinks please.' This request left Amit wondering if the lure of a free drink existed at every level.

'I know when I announced Gowri's move you were extremely upset with me. I was looking at your face and saw it go red with anger. I would be lying if I say that I didn't expect it.'

'Anyone would, Aditya.'

'I know. However, I had expected that given our relationship you would give me the benefit of doubt. Maybe I had a thought behind it.'

'Sure.'

'Then when I saw your message, I realised I had to speak with you.'

'Thanks Aditya. When I saw your response, I did feel relieved.'

'That was the intent.'

Amit just smiled in return.

'There has been a larger realignment in the entire bank globally. The move of the NBFC and other subsidiary companies into my span of control is only one of the changes.'

Amit just nodded.

'I could very easily have given Hari's role to you. I even know that you would have done this brilliantly and made me proud. I always did and still have that faith in you. But remember, our association is a long one. I have to worry about you not for the next one or two years, but for the rest of your career. We have to go a long way together. I will never compromise you for any short-term gains.' If only Natasha had been around, she would have choked. She never believed Aditya when he gave this line to anyone. She was sure that he faked concern. But to Amit that night, it seemed for real.

'Everyone knows that Gowri has complete control on the branch managers and key people in NFS. It's not classified information.'

Amit just nodded.

'We had to release Hari and that too very quickly, because he was getting a wonderful opportunity and you know I don't stand in the way of career growth, even if it comes at my expense.'

'Ya Aditya.' Could he have said no?

'The options in front of us were either Gowri or you. It had to be one of you and no one else. Do you agree?'

'Yes.'

'What would have happened had we given it to you? Gowri would have quit.' Aditya looked at Amit and then added, as if an afterthought, 'Well, probably quit, though it is also highly possible that he would have stayed back and created problems for you. More importantly, he has built this team. The people are his. The team is his. If he goes, they will also go. And without people there is no business. It would have been too much of a risk for the organisation to take. We do not have a choice but to tolerate that asshole for some more time.'

'I understand that complication Aditya. But what happens to me? I need to worry about my career too.'

'I am there. You need to trust me and understand that I will do what is good for you. I have never let you down even a single time. What makes you think I will now?'

Amit just nodded. He was not even looking at Aditya. His gaze was wandering around some insignificant corner at the other end of the hall. 'I know you do not believe me now. But when you hear what I am going to say next, you will definitely agree with what I am saying.'

'Are you with me?' Aditya sensed that Amit was not completely in sync with him. He seemed to be in a world of his own. Aditya jolted him back into the conversation.

Forty-five minutes, eight pegs and quite a few stares from the people on the sane side later, both of them managed to barely stumble through the door of Out of the Blues and wobbled their way towards Carter Road. A Honda Accord drove past them and stopped a few feet ahead.

'I got to go,' said Aditya as they approached the Honda Accord.

Both of them walked up to the front seat on the passenger side. Amit opened the door and held it for Aditya. Aditya managed to somehow fit himself into the seat. While his hands were trying to grab hold of the seat belt and then miserably attempted to strap it across his chest, Amit peeped in.

'Hi.' It was a familiar voice and a familiar face too.

'Hi,' said Amit and the door shut. The car drove off.

'What was he doing in the car? How come he picked up Aditya? Does he know? Probably he would. Aditya was a deal maker. Otherwise he wouldn't be there,' thought Amit. Things were happening too fast for him. 'That's the way he is,' he muttered to himself as he walked back home.

Chanda was not too pleased when she heard about the discussion at Out of the Blues. But this was a part of a wider game plan. Unlike Amit, she did not have blind faith in Aditya. 'Women are more suspicious,' Amit would often say whenever she expressed her doubts about Aditya. That aside, he knew that Chanda was the staunchest supporter of Aditya at one point in time. However, the recent turn of events had probably made her more bitter.

Late that night, Chanda called her mother in Jamshedpur and they had a long conversation on Amit and Chanda's plans. Amit was not too happy about the immediate relay to Jamshedpur, but over the years, experience had taught him that it was not too safe to poke his nose into a daughter's relationship with her mother.

The excitement levels in office the next day were out of the world. Gowri's room resembled a rose garden. Almost every branch in the country had sent him a bouquet of flowers. And he loved it. Getting an ego massage always made him feel good. This was the only chink in his armour that was publicly visible. He was vulnerable to people who knew how to exploit this fissure.

When Amit arrived in office he had to literally watch his step. He tip-toed his way through a sea of flowers, trying not to crush any of them under his huge shoes, and then jumped into his cabin.

Sangeeta was standing at Gowri's cabin door. 'Gowri, I did not know you were so popular. Look at the number of flowers.' It was clearly aimed at making him bloat with pride. 'No. No Sango. I am what I am because of all of you.'

'Sick!' muttered Amit under his breath as he turned towards his laptop, trying to answer a few mails which had come in.

The announcement was to come in that day. They were headed into a weekend and if it missed today, it would get released only on Monday. Amit didn't mind it coming on a Monday though.

Chanda was waiting to see everyone else's reaction. There were quite a few from Sangeeta's camp, even Sangeeta herself who had once walked up to her to ask what would happen to Amit. The gossip around was that Gowri would soon get after Amit and make life miserable for him. In response, Chanda stoically maintained that Amit would continue doing his current role.

And then the message came. It was an email announcement from Singapore, the regional office of NYB. It said:

> *Consequent to the Global Retail Bank conference and the focus the organisation is affixing to the growth of the Loans business (credit cards, personal loans, home loans and consumer finance), I am happy to announce the following organisational changes. This is in line with recommended global changes and will be taken forward with immediate effect.*
>
> *At NFS the Credit and Collections function currently reports to the Managing Director. However, given the focus on the growth in our Loans business, it is imperative that we ensure this function is not biased by business pressures and hence it has been decided to spin it off into an independent vertical. Going forward, the Head of Credit and Collections for NFS will report to the Country Risk Manager of New York International Banking Group in the country, and not to the MD of NFS. This will ensure that we do not compromise on the quality of the loans that we write even as we look to aggressively grow our loans business.*
>
> *A credit centre of excellence is being set up in Singapore for the entire group in Asia Pacific. Manish Kakkar, Credit Director NFS, is being challenged with the task of setting up this unit. This is a challenging assignment and I wish him all the very best as his endeavour.*
>
> *His position in NFS India is being taken up by Amit Sharma, the current head of Mortgages business. Amit is a seasoned resource with widespread experience in the loans business.*

Manish Kakkar will report to me and Amit Sharma to Uma Shelar (India Head of Credit and Risk – NYB) in their new roles. They will be announcing their individual organisation structures in due course.

Gordon Greene   Aditya Bhatnagar
Asia-Pac Head of Credit   CEO – India

It was a defining moment in the history of NFS in India. Credit and collections which was being managed by Manish Kakkar was being spun off as a separate unit and was to report to Uma Shelar who was the head of credit and collections for the New York International Banking Group in India. And Amit Sharma was moving into Manish's role.

Amit saw the global announcement. It was forwarded to all of them by Aditya, with a small message saying, please join me in congratulating Manish and Amit in their new roles. His lips curved upwards in a smile. 'Aditya is an amazing manipulator. Manages to pull off almost whatever he wants to,' he said to himself.

The message meant a lot to him. First and foremost, he was moving into a new role which did not require him to report into Gowri. Secondly, it put him in a position of strength with regard to Gowri. And lastly, Gowri had no clue about this change. Amit's mind started imagining the expression on Gowri's face when he would read this message . . . priceless is the word! He so wanted to be in front of him and capture that expression forever. He came out of his room. From the passage outside his room, he could clearly see Gowri's cabin.

Gowri saw him, and called out to Suzanna. 'Please ask Amit to see me.' Amit was sure he hadn't seen the message yet.

Amit walked up to him, even before Suzanna could call him. He had heard the instruction which was given to Suzanna.

'Ya Gowri?'

'Amit, I needed to speak to you on an interesting proposition. This is something I have been wanting to do for a while, but I have not been able to because of Hari. I think there is merit in formally putting all branch businesses, i.e. personal loans, mortgages, auto loans, etc., under one individual who will be the branch network head. Today, in any case, the branch managers support all the other businesses, but after you have come in, they don't really get the credit for their contribution to other businesses. They are not as involved as they used to be. And in the process, business is suffering. I know you are not really in favour of this, but I am a strong advocate of single accountability. The business managers can then focus on managing the product and the brand. What do you say?'

Aaah, so that's the plan. The bastard wanted to formally club the entire sales in the company under his sweetheart Sangeeta and marginalise everyone including Amit. He couldn't make out if he was serious about it, but he knew for sure that he was making an attempt to spite him. 'I am going to play along,' he said to himself.

'I think it is a great idea.'

'Do you?' Gowri looked up with eyes that disclosed wonder and surprise. He never thought that he could get his kill so easily. 'Your view was quite divergent earlier,' said Gowri, more as a question than a statement.

'I know, but I've changed my mind now. Better sense has prevailed and I think it will be a good idea. It will bring in greater synergies between businesses. And more importantly, if you strongly feel so, it should be done. It will be good for the organisation if the new CEO gets the structure he wants. Don't you think so?'

'Oh, yeah yeah. You're spot on,' said Gowri with his infamous American accent. He had this disgusting habit and it usually came on when Gowri was not too sure about what is happening. Despite Gowri being so sharp, the sly fox somehow failed to recognise the sarcasm in Amit's voice.

'If you want I can draw up the new structure and give it to you. You can refine it with your thoughts and then we can see how it goes.' Gowri looked at him. He had a look of disbelief on his face.

Slowly he nodded his head and moved away from his laptop. 'I would love that.'

At that very moment Hari walked in. It was his last week in office in India and he was moving out of the country to his next assignment early next week. He looked at Gowri and a smile appeared on his face. 'Hey buddy! Congrats man!'

Hari gave a strong handshake and hug to Amit. Gowri had a bewildered look on his face, wondering why this guy was congratulating Amit. He stood up from his chair. What's going on? He had no clue. Seeing Gowri's puzzled expressions, Hari figured out that Gowri did not know about it. 'Haven't you seen your mail box? Please read and then congratulate this man here.'

'What for?' he thought to himself. Anxiety was gripping him by his jugular vein as a voice inside him was saying that something is just not right. He frantically signed in and began searching for the mail. It is usually at such moments when you really want something that very second, that the computer tries all its tricks with you. Gowri's computer was no different. Three minutes of slow internet connection and two minutes of the computer hanging later, he finally found the mail. 'There it is,' he whispered as he opened it. Amit wanted to be in front of him to see his first hand reaction and thanks to Hari, his dream was just about to come true. According to Amit's over-imaginative brain cells, Gowri's eyes popped out like Bugs Bunny, and his jaw dropped down on the floor while he went through the mail.

He turned around to face Amit. The look on his face belied his thoughts. 'Congrats' through gritted teeth was all that he could manage to say.

'Thanks Gowri. Do you still want me to come up with the changed organisation structure? I can still do it for old time's sake.' This time, the sarcasm didn't miss Gowri. He didn't like what he saw and heard. Gowri was looking forward to pinning Amit on the mat, but the guy had escaped from his clutches.

Satisfied to the core of his heart, Amit came out of the room. He picked up his phone and sent two messages. The first one was to Chanda. Chanda saw it and smiled. It said: 'Love you'. The second was to Aditya: 'Thanks Aditya for being what you are. I know I should not have doubted you. Apologies. I am human too. Thanks for all that you have done for me.'

With a spring in his step, Amit walked back into his room, closed the door and crashed into his comfortable plush leather chair. Rocking backward and forward, Amit's mind started reflecting on all that had happened in the last few years at NFS. Life is a big leveller. You win some battles, you lose some. As long as you win more than you lose, you are doing okay.

His thoughts went back to the night at Out of the Blues with Aditya . . . the moment when Aditya told him about the proposed change. He was not very gung-ho about this till Aditya told him it was to be an independent function that did not require him to be reporting to the MD of NFS. That had swung it for him.

'When I heard the imminent structure change at the global conference, it was a great opportunity for me to fix all issues in one go. You and Gowri had problems, Manish wanted to move on . . . he has done the role for too long. If I had to give you Manish's job, it was essential for Manish to move on to get the Singapore job. It ends your pain and Gowri gets to run what he built. Everyone, with the exception of Gowri will be happy when they see this.' Aditya had told him that night.

He was a great manipulator. A people's guy, who would do anything to ensure that his people remained happy. At least his people thought so. Thought detractors argued that Aditya always did things for his own good, and in the process ended up incidentally helping a set of people.

Amit's train of thoughts rushed back to the night he had dinner with Aditya. On the way out when he had opened the door of the Honda Accord for Aditya, he heard a familiar voice from inside. At that time he had wondered what Manish was doing inside the car. But he quickly realised that he was a link in the chain – a critical one if everything had to fall in place. Aditya had influenced three moves in order to make life easy for him.

Beep-beep. The beep of the cell phone interrupted his thoughts. It was a message from Aditya. 'Call me.' He instantly dialled the number.

'Aditya, thanks for this. I will not let you down.'

'If I had any inkling of that sort, you wouldn't be here my friend.'

'Thanks Aditya.'

'Listen Amit, stop being so grateful. There was a vested interest for me in this entire deal. I need you there. As much as you want the job, I necessarily want someone there who can counter Gowri. Who can fight his aggressive persona . . . someone who can push him back. A balance is required in that organisation, or else Gowri will go on a rampage. Who else can do this but you? Given your history I do not think Gowri will screw around with you. He would have walked all over Manish Kakkar despite the change in reporting lines. With you at the helm I don't think he can do that. It will only help my business.'

Amit smiled. He knew that Aditya always had a rationale for everything. Just when their discussion ended, Manish walked into Amit's office. The usual bonhomie, the excitement, and the rara followed suit. The only one with a sullen face during the entire episode was Gowri.

Over the next thirty days, Hari and Manish transitioned authority to Gowri and Amit and moved on. The NFS they left behind was a potentially volatile, but hugely viable business. If run properly it could be a cash cow; however, the Amit–Gowri personality issue held in it the potential to derail the company while also holding an opportunity to make it soar to greater heights.

2005/2006
NFS
Mumbai

Aditya's intent at putting Amit in there as a counter balance for Gowri seemed to be working. Seldom do you get such powerful personalities working in opposition to each other, and yet collectively accountable. And if you do, it would always lead to clashes, difference of opinion and eventually to an overall improvement of the organisation. Some would call it positive turbulence . . . Aditya surely did when he put them together . . . or was it, against each other?

Amit and Gowri spent the first six months in trying to get at each others' throats. For the first time they were real adversaries with a difference – this time they couldn't take undue advantage over the other. In round one, Gowri held the edge. He was the one who had things under his control and unfortunately, at least in the beginning, Amit had to use all the tricks he could think of to wrangle things out of Gowri's stronghold. Not anymore though.

This was a stage where both of them were equals. Gowri ran the sales and business side which he controlled tightly and Amit ran the credit part, which in turn acted as a check on Gowri.

Both of them set about strengthening their own empires. Gowri already had one – an entire empire, of sales guys, branch guys, service personnel . . . in effect, he had the entire branch team eating out of his hands. Amit inherited Manish Kakkar's team, which was also spread out all over the country in the branches of NFS. This team of credit and collection managers was involved in processing of loan applications, approving the loan applications and even in collecting the money back from customers who defaulted on their loan commitments. This being a role that Amit had never undertaken before, the learning curve was enormous and the power to control was addictive.

Initially, his team was apprehensive. In the past, they were used to listening to the branch managers. Even their performance appraisals were indirectly controlled by the branch managers. For them life began and ended at the branch manager's doorsteps. Gowri, had all along been seen by all of them as the person to please . . . the person who held the reigns to their career and could determine the pace at which they could gallop from one level to the other.

Amit had to change all this. He had to build a certain amount of trust in his team. To get them to start functioning without being dependent on the business guys was not easy. The team lacked self-confidence and he had to make them believe in themselves and build their own distinct character. The credit and risk team had to have a separate identity as against the branch network.

This change couldn't wait. He got down to work, the day he took over. Sitting down at his table late at night he typed out a message. It was his first day in the new role.

Dear Team,

We are at a stage where the organisation has in its wisdom made some sweeping changes in the way we do our business. As you are aware, we have decided to bifurcate business into two independent verticals – Sales and Credit & Risk. This has been driven by the need to balance and the necessity to grow quickly with adequate controls – checks and balances. We do not want the aggressive growth plans to pressurise the credit team into approving loans which they should not be approving.

I know in the past many of you have been operating under the instructions of the branch managers and at times have even been rubber stamping whatever the branch managers wanted you to approve. This will not be tolerated anymore.

You need to change the way you work. All of you are now a part of the credit function and to that extent you are different from the sales guys.

I am hereby enclosing the revised organisation structure. Your lines of reporting and governance model is attached hereunder.

With immediate effect, all the loan approving authorities of the branch managers are being withdrawn. Only the credit team in the branches will have the authority to approve these loans. Anyone succumbing to pressure from the branch managers and approving loans under the influence of the sales guys will be dealt with appropriately. You will only approve loans which fall under the prescribed policy.

If anyone has an issue with this, please discuss with me. I expect this to be implemented in true spirit. Any deviation will not be tolerated.

Regards,
Amit

He copied Gowri on the mail which was sent to the branch managers and to the entire credit team. Gowri, as usual, seriously objected to the manner in which the mail was written. Like one of those irritating kids in school, he immediately rushed to Aditya, his new boss, whining and complaining about Amit. But Aditya asked him to lay off. Being the proactive guy that he was, Amit had run the mail past Aditya and taken his sign-off before he released it.

This mail did two things for the team. Firstly, it established complete clarity on the reporting structure. And secondly, by taking the authority out of the branch manager's hands, and putting it solely with the credit guys, it elevated the status of the credit folks in the organisation. Now the branch managers were at the mercy of the credit folks. Earlier it used to be the reverse.

Credit in any organisation is supposed to be made up of guys who are not capable of being in sales. Such was the perception of the credit department in NFS in those days. There were many other organisations in India where credit guys had moved on to become more dynamic and aggressive, but in NFS it was boring . . . boring because it consisted of people who had no energy, no drive and who preferred to live in the shadow of sales. Amit tried to change all that. His experience in sales helped.

First month in office, he roughed it out on the field. He travelled to every corner of the country. He met the sales and credit guys in one forum, in which he discussed sales-related issues and also what sales needed to do to ensure that the credit team is able to do their job better. No one in NFS had done anything like that before. It always was about what credit should be doing to make the job of sales better and easier. He brought in a fresh perspective.

At NFS, conferences and sexy off-sites were reserved for the business guys. The people in the credit and collections departments were invited on a need basis. Amit turned this system on its head. He organised off-site get-togethers and parties for the credit and collections teams and invited a few guys from sales to be a part of it. He charged up the entire team towards a cause. Manish Kakkar did not have the luxury of an independent team. He always lived in the shadow of Gowri. Amit did not need to. He had a mandate from Aditya and he went about executing his mandate.

Amit also infused fresh talent from outside. It suited him because they didn't come with any history in NFS and were from the beginning, more aligned to him than to the branch managers, Sangeeta or Gowri. It was easier to mould them to his vision than anyone from within the organisation.

He went about meticulously creating an organisation which was conscious about quality, integrity and controls even if it meant conflicting with Gowri's aggression. The credit team, over a period of time, started to look up to him and began to believe in his words and leadership.

Rajesh Krishnamoorthy was one such talent that Amit discovered. The latter was with GE as a branch credit manager in one of their branches in Delhi. After a lot of persuasion, Amit managed to convince Rajesh to shift from there to NFS. Rajesh too had heard a lot about Amit and that was one of the reasons why he joined NFS. Otherwise, from his perspective the brand pull of GE was much stronger and more attractive. Wanting to be a part of a revolution, he took a leap of faith and joined Amit's bandwagon. Amit was out to change the organisation and Rajesh was keen to participate in the process.

Rajesh joined as the regional credit manager for Chennai. With twelve huge branches in the city, the business of NFS was very well established in Chennai. As in any other city, the branches in Chennai too were run by individual branch managers who reported to Jagmohan Awasthi, better known as 'Jugs'. He was the regional sales manager for the Chennai region. At Gowri's behest, Chennai was carved out as a separate region . . . only to elevate Jugs to the position of a vice president. In the process, Jugs became the only city head who was of the cadre of a vice president in the organisation. His closeness to Gowri was known to everyone. Even Sangeeta, to whom he reported, had little control on him.

Jugs was a cow-boyish clone of Gowri and believed in pushing the credit folks to the extreme to approve loans irrespective of the merits of the case. Normally, most sales guys do that, but as you reach the level of a vice president, one is expected to exercise some restraint and balance. However, Jugs belonged to an entirely different species. He did not know what restraint meant. He would go after the credit guys asking them to approve every case, every application and often fire from Gowri's shoulders.

Rajesh was the new guy in the picture and early on he was pitted against the aggression of Jugs. Being an amenable and practical person, he would argue every loan case logically and if questioned, would come out with a rationale on why the loan applicant was declined. Rajesh's logic was often sound and couldn't be questioned under normal circumstances. This led to some friction with Jugs, as Jugs could no longer have his way . . . and soon, it started impacting business.

The Chennai sales numbers started dwindling. Jugs, a man who had never been behind on his monthly targets ever in his career, started feeling the heat. Gowri began asking embarrassing questions to Jugs for which he couldn't provide any retort. Conveniently, he started putting the blame solely and squarely on Rajesh. For Gowri, it was difficult to absorb the fact that a credit guy was impacting the business numbers in Chennai and as a consequence, the Jugs–Rajesh war got escalated to Gowri and Amit. When it reached their levels, they had to take stands. Each one protected his own guy. Amit backed Rajesh to the hilt; after all, he had hired him in the system.

When Gowri couldn't influence Amit to do something about Rajesh, he was pissed and asked Sangeeta to do a review of all the loan applications which had been declined in Chennai and figure out if any of them could have been approved, if at all. Sangeeta flew into Chennai for a couple of days, picked up all the rejected applications and sat down with the credit team to review them. The due diligence with which they had executed their work (thanks to Amit) was so thorough that she just couldn't pick out anything to complain for. Despite not wanting to, she had to go back to Gowri with a report that the loans which had been declined deserved to be declined and that they needed to change the way they sourced their applications for loans.

'Our DSAs in Chennai are not sourcing the right kind of loan applications. They need to be trained to source quality customers,' said she in her report to Gowri. She also made it slightly caustic because she didn't like Jugs' closeness to Gowri. In this case she saw an opportunity to get back.

DSAs – Direct Sales Agencies are the backbone of the loans business for any bank in India. They contact the customers, get the applications filled, and mediate between the customer and the bank. The bank pays them a commission based on the value of the loans that they source.

This, over the years, has led to the mushrooming of many fly-by-night operators who masquerade as DSAs and pump in fraudulent loan applications into the banking system. These customers then avail of loans and after paying a few monthly instalments disappear, never to be traced again. Banks are then forced to write off these loans and incur a loss. To get over this menace, banks manage all direct sales agencies and oversee the executives working in the DSAs very very carefully. They even lay down a list of do's and don'ts for the DSAs and conduct regular audits to see if the DSAs are following the processes outlined by the bank.

They also hire fraud prevention agencies which in fact put in fraudulent applications into the DSAs to see how the channel reacts to it. (They are referred to as 'seeding of applications' in banking parlance.) This helps the bank identify weaknesses in their control process. If a seeded application makes it to the approval stage and does not get identified as a fraud and declined before that, it indicates a weakness in the bank's approving process. The bank would then work on fixing the gaps. This process is useful in exposing agencies which indulged in unfair practices to get these applications through. If any executives are found to be indulging in frauds, they are normally dismissed immediately and blacklisted. Banks do not accept any further applications from such executives and even applications from this executive which are in various stages of processing are declined immediately. The logic for this is very simple. All applications received from a fraudster sales executive, are very likely to be fraudulent and hence banks do not risk their money by giving out loans to applicants who have come through executives who have been identified as frauds.

NFS, given its nature of business, also had a very interesting manner of evaluating a customer's credit worthiness. Every customer who wanted a loan would be called to the branch and met by credit officers. They would meet him, check his documents (bank statements, documents which support his source of income like pay slips, income tax returns, etc.) to ensure that they are not fraudulent, interview him, draw up a detailed income and expense statement for the customer and on the basis of that, if they conclude that the customer would be able to pay the instalment for the loan, they would approve the loan and give him the money. Else, they would decline it. They would also refer the customer to a credit bureau to check his performance on loans with other lenders to ensure that he was not a defaulter with them. A rather manual way of doing it, but in a country like India there is no other alternative.

On an average, about two hundred customers walked into the T-Nagar branch of NFS on a daily basis, making it one of the largest branches in the country in terms of customer traffic.

Rajesh, on one of his branch visits, landed in the T-Nagar branch that day. He finished speaking to his team of customer facing credit officers and was walking towards the back end processing shop when he heard some commotion and turned back. A customer was screaming at a credit officer and was creating a fair bit of hullabaloo in the front office. Sharada, a credit officer in Rajesh's team was trying to explain to the customer that his loan application had been turned down and the customer was getting furious. Rajesh walked towards Sharada. He had a soft corner for her and this gave him an opportunity to be the knight in shining armour. Avoiding walking straight into the fire, he indicated to Sharada to step away from the customer and come to him. Sharada understood his gesture and excused herself to join Rajesh in the conference room.

'Rajesh, this is a declined case. I told him that we cannot give him the loan and he started screaming. I did not do anything.'

'Show me the customer file.'

Sharada stepped out and brought the file for him to see. Rajesh looked at the file. The credentials as mentioned in the application form seemed okay. The customer's documents seemed to be in order. Even the bureau check was not negative.

'What is the problem? This seems doable.'

'It's a fraud case.'

'Fraud?'

'He looks decent? The documents in the file also seem okay? He can't be a fraud. What is the reason for declining the loan?'

'Yes Rajesh. It is a doable case. But this is Shanmuga's application.'

'Shanmuga . . .?' Rajesh couldn't connect.

'We blacklisted him last week. He had made an incorrect declaration on the application form on behalf of the customer. The customer did not fill in certain fields in the application form and he filled it himself. We strictly prohibit sales agents from doing so. He is from an agency called Insta-Money.'

'Oh, so we have declined him because the executive through whom this case came in was a fraud.' It was now clear to Rajesh.

'Yes sir,' Sharada nodded. 'That's the normal process. If we sack a sales executive for fraud, we decline all the other applications which have come in through him and are in the pipeline. We assume that if the sales executive is caught indulging in a fraudulent practice, the likelihood of all other applications which he has brought in being frauds is very high. That's standard operating procedure. Do you want us to over ride that and process his application?'

'No, don't do that. Let me talk to him.' He walked up to the customer and introduced himself.

'Sir, we have a small problem with the agency that your loan came through. Shanmuga, the sales executive through whom you have applied for this loan does not work with us any longer. We need a little more time to do the various verifications that we normally do. Can we get back to you sometime early next week?'

'Shanmuga? Who is Shanmuga?'

'The same sales guy through whom you applied for the loan.'

'I don't know any Shanmuga. I had walked directly into your branch to apply for a loan.' By this time, Rajesh's demeanour had cooled down the customer. 'You do your checks and verification. I will come back next week. Or you call me when you are through. But it is not good to harass a customer who has left all his work and come to your branch.' And he walked out of the branch.

'Maybe there is some mistake. Do all the verifications. Send the documents for fraud check. If it is clean, do the loan. He seems to be a nice guy.' He smiled at Sharada, gave her an affectionate look and walked away. Sharada also seemed to like talking to him.

The next day at around five in the evening, Rajesh's mobile rang. Rajesh picked it up almost instantaneously. Sharada's call was always special to him.

'Rajesh, the customer's fraud check reports have come in. All clear.'

'Hmm . . .'

'All his documentation is fine. We can go ahead and do this loan.'

'Go ahead. I am fine with it. Do this loan. Life is all about taking risks and I am happy to do it in this case.'

'Do you have some time? There is something else I wanted to speak to you about.'

'Go ahead. I have all the time for you.' And he smiled, clumsy flirt he was.

'There are three other customers who walked in today. We had earlier declined their loans. They all seemed to be of a decent profile, except that they are also applications sourced by Shanmuga. Should we go ahead and put them through fraud check before we process their loans too.'

'Four in two days. Seems high. Any other observations?'

'Like yesterday's customer, they too said that they don't know Shanmuga. Actually that's what all of them say, when cornered. Who knows . . . maybe Shanmuga himself has cautioned them and told them to say that they don't know him.'

'Did you specifically ask them how they applied?'

'Yes I did. The ones who came in today said that they walked into the branch and filled in the application form. They claim that they didn't come through any DSA.'

'The same response that yesterday's customer gave?'

'Yes Rajesh.' Then there was silence at the other end.

'Rajesh . . . are you there?'

'Yes, yes. Give me a minute.' There was a brief silence at the other end. Sharada was wondering what was going on and was about to disconnect and call back when Rajesh reappeared on the call.

'Hello'

'Am there . . .'

'OKAY. Tell me, are those customers still there or have they left?'

'They left long back. I was slightly tied up. Couldn't call you earlier. Tell me . . . you want to meet them. I can call them again if you give me some time.'

'No no . . . you do have their phone numbers right? Obviously you will. What a stupid question?'

'Ya.'

'Call them right now and ask them for the date and the approximate time they came to the branch to apply for the loan.'

'. . . and then?'

'Do as I say. Call me once you find out . . .' He had a plan which he did not want to reveal.

'Okay . . .' there was very a confused voice at the other end before the phone disconnected.

Within fifteen minutes Sharada called back. 'I have the date and time of all four of them. Now what?'

'Every branch must have an "In and Out" register, where every walk-in customer is tracked. Their time of entry and time of exit must have been noted down. Go to the security desk at the reception and from the "In and Out" register there, check if the date and time matches. Find out if there is an entry in the names of the customers, on the mentioned date around the time these customers stated. If there is, they are not lying. They have indeed come to the branch on the mentioned day. If there isn't, then they haven't come into our branches and are just fibbing to get their applications through.'

'Okay. I am walking towards the security. Hold on. I will tell you right away.' And she started walking. The main door was a few metres away and the security desk with the "In and Out" register was right there.

'Register *dena*,' she whispered to the security guard and took the register from him. While on the phone, she took the register from the security guard and started flipping through. It had the entry and exit times of every single customer who walked into NFS. After a couple of minutes of flipping through, she muttered a 'thank you' that was obviously for the security guard.

'You are right. All the names are there.'

'That means someone is screwing around.'

'Sorry.'

'Pardon my language . . .'

'We are used to it. We have been mentally conditioned to ignore uncomfortable talk and unparliamentarily language. It's okay.'

'Someone has been swindling the system. We need to get to the bottom of it.'

'Should I call Jugs and tell him?'

'No. Let me come there tomorrow. We will figure out what to do. Please do not speak to anyone on this.'

That night Amit called Rajesh. Normally Amit spoke with his key guys at least once a day. During the course of the discussion, Rajesh mentioned the happenings to Amit.

'I know what this is.' Amit's sales background made it simple for him to comprehend what was going on. He went on to tell Rajesh what he should be doing about it.

'Just be careful. Don't let people know till you are sure. Update me tomorrow.'

Rajesh was in the T-Nagar branch the next morning. Sharada too was there. In fact Rajesh had text messaged her to come in early. He went through the application forms and the supporting documents of all the four customers. All of them seemed to be perfectly in order. He saw the fraud check reports. They were perfect. He even saw the gate register with the security guards. The customers were not at fault. They had in fact come in on their own and put in their applications.

'All these customers had been allocated to Reuben.' When Sharada said this Rajesh's eyes lit up. There was the answer. 'He is the culprit!' exclaimed Rajesh. He seemed like an amateur detective who had just solved his first murder mystery.

Reuben was the customer service executive who had been working in the branch for over three years. He was one of the first employees to be recruited and a trusted one too. Rajesh was quite flabbergasted at the very thought that this guy could be involved.

At around 9.15 a.m. Reuben came into the branch. He was quietly whisked away into the conference room by Rajesh. Sharada stayed out of this. She was too junior to be involved directly.

Getting Reuben to confess was not too difficult. Rajesh confronted him with the facts and also threatened to bring the customers face to face with Reuben. The rest was easy. Reuben quickly realised that his game was over. 'I just passed on the lead to the DSA because it would have been easy from the customer's perspective. If a DSA follows up on a case, the customer is saved all the trouble. He doesn't need to run around. Had he given us the application to process, he would have had to run around himself. Now the DSA would do everything for him and help him get his loan approved.'

At that instant, Jugs walked in languorously into the conference room. 'What's happening?'

Rajesh told him the entire story. Not surprisingly, Jugs was extremely dismissive and said, 'Okay, leave this to me. I will manage.'

'But you know this is a fraud, don't you?'

'I will figure that out. You have no right to speak to my team without MY permission. I said, leave it to me.' Being one of Gowri's cronies, becoming an arrogant bastard didn't need too much of an effort.

Rajesh did not have a choice and he left. Jugs was right. Reuben reported to Jugs and protocol demanded that he should have spoken to Jugs before he questioned Reuben.

Once out of the conference room, Rajesh called Amit and spoke to him about the incident. 'It's fine. Let's find out more about this. Get someone to call all customers who walked into the branch and were allocated to Reuben in the last three months and see if there is a trend.'

Within three hours, Rajesh called back. 'Amit, I mapped the names of customers who came in and were handled by Reuben in the last 90 days with the list of customers who applied for a loan and found that there is a 100% match in 344 cases. In other words, 344 applications have come in from customers who have walked in and met Reuben in the last 90 days.'

'Wow. That's a big number.'

'And wait. You will fall off your chair when you hear this. All of them have been logged in as applications which have been sourced by Shanmuga of Insta-Money.'

'OKAY. Interesting.'

'And out of this, 238 applications have been approved and loans disbursed.'

'Any idea about how much we pay the DSA for every loan?'

'It works out to approximately Rs 5000–6000 per loan.'

'In other words we have paid approximately Rs 5000 for each of the 238 loans, to Insta-Money for loans which they had no role in sourcing. Wow. 15 lakh paid to the DSA, Insta-Money, without them having to do anything. This is nonsense. Someone has to pay with his job. Ridiculous!' Amit was screaming now. He was passionate about his job.

'Yes it is Amit.'

'I will send a note to Jugs asking you to investigate this. I don't care if anyone wants you to lay off. You will not.' Jugs had just managed to stoke the fire. Amit was seething with rage and that came out very clearly in his tone.

'OKAY Amit,' said Rajesh trying to counter-balance Amit's mercurial temper with his calm tone.

In the meantime, Jugs being the whiner that he was, had run cribbing to Gowri about it and Gowri came charging into Amit's room just like a bull that had just seen red!

'You have asked your bloke to investigate Reuben?'

'Yes,' came the calm and half-mocking reply.

'Don't you think any investigation against staff needs my approval?'

'Not in the case of a process fraud. Only if staff integrity is concerned I need your approval. In this case I was interrogating him for what looked like a DSA fraud.' It was a technicality, but Gowri couldn't do anything.

'I want you to stop this investigation right now. I will ask Sangeeta to do it.'

'She can join in if she wants. Rajesh will be leading this for me,' he said with a straight face.

'I will ask her to speak to you,' said Gowri in a dramatic whisper that was meant to be screamed and went away in a huff. He hardly spoke with Amit. The tension had not died down yet. Whenever they crossed paths, every minute seemed like Diwali with a vengeance!

Rajesh was in the thick of action again. Within hours, the interrogation of Reuben resumed. Things were crystal clear now. Reuben's dirty doings were out in the open – it was not out of goodwill that he had passed on interested customers to Shanmuga. He was not too concerned about the fact that going through the DSA would make life easier for the customer. There was clearly a personal consideration involved. The money paid to the DSA had clearly made its way back into the hands of people in the bank. Who was it? Was it only Reuben or were any others involved? These were the questions for which they needed answers.

As the interrogation progressed, they decided to bring in Shanmuga. Rajesh called him on his mobile, summoned him to the office and Shanmuga didn't seem to have any reservations. Normally if you are sacked for fraud, you would hesitate going to the same organisation again. Not Shanmuga. Something in the conversation told Rajesh that Shanmuga was being made a scapegoat. The latter was in the same neighbourhood and agreed to come in straightaway. This biased Rajesh who after the conversation sensed that Shanmuga could be innocent.

Within the next sixty minutes, Shanmuga strode confidently into the T-Nagar branch of NFS.

Again like the four customers who came in earlier, Shanmuga didn't look like a fraud. He seemed to be a nice and honest guy. A typical Tam-brahm. If he wasn't, why would he come in within sixty minutes, especially considering the fact that he had been sacked a week ago. He could have shown them the finger and stayed away.

When confronted with the facts Shanmuga had only one thing to say – 'Look, I don't know any of these customers. I haven't met any of them. Ten days ago, Sharmila called me.'

'Sharmila. Who is Sharmila?' asked Rajesh.

'She is a credit officer here,' said Sharada and almost instantaneously Shanmuga also echoed, 'she is a loan approving officer with you.' Rajesh could be pardoned for not knowing any credit officer in the branch apart from Sharada.

'Oh. OKAY.'

'Sharmila had called me for some information on one of the customers who she said that I had sourced. I was surprised . . . because I had no idea who this customer was. I hadn't put in these applications. I told her that and even came to your office and met her. On asking her for a list of customers against my name, she printed out a list of twenty-six customers whose applications were in process and I was baffled to see the list. Only four of them were applications that I had logged in. I had absolutely no clue about the others. Maybe it was a data entry error. I asked a few other sales executives in my team and no one knew these customers.'

'So someone else is logging in files in your name. Why would they?' asked Rajesh.

'Sir, if they are against my name, tell me, shouldn't I at least get incentives for them?'

'You should,' Rajesh nodded in acceptance.

'So I went back and asked Murugan . . . '

'Who's Murugan?' Rajesh interrupted, his eyebrows knitting together to form a curling V.

'Murugan is the proprietor of Insta-Money. He didn't entertain me and refused to pay me any incentive for those loans. I let it be because in any case those were not my cases. However, during my next visit to NFS T-Nagar to login some other applications, I met Jugs sir. I thought I would try my luck and ask him.'

'Did he help you?'

'Not at all. When I told him the story and asked him to speak with Murugan, he got so furious . . . so furious that I really got scared.'

'Why, what did he say?'

'He said, "why should we pay you for customers who are walking into the branch" and walked away without holding any further conversation.'

'What did he say? What did he say?' Rajesh suddenly got interested.

'He said, "Why should we pay you for customers who are walking into the branch?" And the next thing I know is that I have been terminated. I didn't know what to do. I've not even got my salary. Please help me.' Shanmugan looked genuinely distressed. His panda eyes showed thin red veins and revealed nights spent without sleep.

Rajesh was shocked. He was recording the entire conversation in the audio recorder of his cell phone. Once the conversation was through, he downloaded the conversation on his PC and sent the audio file as an attachment to Amit. Amit heard the entire conversation. He wasted no time and called Jugs immediately.

'Jugs, what's going on in Chennai?'

'Means what?' Jugs was arrogant.

'What's going on in Insta-Money?'

'He is a DSA. Why? What's the problem?'

'Don't be so naïve.'

'You paid him 15 lakh of excess payout in the last few months . . . that too for loans he didn't even source. What's your cut?'

'You are insinuating that I am hand-in-glove with the DSA? Are you suspecting my integrity? I don't think I should be talking to you, if you don't have any respect for people who have worked in this organisation for over a decade.'

'Fuck off! Tell me the truth, you scoundrel, before I make life miserable for you.'

'I am sorry. I refuse to carry on this conversation. If you have an issue, please speak with Gowri.' Saying that, he banged the phone leaving Amit fuming.

By the time Amit walked into Gowri's office, Gowri had been sufficiently briefed on this conversation by Jugs. Gowri looked at him, a smirk on his face. 'What's your problem man?'

'Oh good. So I don't need to repeat the story. Great. Now hear this.' And he played the conversation with Shanmuga. Amit was carrying his own laptop with him and so it was easy for him to play the recording of the conversation Rajesh had with the sales executive.

'What's there in it to get so excited about?'

'I will tell you. I never mentioned to Shanmuga that these were customers who walked in on their own. So he had no way of knowing that these were customers who walked into the bank. The incentive payout made to Shanmuga which we control, has been checked. Sharada has got the entire incentive payout details verified. Shanmuga has not been paid incentive for these loans. Which proves beyond doubt that these are not customers whose applications were brought in by Shanmuga.'

'So?'

'You heard the conversation. Shanmuga says that Jugs told him they will not pay any incentive for walk-in customers. How did Jugs at that time, when Shanmuga went to him, know that they were walk-in customers? Unless of course he himself was involved and knew about it before hand. You give me the answer to this question and I will go away.' Gowri knew that Amit was right. It was clear to him that Jugs was fucking around in this case. But his heart was not willing to let go.

'What do you want?'

'I want permission to investigate on Jugs. A proper staff investigation. I suspect his integrity. He is on the take.'

When Gowri did not respond, he added, 'A part of the 15 lakh that is being paid to the DSA every month is coming back to feed

Jugs and I am sure of that.' Amit was bang on. All customers who walked into the branch were to be serviced by the customer service officers in the branch. What Jugs was managing to do at T-Nagar branch was a big fraud. Jugs and Reuben were hand-in-glove. All customers who came to Reuben were being logged into their records as applications sourced by Insta-Money. Given that all applications from the DSA had to come in with the name of the sales executive, they had pulled out a name at random and that name was Shanmuga. All such applications were logged in under Shanmuga's name. At the end of the month, Insta-Money would get paid for all loans done in this fashion. This amount for the last three months was over 15 lakh. Part of the amount was being paid back to Jugs and Reuben by the DSA. Clearly Jugs was siphoning off money in this manner. Gowri didn't need to be too much of an expert to figure this out. He knew that Jugs was cornered.

'I will speak with him.'

'Not acceptable Gowri. If you don't want an investigation, he has to resign today and must be relieved NOW.' And after a pregnant pause added, 'Else, I will escalate this request for an investigation.' Amit then walked out. He felt victorious and he knew that he had cornered Gowri. If only there was some sazzy background music that could accompany him like the scenes in Bollywood movies, the picture would have been complete!

Jugs' resignation was announced to a small group that evening in a cryptic message from Sangeeta. Word got around to Amit that the mission has been accomplished and he didn't raise stink. He followed a bit with Rajesh to ensure that Insta-Money was also terminated as a DSA. Reuben didn't attend office from that day onwards.

Gowri's most trusted lieutenant had been sacked, and this was the second time something like this had happened. Earlier his aide in Raipur too had been sacked at Amit's behest. Gowri was simmering, and dying to get back at Amit. Had Amit not gotten involved, he would have managed it. However, the entire issue got messy with his involvement. Somehow he had to get rid of that guy. Wasn't he getting too powerful? Too big for his boots?

Apart from the irritant that Amit was proving to be, everything else was like a dream come true for Gowri. Business was beginning to rock. NFS was on an expansion spree. It was opening two new branches every week! By early 2007, Gowri had set up a distribution network of over 350 branches. He was the toast of the town.

His team was happy. When an organisation grows from 150 branches to 350 branches in 18 months, people are bound to be happy. It had only one meaning for everyone – career progression.

Young officers from existing branches were promoted to branch managers, and branch managers to regional managers. Pay hikes, promotions and parties were the order of the day. Even Sangeeta, who was good for nothing, got promoted to a senior vice president.

Business volumes were galloping. The company was doling out over Rs 200 crore of loans every month. In the global forum, it made Aditya look very good and he too was thrilled. At the New York Analysts forum the NFS branch expansion was a testimony to the groups commitment to an emerging market like India. It kind of worked for everyone. Almost everyone.

The unabashed growth was giving Amit sleepless nights. Many a time, at various forums he tried mentioning to Aditya and to Gowri that this growth would come at a cost and that when the repercussions hit, there will be blood on the streets. Aggressive growth in loans often come with back-ended losses. Revenue comes first and losses come thereafter. No one was willing to listen. The growth story that India was, camouflaged every single need to be cautious and 'grow at any cost' seemed to be the mantra, much to Amit's displeasure.

'There ain't any coal in a gold mine, my friend. You are in a gold mine now, look for gold,' Gowri had once told him. 'If you are so scared, you should be somewhere else.'

To which Amit had retorted, 'You are pissing on an electric fence, watch out!'

Amit was worried that this unabated growth in the lending business would boomerang one day. His view was that such growth would not be without its implications. It would come back to hit NFS in the form of high delinquencies and would ultimately impact their long term profitability. Whether it would or wouldn't, only time would tell.

The New Angle
Hyderabad
December 2007

It was the fifteenth of December. Tulsiram was walking back slowly. His house was in the Indira Park area of Hyderabad – very close to the Tank bund and just overlooking the Marriott Hotel. Everyday the hotel bus would drop him back at the closest point accessible by road. But today was not one of those days.

On any normal day, his grind at the hotel was simple. He would accept the keys from anyone who drove in, give them a receipt of acceptance and say, 'Thank you sir. Welcome to the Marriott'. He would then get into the car, admire its interiors for a few seconds and then drive on to the parking lot, with the keys to another car in his pocket. From the parking lot, he would drive back to the main porch in a different car, hand it over to a waiting customer, accept a meagre Rs 5 or 10 as a tip and then wait for the next car . . . or the next customer.

That day he had gotten off early from work. Even though the shift got over only at 10 p.m., he was off from work at 7 p.m. He was not keeping too well. The call from his wife earlier during the day had disturbed him. She had called him from a local phone booth. The news was not good.

He slowly walked, probably towards his house . . . it was more of a hutment. One could probably call it a high end slum. His legs felt like concrete. Every step seemed to need every ounce of energy left in his body. His steps were dragging, pulling him back. He did not want to go back home. What should he be doing? How could he manage what was expected of him? His thoughts went back to the youngest of his four children. She was just three months old. His wife had returned only the week before, from Narsapur where she had gone for her delivery . . . hoping that after three girls, the fourth one would be a boy. The baby turned out to be a girl. Luck deserted this time too . . . or so he felt.

It was getting shadowy. His pace was getting slower and slower. The road turned narrow and inched upward. It was becoming dark and the thorny bushes on the sides added to the bleakness of the night. The absence of the street lights made it a difficult terrain to manoeuvre. He pushed his way up the path. There was a huge mound of mud in front of him. Pausing for a moment he surveyed the road ahead of him. Fifty metres from where he was standing, the road turned into a muddy track. A deep breath later, he marched up the road, stopping intermittently to give his lungs some rest. His tired lungs forced him to stop to gather all the breath they needed . . . panting and making scary sounds . . . each breath reminding him in the bargain that he was a misfit.

'It doesn't matter,' he said to himself as he stepped forward. Midway to the top, he stopped and sat down, clutching his head in his hands. His heart went out to his four daughters. He wiped the tears which had for a long time been trying to squeeze themselves out of his eyes.

The slippers came off, and he carefully placed them by the side. He got up and walked a few more feet. One could feel an unpleasant chill in the air. There was some water nearby. One could smell the dampness. He removed his trousers and shirt and walked a few more metres. The walk became even more slow. He wondered whether he was actually tired or was it fear . . . it could have been both. The path was now reduced to a small lane of mud in the midst of a thick overgrowth of bushes.

A few more steps and he stopped. He looked around. First to the right, and then in front of him. He strained his neck and looked behind to see if someone was following him. There was a thick growth of bushes to the left. A strange fear overtook him. There was a numb shiver in his body . . . probably the chill in the wind . . . probably not. He closed his eyes. Mumbled something that looked like a prayer, and then he let go. His body lunged forward, while his legs remained static. His body kept moving, using his toes to swivel till a point when his legs were lifted off the ground and they followed the head as it plunged deep down into the Hussain Sagar Lake. A splash killed the silence in the area. But there was no one around to get disturbed by it.

His body was found the next day by morning walkers, who called the local police and informed them about a body floating in the lake.

Tulsiram was dead by the time he was taken to the hospital. The police dismissed it as a regular suicide. When they checked with his colleagues at the Mariott, even they had no clue. Tulsiram had never shown his frustrations to them and so, they were not aware of what was going through his mind.

His wife was distraught. Four daughters and herself to manage. She had no clue about how she was going to survive. Tulsiram never told her about his problems. Was there something fishy? Was there a conspiracy she was not aware of? Questions after questions clouded her mind, but she did not have answers to any.

The next day in the morning, when one of her neighbours went to check on her, they were in for a rude shock. She was found lying on the mat, wrists slit. Next to her, lying on the floor, were her four daughters . . . dried froth stuck to the sides of their mouths. They were all dead. Tulsiram's wife had killed all four of them before slitting her own wrists. Why she chose to poison them and take the difficult route of slitting her own wrists was a mystery to everyone in their neighbourhood. Limited supply of poison maybe?

The city police was shaken out of its slumber by these five suicides. The force which had refused to act when Tulsiram's body was found floating in Hussain Sagar Lake, was now forced into action when faced with five more deaths. Public outrage at the loss of these six lives forced them to move out of slumber. They went into an overdrive.

Tulsiram's house was sealed. The cops searched every nook and corner of his hutment. The search didn't take too much time, because it was only a one room house. They couldn't find anything that could throw light on the reasons for the suicide. Finally, a search of the Marriott's driver room was undertaken. The lockers were sealed and searched.

And there it was. Inside Tulsiram's locker, in a sealed cover was a two page note. It was in Telugu. The police could not read it properly as it was scribbled and the person seemed to have written the letter in an inebriated state. Experts looked at the letter and translated the same into English. The note was addressed to his wife.

Dear Nagamma,

I am sorry. I married you hoping to give you a good life. I brought you from the village expecting you to be happy with me. Year after year I hoped that our financial standing would improve. I hoped to earn more money and live comfortably. Alas, that was not meant to be.

Our four beautiful daughters have come into this world hoping that life will give them something exciting. Stars in their eyes they would have hoped to live for something great. I can't even give them a normal life.

The salary I get is not even good enough for all of us to lead an average life. Amma and appa are struggling in Narsapur. I am not even in a position to send them money. Their cows died last year and I had to borrow money from CitiFinancial to help them buy another cow. I also helped them get their land released from Reddy. I have not even been able to pay the loans that I took to pay for your fourth delivery. I have a huge debt on my head and I am now not able to service the instalments. These guys are now threatening me.

Yesterday the guys from NFS landed at my office. They threatened to kidnap our children if I am not able to repay the loan. They demanded three instalments from me. How can I pay three when I don't even have the money to pay one? Not only that, the moneylender's guys also came to me this morning asking for their money. I don't know what to do. How can I come in front of you when I have not been able to provide for you? Even the bangles which your mother gave us on our wedding are with the sahookaar. I have been promising you for five years that I will get them released.

You have been so good to me. What have I done in return? Nothing. Only made life miserable for you. I have not been a good husband, a good father or even a good human being. By the time you read this letter, it might be too late. Please forgive me Nagu. I love you and our four sweet daughters. I can't see you in this plight. I am freeing you from my clutches.

Please forgive me.
Tulsiram

That was it. Beginning of mayhem. All hell broke loose.

'Mercenary Recovery Goons wipe out entire family'

This line screamed out loud from the front page of a mainline daily.

'Who is to blame – Tulsiram or NFS recovery agents?' said another. All these stories went on to blame the recovery agents for the deaths of Tulsiram and his family.

The story became the scoop of the year for the media. Overnight, Tulsiram became a rallying point for all the politicians. In his life he couldn't become more than one poor nondescript soul. In his death he became a star. Newspaper after newspaper exploited this story. The television channels kept it alive. The media consistently portrayed Tulsiram as the poor exploited common man who was pushed into committing suicide by the loan brokers of the country. NFS figured prominently among them.

The opinion makers of the community started doing what they were good at – 'Voicing their opinion'. In our country, if a rickshaw hits a motor car, the blame is almost always taken by the one driving the car, even if the rickshaw puller is in the wrong. It is quite easy to guess that in the battle between the affluent and the poor, who is to face the brunt. The same thing happened here as well. No one questioned why Tulsiram borrowed so much and lived beyond his means, why he gave birth to four children when he could not afford to bring up even one? Questions were only raised on the recovery means employed by banks and finance companies, specifically NFS to get back their legitimate dues.

Elections were due in the country in the next eighteen months – an election that would decide who gets to run the second largest democracy for the next five years. The elections always came with the potential to become a debacle of many sorts. Appeasement of masses is but natural at this time. If one tried putting his brains into the kind of statements that the political leaders made, one would be left with no doubt that our dearest 'selfless' politicians consider the janta to be nothing less than fools! Everything hinged oп votes . . . and would the scheming politicians ever miss such a wonderful opportunity? They got active too. And unfortunately if the politicians get involved in anything in India, it becomes an unmitigated disaster. It only adds to the confusion and adds dollops to the already high frustration levels. One thing leads to another and everything collapses like a pack of cards. Disaster was lurking in the shadows. Could it be far behind?

Questions were raised in the assembly if the government was doing enough to protect the poor farmers, villagers and the low income group from the atrocities of recovery agents. It became a PR nightmare for the involved banks and finance companies. A tragic one off instance had turned into a big political agenda, a battle between the 'Have's' and the 'Have nots'. Not surprisingly, the political parties went all out to back the 'Have nots', a tried and tested vote bank politics strategy.

NFS was facing the brunt of this chaos. They became the poster boys for ruthless collections and were being solely held responsible for these mass suicides. Even though Tulsiram's letter talked about loans from moneylenders and other financial institutions, NFS seemed to be the only one being singled out in this so-called democratic exercise of right to protest. Their branches in the city were shut down, security beefed up at all their branches to prevent loss to property and most of the employees were asked to stay at home to ensure their safety. Though it was shut down for business a few branches were kept open for the management team to visit and meet to work out damage containment strategy, albeit access was through a side door, away from public and media glare.

It was in the midst of this chaos that Amit landed in the city. When he had heard about the multiple suicides, he was shocked. An uneasy feeling kept lurking in the pit of his stomach. It felt as if something was taking somersaults inside and it just stopped short of making him throw up. It was not a good sign.

Why us? He thought even as he decided to be on site and marshal his resources himself. A senior management visit in such situations definitely props up the team at ground zero. Who knows what challenges they might be dealing with? He packed his bags and landed in Hyderabad. 'I hope it ends well,' he had mentioned to Chanda that day, before he left. The shiver in his voice was something Chanda had felt for the first time.

The plane landed at 7.55 a.m. He stepped out of the aircraft, walked to the luggage belt and waited patiently for fifteen minutes for the luggage to arrive. 'Why can't it come on time?' he cursed under his breath, as he bent down to pull out the trolley. A few muscles in his back revolted, making him realise that he hadn't been to the gym for quite a while.

His eyes scanned the endless list of taxi drivers to find a placard with his name. As he was looking around, someone thrust a pamphlet in his hand. It was about Hyderabad airport shifting to a new site in the next three months. 'A larger and better airport, built to international standard and style,' it said. 'Who the fuck cares?' he thought and threw it into the nearest bin.

There was only one thing on his mind. He wanted to be sure that in Tulsiram's case, NFS came clean. He had done his research on the case and he was surprised at the allegation made by Tulsiram.

Back in Mumbai, when the Tulsiram case first blew up, the first thing he had asked for was Tulsiram's loans statement of accounts. It clearly showed that Tulsiram was not a delinquent customer. He was up-to-date as far as his payments were concerned. In the books of NFS, there were no overdue payments from Tulsiram. Even though Tulsiram had bounced a few of his EMI repayments, he had paid up every single instalment on subsequent follow up by the NFS collection agencies.

'Then why all this noise about not being able to pay three EMIs to NFS?' he wondered. 'Probably, Tulsiram's state of mind caused him to get the name of the finance company wrong,' he thought as he got into a waiting white Hyundai Accent cab. He also immediately realised that his mind was making its best efforts to console and stop the sickly feeling in his stomach.

'Somajiguda branch,' he said to the driver, who just nodded. The driver was a regular and hence knew where to go. The drive was a comfortable one as it was relatively early in the morning and there wasn't much of traffic on the road. He was casually looking out of the car window. Shops were flying past in the reverse direction. Buildings were coming up on both sides of the road. Hoardings were hopping behind. 'What a city?' he thought. 'Why the hell do they screw up the city skyline by putting up hundreds of hoardings? Why doesn't someone do anything about them?' he thought even as he compared the hoarding menace to that in Mumbai. City people love to complain about and compare the problems in their city with those of others. 'Amchi Mumbai has left no stones unturned either. The menace comes with double the force there,' said his interior monologue.

Flying past him in the reverse direction were a mix of large metal hoardings and a number of small untidily tied cloth banners. Back in Mumbai, the cloth banners were banned. They were unauthorised. However, nobody ever gives up. Every night, some unscrupulous vendors would put up tens of hundreds of cloth banners in Mumbai . . . across roads, along railway stations, between electric poles, in the market, in every conceivable place, only to be removed the next morning by the municipal corporation. The huge numbers of banners across Hyderabad streets made him feel that maybe the corporation was not as effective in Hyderabad as in Mumbai.

In the midst of all this, there was one banner which caught his attention. All along the route he would have seen over a hundred of that particular type of banner. It was in Telugu, the local language, and hence he could not make head or tail of it. Every banner had pictures of two individuals on it. One of which was constant in every banner. The second picture changed every two to three kilometres. There was a symbol at the bottom, that looked like an election symbol, making him realise that it was a banner put up by a political party. However, he had no clue of what was written on it. There was something about the banner which gave him an uncomfortable feeling. In fact, there was an eerie sense of familiarity about the banner, but he could not figure out what it related to.

Victor was waiting for him at the Hyderabad branch of NFS. He was the head of collections for NFS for the state of Andhra Pradesh. Victor had taken over the head of collections role for the province around the same time that Amit moved to his new role in NFS. He was Amit's man.

The main door of the branch was locked. Victor led him inside through the back door. The collections team was waiting for him. All of them looked worried. After the initial round of discussions and updates, he stepped into the conference room.

'Show me his file.' Amit asked for Tulsiram's loan application set.

'In a moment,' said Victor as he stepped out of the room. Within minutes he was back in the room with a copy of the customer file. Amit reached out and took it from him. The first sheet of paper in the document set was the application form that Tulsiram had filled. A photograph of Tulsiram was pasted on the application form – Tulsiram in his driver's uniform, photographed outside the Marriott. Seemed to be a decent chap. A nice photograph is often a positive when you evaluate a loan application form. A pleasant looking photograph often disposes the loan officer favourably towards the applicant.

'There is something very familiar about this guy. I have seen him somewhere,' thought Amit. 'Maybe at the Marriott. I have stayed there so many times in the past,' and he dismissed the thought as he moved on to critically examine the customer file. The salary slip seemed perfect; the bank statements were in order and the verification reports were fine. The entire due diligence process seemed to have been followed. In the normal course something like this would definitely have got approved. So giving him a loan was in line with the policy of NFS. It was not an error. Nobody had committed a mistake in approving a loan for him. As he closed the file, he suddenly chose to have one last look at Tulsiram's application form. And then he shut the file. Something was nagging him.

'Give me the detailed collections report,' he said, wanting to see if there was any instance of collection excesses on Tulsiram. He knew that everything was in order; however, he wanted to double check. It was a sensitive case and could blow up anytime. Hadn't it already?

While Victor stepped out to get it, Amit walked out to the wash- room. The washroom in the Hyderabad branch was in one corner of the floor – a small niche converted into a washroom, overlooking the main road. It had a small hole in the wall which was a window now . . . it probably would have housed an exhaust fan in the past.

He managed to squeeze himself into the washroom and looked at the mirror above the wash basin. Age was beginning to show on his face. He splashed a few drops of cold water on his face and looked up again. The water was a relief from the heat that he was facing in his professional life. The tissue box was hung on the left of the mirror. He reached out and pulled one. Beyond the tissue box was this small window, through which he looked out into the street below. He casually looked at the passing cars, the struggling rickshaw puller, the beggar at the traffic signal, and then moved his gaze up to the mall across the street. The mall housed a large Louis Phillipe store. Next to it was a fancy showroom. He could see the front façade where the words 'SALDI' were written in bold red, multiple number of times. He tried to guess the brand, but a large banner was blocking his view. Straining his neck, he tried to look over and around it, but couldn't make out which store it was. He washed his hands still trying to figure out the brand.

'Up to fifty percent sale is not bad. Maybe I should look at it before I leave the city,' he thought as he turned back. And suddenly, as if hit by lightning, he craned his neck to look back at the road again. There it was. The nagging feeling was not without reason. He hurried back to the room. Victor was already there. He quickly opened the file and turned the papers to get to the application form. He looked at Victor, 'This guy. This guy . . . what is he doing on the banners there? All the way from the airport to here, I saw this guy's photographs on banners. They are all over the place. Why? What's written on those?' Worry lines conquered his face while the colour drained out of his cheeks.

Victor's expression was a give away. He squirmed a bit and said, 'Amit, I was about to tell you. The opposition party here has taken Tulsiram's story to town. They have put up posters all over, publicising this suicide, especially in poor localities.'

'What do they say? I can't make out a word of it. It's in Telugu.'

'The banners which have been put up by the Telugu Rakshana Party, a local fanatic party, implore people to contact them in case recovery agents were to harass anyone. They have offered to help them deal with the recovery agents. They have put pictures of all their politicians alongside Tulsiram . . . one-by-one. Tulsiram has become a sort of a cult figure for loan defaulters. With elections due in twelve–eighteen months, this seems to be an issue that can be converted into a vote magnet.'

'Goodness me! Have they named us in these banners? What's the impact?'

'Thankfully, not yet. They are quite generic and do not single out any particular bank. It has however impacted our ability to collect. The collection agents have not been able to go into the field to collect from defaulting customers. Last evening, four of our collectors got beaten up. The rest are now reluctant to go and collect. And . . .' he hesitated.

'And what?'

'This morning before you walked in, six of my agents have resigned. Their families do not want them to be in collections and risk their lives,' Victor added. Amit was reminded of his mother's call, the night before he was due to take up the new job. 'Don't take it up beta. This is a dirty line,' her voice echoed in Amit's head.

'Where will they go? Don't they need their salaries?'

'That's not a problem, Amit. The mall mania is taking its toll. All these guys will find jobs in numerous new shopping malls that are opening up. Maybe even at a higher salary. They get to work in a less intimidating environment and an air-conditioned atmosphere. Personal security was never an issue thus far, you see. Now it has become one. It's normal for families to be concerned and parents stopping their wards from working in collections.'

'That's bad news.'

Victor nodded in acceptance. He had a sombre look on his face. 'Do you think meeting with the higher ups in the police will help? I can meet them today and argue our case,' asked Amit.

'No, it won't. This issue has become so big that the government is not going to let it die down so easily. As I said, elections round the corner. The police will not do anything which will attract an adverse reaction from the masses. The police is under their control and will follow their instructions. We must not do anything proactively. In any case they have asked for the name and address of the head of collections for all banks who have doled out loans to Tulsiram. At this point I do not think it will be an issue for us because as far as our records show, he is not a delinquent customer. Why should we go there on our own and make it an issue for ourselves? Fortunately, they have not singled us out, though initially most of the newspapers tried to exploit our MNC status and make us the torch bearers of inappropriate collections practices.'

'Hmmm . . .' was all that Amit could say.

After another forty-five minutes of reviewing, Amit was convinced that it was not worth risking aggressive collections in this environment. Not only would it put the entire collections team at risk, it would also put the NFS franchise at risk. The brand would come under the media glare and that was not a good thing. He was also convinced that they were not in the wrong. Their name just happened to be mentioned along with a few others because they had lent money to Tulsiram.

'OKAY,' he said as he prepared to leave the office to catch a flight back to Mumbai. 'Tread carefully. Don't send your collectors out to collect from difficult customers. Lie low for a couple of weeks. We will take a hit on delinquencies and portfolio performance for a month or two. I will sensitise everyone and manage expectations at the management level. We will try and cover up for this month's performance shortfall when the situation improves. And no media interviews or discussions please. All queries from the media to be directed to the public affairs team in Mumbai. Tell your team too.'

He got into the car and left for the airport. En route he passed a procession – a long one – wherein people were carrying placards and banners and were screaming at the top of their voices. This time around he recognised the picture. It was none other than Tulsiram. 'Tulsiram, what did I do to you? You have become such a pain for me,' thought Amit, even as he felt sorry that the entire family had got wiped out in a span of two nights. 'Maybe it was good. In any case, they would have struggled without Tulsiram' was his last thought of justification and consolation before he closed his eyes for a short nap. He couldn't sleep. The airport was forty-five minutes away.

He had a disturbed flight that night. The flight was smooth but his mind was going through a fair bit of turbulence. The air traffic congestion at Mumbai added to the chaos. The flight took over three hours to land in Mumbai . . . something which should have taken him less than two hours. 'Flights are meant to catch up on sleep,' he would normally say. Not today. He was wide awake. He ignored repeated offers from the crew for dinner and kept staring at the back of the seat in front of him. He was not getting a good feeling about it. A voice at the back of his mind kept telling him,

'Something is going to blow up somewhere, watch out'. If only he knew when and where . . .

Chanda was awake when he walked in. The tense look was not lost on her. She still cared for him. Initially when she heard about his role in collections, she had been worried. So were both their parents. But once he had made that decision under Aditya's influence, she had supported him wholeheartedly.

Amit tossed and turned in bed almost the whole night. She had never seen him restless like this before. In the middle of the night, she woke him up. Actually she didn't need to as he was wide awake. She sat up with him and humoured him for over an hour. They spoke about his career, his college days, his bank, their parents, etc. What a conversation to have in the middle of the night! Amit had put on some weight off late and Chanda was worried about his cholesterol level. When Amit kept tossing in bed, Chanda's mind started working overtime, making her feel that these could be sure-shot signs of an emerging cardiac problem. Just to ensure that it was not so, she decided to stay awake with him for some time. It was a long never-ending night for both of them.

The Next Day
20 December 2007

Rakesh Srivastav arrived the next morning. When he showed Amit the non-bailable arrest warrant, it had shocked Amit. Why him? What had he done? Why should he be arrested for something which he couldn't be held guilty for? These questions had no answers. He was taken to the Bandra police station, where after a prolonged discussion between the Bandra police and Rakesh Srivastava, he was lodged in prison.

Rohan Naik had promised to do something for him. The bank has clout he had said. 'We will pull you out. Do not worry.'

He was hoping that those words didn't remain mere words when the knock on his prison cell woke him up. He had shut his eyes and was trying to get away from the world of pain. Tulsiram would have felt the same. Helpless. The thought of Tulsiram, his family, his pain and the utter poverty which would possibly have driven him to commit suicide crossed his mind. The big clock in the hall started ringing its hourly note. He counted the number of hits of the dong, and that told him that it was only ten at night and he had a long night ahead.

'You have visitors,' a constable with a handle-bar moustache said in a voice that was softer than the other voices he had heard there. Amit looked up with eager and hopeful eyes.

Behind the head constable's desk, sitting on the same bench where he was sitting in the morning, he could see Chanda. Along with her was the other gentleman who was solely responsible for getting him into all this. Actually why should he be blamed? Amit had the option of not taking up this assignment. No one forced him. Hadn't he taken it up on his own free will? The constable opened the cell door and disappeared. The cell he was lodged in was not a prison meant for normal prisoners. It was just an overnight lodgement area found in most prisons for convicts to be put up before they moved to formal prisons and long-term cells. He walked out into the main hall of the police station. Chanda ran up to him and hugged him. She had tears in her eyes.

'Ma called,' said Chanda amidst short sniffs.

'Don't tell her about this.'

'No I won't.'

'Don't worry Amit.' It was Aditya. 'I will personally take care of this and ensure you come out with your reputation intact.'

'I hope so too Aditya. I don't even know how they could arrest me on abetment to suicide.'

'We will have to wait and see the charges that they have filed against you.'

'We are moving a stay petition tomorrow morning in the High Court. My first priority is to get you out of here. How to handle the Tulsiram issue is something we will think about later.'

'Who is working on this?' Amit asked.

Aditya reassuringly replied, 'We have got Subramanian & Co. to work on this. Ravi Subramanian is looking at this case himself. I have personally spoken to him. Naik is currently at his office drafting the petition to be placed in front of the magistrate tomorrow morning. You do not need to worry. I am on top of this now.'

'Chanda, it will be fine. It's going to be OKAY,' said Amit while holding her hand as a gesture to reassure and comfort her. Chanda looked distraught and ready to break down any time.

'Amit, tell me, do you think we were at fault in Hyderabad?' Aditya interrupted their romantic embrace.

'No Aditya. Tulsiram is not even a delinquent customer with us. The suicide note says that the recovery agent asked for three EMIs from the customer. There is not a single payment overdue from the customer at this point in time. How could we have gone and demanded three instalments? Obviously a recovery agent from some other financier has gone to the customer and he is confusing him with ours. He has multiple loans and is defaulting on most of them. It could be possible that he mixed it all up, given the confused and depressed state that he was in at that point of time.'

'How confident are you that our agent was not involved?'

'Quite confident, Aditya. Why do you ask? Is there any other twist to the tale?'

'Jaldi, jaldi . . . khatam karo . . . finish, finish . . .' a constable started heckling them before Aditya could answer Amit's question. Aditya looked at the inspector sitting in a corner and waved at him.

'Ae pandu, let them be. Wo hamare aadmi hain. They are our people.'

The police in Bandra were quite helpful. The NYB security team had managed to influence them through the seniors at the IG's office. Unfortunately, the arrest warrant for Amit was issued in Hyderabad and hence unless it was quashed, the Mumbai police could do nothing about it. At best they could extend basic courtesies to Amit.

Rakesh Srivastav had himself come down from Hyderabad to arrest Amit. The warrant was issued late last night and Rakesh Srivastav had flown to Mumbai the same night to execute the warrant. The irony was that even Amit was on the same flight to Mumbai the previous night.

'Ya Amit, you were saying that we are not to be blamed,' Aditya restarted the discussion after the temporary intrusion.

'That's correct Aditya.'

'What if I say we are?'

'Sorry?'

'What if I say we are?'

Amit couldn't believe his ears. 'Aditya, this is not the time to joke. I returned last night from Hyderabad after taking stock at the ground level. I have no reason to believe that our team is at fault.'

'Amit, I am sorry, I couldn't see you earlier, but I was in Hyderabad this morning. And I think we have nailed the issue.'

'You were in Hyderabad?'

'Hmm . . .'

'Why? Why did you have to go?'

'I knew this was serious and could blow up. We have never faced such a situation in the bank. So I decided to go there myself. Went with Manish.'

'Manish who? Kakkar?'

'Yup. He came in directly from Singapore.'

'You should have told me. I would have stayed back in Hyderabad.'

'And would have got arrested there. At least we have some say in Mumbai. Who would have helped you there? Jails in Hyderabad are worse.'

It brought a smile back on Amit's face. Chanda remained frozen. She didn't like the looks of whatever was going on. She wanted the nightmare to end soon. She had picked up some food for Amit on the way. She opened the packets and they sat down on a bench in a secluded corner of the police station.

Amit was wondering what was it that Aditya knew and he didn't. How was it that he always knew more than the others? Maybe that's why he was the CEO. 'I did not know Manish Kakkar was in Hyderabad,' he said to Aditya, but the latter did not react.

Aditya guessed the thoughts in Amit's mind. 'Don't worry. Eat first. I will tell you the story. You might be hungry. Your brain normally reacts slowly when hungry.'

'Will he get out of jail Aditya?' Chanda queried.

'I am not the judge lady, but I can tell you it looks like he will tomorrow.'

'I am confident he will.' Ravi Subramanian had just walked in with Naik. 'There is no case against him. It's a knee-jerk reaction by a desperate government wanting to capitalise on this calamity for electoral gains. They want to sensationalise this issue and we will not let them party out of someone's misery.'

'Hi Ravi! Meet the man, Amit Sharma.' And then he looked at Amit, 'Amit, the man here holds the key to your fortune. So better be nice to him.'

For once Amit smiled and acknowledged him.

'Our papers are ready for filing, early tomorrow morning. We get to go first tomorrow. Have informal confirmations on this from the court. Hopefully you should be out of here by early afternoon tomorrow.'

'What will be our defence?'

'We will argue on the grounds that you in Mumbai cannot be held accountable for a transactional lapse that may have happened in Hyderabad, even if for a moment you assume that there was a lapse. You don't even know the customer or his family. Incidentally, we have heard that similar warrants have been issued against people holding your position in Citibank, GE and other organisations too. Heads of all organisations which gave out loans to Tulsiram are in the dock. But those guys got wind of this early and they went into hiding. Their petitions are also coming up tomorrow.'

'Oh . . . OKAY.' This sounded reassuring to Amit. He was not alone in this.

'We will also ask for evidence on the basis of which they have issued this warrant. I know that they don't have any. I have also spoken with Rakesh Srivastava. Met him outside the police station. He is not too keen to oppose the motion.' He then looked at Chanda. 'I presume she is the wife. You can sleep well tonight madam.' He looked at his watch and added, 'Whatever is left of it.' And there were smiles all around.

Ravi Subramanian needed some signatures from Amit on the court documents. Once they were done, he wished both of them and went back home. He needed some sleep before the courts opened. Normally in such a case, he would have sent his assistant. However, after meeting both Amit and Chanda, he decided to go himself.

Aditya sat down with the two of them after the lawyers and Naik had left.

'Aditya, you were saying something about us being at fault?'

'Oh yes. It's crazy. But we could have an issue on our hands in Hyderabad.'

And he started telling them the entire story and what he had found out about the Hyderabad incident. It left Chanda speechless and Amit looked surprised too.

'It's therefore important to back the right people,' Aditya said. 'I will always back you my friend. I have said that in the past and will say it again. You will never find me letting you down.' And he walked away. He was close to the jail door when he turned back. 'And Amit, my wife never believed me. She thinks all along I batted for you, for my own gains. Sometimes yes, I did it for my benefit, but at other times, I wanted to genuinely see you prosper. I hired you in the bank didn't I? My wife never believed me when I told her this. And . . .' He paused. 'I think your wife here doesn't believe me too. I will ensure both of you do well in life . . . God bless,' and he turned and walked away.

'Was that the shine in his eyes or were there tears in them?'

'Maybe both,' said Chanda as she rested her head on Amit's shoulders. Both of them sat there holding hand-in-hand, on that solitary, hard bench. The station staff didn't harass them or ask

Chanda to go back. Amit was not asked to move back into the cell. They just let them be. Naik and Rakesh Srivastav had given instructions not to hassle them.

Neither of them got a wink of sleep that night. It was the second sleepless night in succession for Amit. They were just waiting for daybreak, so that they could go back home, back to the safe confines of their four walls.

Epilogue
20 December 2007
Hyderabad

Manish Kakkar landed in Hyderabad in the wee hours of the morning. The Singapore Airlines SQ 187 was late by an hour. By the time he reached his hotel it was well past 2 a.m.

The check-in counter at the Grand Kakatiya had a message for him. It was from Aditya. 'Call me when you reach. Irrespective of the time. I am in room No 1209.' He knew that Aditya was also staying in the same hotel.

'Will call him from my room,' he said to himself as he made his way to his fourth floor room. Aditya's suite was on the more anointed and exclusive twelfth floor. He was the boss and an executive suite was his privilege.

Aditya picked up the phone on the first ring. He had been waiting for Manish to call. 'Come up to my room. I need to see you right away.' When he heard this, Manish took the lift to the twelfth floor and walked up to the room at the far end of the corridor. The door was open. He walked straight in.

'Hi Manish, how have you been my friend?'

'Great Aditya, what's going on?' asked Manish while he surveyed the room. The TV in Aditya's room was playing the news hour on CNN. An inane newsreader was mumbling something which was related to a red band at the bottom of the screen that screamed 'Breaking News'.

'Oh. Another car bomb in Iraq has blasted seventy-four people.'

'No Aditya. I was asking about what's going on in Hyderabad? You called me in such a hurry. I just hopped on to the first available flight. I knew that there would be an emergency. Else, you wouldn't call me in this manner. What happened?'

'Manish, years back, when you guys were just setting off on your career, there was a collections disaster. We had repossessed a wrong car that had caused nuisance to someone who hadn't even borrowed from us. That hit the front pages of the *Wall Street Journal* hours before our annual results were to be declared.'

'Yes. I know the story.'

'It cost the key people in the company their jobs and extreme loss of face for the organisation. Some even went to the extent of saying that the timing of the story was dictated by our competitors, with the sole intention of embarrassing NYB.'

'I know.'

'We seem to be heading towards a similar disaster again.'

'You are obviously referring to the Marriott driver suicide case. What's the development there? Are we clean?'

'Manish, it does not matter whether you are clean or not. What matters is what the public perceives and what the media states.' Manish nodded in response.

'A day after this guy committed suicide, the family too committed suicide. The wife and the four children. She poisoned the children before killing herself. This has already blown up in India. Somehow I get a feel that the international media will step into this very soon. I am sure they will . . . sooner than later.'

'I am aware Aditya.'

'I know. I had sent across the incident report to our Singapore office as a matter of routine escalation. However, I do not believe the stories that everyone around is telling me. Everyone is telling me that we are on the right side in this entire episode. But I am not convinced. My job and the organisation's reputation is at stake. I want to get to the bottom of this myself. In such a situation I don't trust anyone around. And that's why I called you. Remember this is in Amit's line of command. Ideally I would have got him to sort it out for me, but given that he might be the impacted party and might have a vested interest in not bringing out the truth, it is important that we do this on our own. An independent perspective always helps.'

'OKAY. So, what do you expect of me?'

'Let me tell you the story in its entirety . . . as we know it . . .' and Aditya began narrating the entire sequence of events. He told him about everything that had happened over the past few days in Hyderabad.

'Aditya, a question,' said Manish when Aditya paused for breath. 'Isn't Tulsiram a customer who has paid all his dues? I was told that all his payments have been made and there is no overdue? That's what the initial incident report said.'

'Yes Manish. You are right. However, here's why I do not trust what is being told to me.' And he handed Manish a sheet of paper. 'I have a small concern here. Don't know if anyone else has picked it up yet. But here, look at his statement of accounts.'

Manish looked carefully at the document given by Aditya. It was a loan account statement of Tulsiram.

Date	Narration	Debit	Credit	Balance
1st August 08	Balance Outstanding			46956
5th August 08	Cheque payment		1979	
6th August 08	Cheque returned unpaid	1979		
22nd August 08	Cash payment received		1979	46591
5th September 08	Cheque payment		1979	
6th September 08	Cheque returned unpaid	1979		
29th September 08	Cash payment received		1979	46213
5th October 08	Cheque payment		1979	
6th October 08	Cheque returned unpaid	1979		
31st October 08	Cash payment received		1979	45823
5th November 08	Cheque payment		1979	
6th November 08	Cheque returned unpaid	1979		
30th November 08	Cash payment received		1979	45419
5th December	Cheque payment		1979	45001

'Cheque returned unpaid means that the cheque which was presented has bounced,' said Aditya even as he looked at Manish and winked.

'Aditya!' The drag on the last few alphabets was a conscious one. 'I have worked in India for over a decade, long enough to know that,' said Manish. Aditya was just having some fun.

Manish went through the statement and looked up at Aditya. 'He has bounced each of his last four instalments.'

'Yes. Except for the December instalment cheque, which he has paid on time. The ones for August, September, October and November have bounced.'

'Not only that. He has also paid up in cash every month before the month end. In August he paid early, but in the later three months he has paid dot on the last day of the month.'

'What does that show?' asked Aditya.

'That the collections team has been pushing him aggressively and getting him to make these payments before the end of the month,' Manish replied.

'In other words these are customers who have a habit of bouncing their cheques but are easy to collect from, with a little bit of follow up. A debt collector's delight, right?'

'Yes Aditya. That's what it looks like. I would also assume that he is a low risk customer as we have been able to repeatedly and successfully collect his dues from him. And you are bang on . . . collectors normally like to deal with customers like these.'

'Agreed. What you are saying could be right. One of the possibilities,' said Aditya.

'What else could it be? You are obviously thinking of something else.' Manish was now beginning to wonder what he meant. 'What's on your mind Aditya?'

'It could be that instead of him, someone else is making the payment on his behalf?'

'Who could it be? And why would someone make a payment on his behalf? Unless you are implying a fraud in the system.'

'Yes Manish. Do you think that could be an option?'

'Hmm . . .' Manish began to ponder. 'That could be serious.' He couldn't say anything else.

'If you go back to Tulsiram's loan repayment, he has bounced his check in the past, before August too, but never with such regularity.

Often, he has paid much before the 30th. Look at August. He paid on 22 August. Prior to that he bounced his cheque in May, but paid almost immediately. On 13 May. The trend in the last three months is strange. Every month he has paid dot on the last day of the month. Why? The cash payments on the same day is too much of a coincidence.'

'I can investigate and find out if your suspicion is true,' added Manish.

'I know. Normally, the only way to check this is to call the customers and check if they have in fact made these payments on the last day of the month. But in this case, there is no way in which we can get in touch with Tulsiram. Unfortunately, Vodafone's network didn't follow him where he went.'

Manish smiled.

'If what I suspect is true, it could be a serious fraud, a big controls lapse and we could be up shit creek,' Aditya continued.

'What would you want me to do in this?'

'I want you to get to the bottom of this. Find out who is responsible, who is screwing up. Find out if at all we had a role to play in abetting the suicide, directly or indirectly. Can anyone link it back to NFS? Do it carefully. I don't want too many eyebrows to be raised. There are not many people who I can trust in this situation. I want you to do it for me. Can you?'

'How much time do we have for this?'

'Twelve hours.'

'What? Twelve hours?' Manish was shocked. It was too short a time frame.

'I am here in Hyderabad for a meeting with the chief minister on a SEZ project funding. Taking the evening flight to Mumbai. I need the report by the time I leave. You don't need to give me a written report. Just let me know your findings. Actually, I think I know what the story is. I just want someone to validate this.'

'Can I get Amit involved?'

'You must be kidding my friend. If he was required, why would I fly you in from Singapore?'

'Got it. Will do my best to close it today.'

'Here are all the papers I have got. I will expect your call tomorrow evening . . . actually this evening. You have my authority to do whatever you want. Call upon whoever you want. Interrogate who ever you choose to. Do what it takes. At the end of the next twelve hours, I want to know if there has been a screw up and if indeed there has been one, I want to know who is responsible. The person responsible for the screw-up needs to go. Whether it is Amit, whether it is Victor, I don't care. I will go by what you tell me.'

'I will call you in the evening.'

'Better still, if you have nothing else to do in Hyderabad, take the evening flight back to Mumbai along with me. I will ask my secretary to book you on the same flight.'

Manish nodded. He knew that now the twelve hour deadline was cast in concrete. He had no means of extending it.

Manish was awake the whole night . . . reading all the documents that Aditya had given him, trying to digest the information and form his own views on what could have happened. For a moment he browsed over the fact that Aditya could have called Amit to do what he was asking Manish to do. Why didn't he? Maybe Aditya did not like him as much as he did earlier. Were there any issues between them? Probably he didn't trust Amit. Anyway it was none of his business. He had to do what was told to him. Period.

By the time he finished going over the sequence of events again and again in his mind – the customer, the amounts due, the instalment paid, the cash on a month end, the suicide and then the mass suicide, the public frenzy and the resultant political involvement – the phone in his room rang. He picked it up. Who could it be at this hour?

'Good morning sir. This is a wake up call for you.' What the hell? A look at his watch told him that it was already 6.30 in the morning, and he hadn't slept even for a minute. Aditya had given him only twelve hours. He quickly showered and was ready by 7.15 a.m. Sleep could wait. He rushed down to the coffee shop for breakfast.

Before leaving Aditya's room, he had sent a message to Victor, to be in the hotel by 7 a.m. He knew that Victor was an early riser and hence would definitely see the message and be with him at seven.

As he had expected, Victor was waiting for him at the lobby. 'Hi Manish. How come in Hyderabad? A surprise visit?' Victor had not expected Manish to be in Hyderabad. As a matter of fact, Manish was known to be a poor traveller and wouldn't visit his operative locations even during his stint as a head of credit at NFS.

'I had to come here to close a deal with a credit analytics firm. We might be buying a data analytics package from this Hyderabad company. That's why I came in yesterday morning,' he lied. 'When Aditya got to know that I was here, he asked me to take a look at the processes that you guys run.'

'I understand. You too are here in connection with the suicide issue? Amit was here yesterday and you are here today.' Victor was not an idiot and was quick to see through Manish's clumsy attempt at lying. Manish didn't respond. He just smiled. Within minutes, they were walking out of the hotel, into Victor's car, on their way to the NFS branch in Hyderabad.

Manish got down to work almost immediately on reaching the branch. The conference room in the front office of the branch was free and became Manish's den for the day.

He asked for the application form, the documents submitted by Tulsiram, the fraud check results . . . almost the same documents that Amit had asked for. All those were quickly reviewed and shoved back into the cupboard in twenty minutes. Nothing fishy there. The receipt books were next on his list.

The collections receipt books are an integral part of any collections process. These receipt books or rather receipt pads are given to all the collection agents. They are sequentially numbered and the collection agents are supposed to carry them whenever they go on their field visits. These are meant to be issued to every customer who pays up his overdue instalment to the agent when they go knocking on the customer's door. The collection agent fills out these receipts in duplicate and gets the customer's signature on them as an acknowledgement. A copy is then given to the customer as a proof of him having paid the instalments to the agent of NFS. The receipts are audited every month to see if receipts are available for every payment collected. The audit needs to validate the receipts corresponding to every payment picked up by the collection agent.

The receipt books ensure that the cash collected by the agents is deposited in the company every day. There are instances where some collection agents collect money from the customers and do not deposit it back in the company. In such a case, a copy of the receipt with the customer is used as a proof to nail the collector. It also avoids conflict between the customer and the finance company.

The receipt book is a very abused, but nevertheless a critical part of the process in collections. Many a frauds in collections surface during the receipt book audits. In all good organisations, a monthly audit of the receipt books is diligently undertaken. To ensure independence and sanctity of the audit, this is done by someone from outside the credit and collection chain of command. The receipt book is the bible of collections and any abuse of the receipt book process is met with instant termination of the officials concerned.

'Victor, can I have the receipt books and the receipt book audit report for the last three months? I want to specifically see the receipts for Tulsiram's payments from August 2007 to November.' And 'Yaaaaawwwwnn . . . I want to see them quickly please. I do not have time . . . Yaaaawwnnnn,' drawled Manish while making a miserably failed attempt at screaming. He was in a hurry and any delay on the part of the Hyderabad team was not acceptable. The long flight and the lack of sleep the previous night, thanks to Aditya, was catching up with him now. He was feeling tired. His eyes were red and burning.

Sitting in front of his laptop all night long had literally made him a mouse potato! The tight deadline had put so much pressure on him that he couldn't afford any rest. The only way to keep awake was to gulp the ever-reliable dose of caffeine. He walked up to the pantry which was towards the rear of the branch, intending to pick up a cup of coffee for himself. He had to cross the back office and the collections bays en route to the pantry. While trying to convince his mind that it was just a cup of coffee away from being bright eyed and bushy tailed again, a glitzy poster stuck on a wall in the bay caught his attention. It had the interesting caption, 'MONEY LAO – DOLLAR PAO' written in large mega fonts. Images of dollars were carefully strewn into a graphic depicting fun and frolic. Seemed to be a promotional poster for a collections contest. He waved out to the guy sitting in the bay, who saw him and came running.

'What's this?' he asked pointing at the large poster.

'Oh this? MONEY LAO – DOLLAR PAO,' and he beamed as if all the dollars had gone into his pocket.

'I can see that. But what is it?'

'It is a collections contest which we are running for our agents. It means collect outstanding dues and take your reward in dollars. Well actually, it's just a rhyming title for promoting our collections contest. We are not actually paying out in dollars. The incentives are being paid out in rupees only.'

'I know that.' Manish was irritated. Why do people always give long answers for short and simple questions? He did not realise that it was his anglicised accent that made the guy respond in the manner he did. Manish always spoke as if there was a plum in his mouth. Indians in corporates normally go all out to impress a foreign visitor and the poor bloke was no different. He was under the impression that Manish was a big shot visiting them from across the seven seas.

'Is it on now?'

'Yes sir. December is the last month for the contest. It's for four months – September to December. We were running behind on our collection numbers for the year. So Victor sir approved a four month contest. This is to help us get closer to the plan numbers for the year by December.'

'Great, thanks. India is the only country in the Asia Pacific region, which does all these contests and builds excitement at the grass root levels. Can you give me a copy of the contest note, for my reference? I just want to know the terms of the contest. Just so that it can be shared across the region . . . you guys are doing a fabulous job. Keep it going. There are a number of fantastic practices here that we need to replicate across our global network.' Saying this, he added a fake smile as a finishing touch, a smile that he had learned to perfect in his role at the regional office.

'It will be with you in five minutes sir,' a fully motivated collections officer replied.

'Great. What do you do here?'

'Sir, I manage the collections MIS and strategy.'

'Oh, so you are the guy who sends out those daily MIS reports for the contests, etc.'

'Yes sir I do. That's my job,' beamed Pushkar.

'Great, why don't you also give me a copy of the various contest MIS that you publish. It would be good to see that as well.'

'Sure sir. I will bring it to your room.'

'Thanks!' Forcing himself to sound pleasant and flashing a grin, Manish went on his way to get himself a much needed cup of coffee. Within five minutes as promised, Pushkar was at his desk with a CD. The CD had the contest note and the MIS deck. Manish inserted the CD in his laptop and glanced through the MIS deck. It had collector-wise details of performance against set targets. 'Useful stuff,' he muttered to himself.

'I thought a soft copy might be useful,' said Pushkar.

'Oh yes it is, thank you.' A happy Pushkar went on his way, back to his workstation.

The collections receipt book audit report came to him in about half an hour and so did the receipt books that contained amongst others, the receipts pertaining to the last four payments made by Tulsiram.

Manish took about an hour trying to put all the pieces of the puzzle together. A couple of times Victor came and knocked on the conference room door. Manish dismissed him and asked him to come back later. Finally, after about an hour, he buzzed Victor and asked him to come and see him.

'Ya Manish?'

'I want to meet all the agents who interacted with Tulsiram and collected cash from him in the last four months.'

'Oh, it's the same guy. For six months now, it has been only Sunder who has been speaking to him. I will try and call him. Poor guy has been interrogated enough over the last few days. Do you want him to bring anything for you to review?'

'Yes. I want him to bring the various reports he had filed after his collections visits on Tulsiram.'

'Sure. Anything else?'

'That will be fine for now. If you can ask this agent to meet me in the next two hours, that will be really helpful. I am really short on time.'

'Will ask him to come right away if I can get him on the phone.'

Thankfully, Sunder was available and came by. Manish met him for about fifteen minutes. He asked a few basic questions and then let him go.

As Sunder was walking out, Manish called him back. 'Sunder, if I have any further questions, I will call you. What number can I reach you on?' Sunder pulled out a card from his bag and gave it to Manish. 'My number is on this card sir.'

'What do you think of him?' Victor asked when he was alone in the room with Manish.

'Nothing in particular. Why?'

'Seems to be a decent chapie.'

'Am sure he does look like one.' The reaction was curt and was an indication to Victor that Manish was not keen on nor did he have any time for unnecessary discussions.

In another hour, Manish was almost through with what he had wanted to do. He had collected all the data he needed. The analysis was done and complete. There were two more tasks to be accomplished, and then he would be ready to present his analysis to Aditya. Aditya had a 7.45 p.m. flight back to Mumbai. 'I have to be at the airport by 6.45 p.m. . . . which means I will have to leave the branch by 5.45 p.m. I have three hours to go,' he muttered, reminding himself that he had to hurry up and close his discussions.

'Victor, I want to meet the guys who normally do these receipt book audits.'

'Let me see who has done these.' Victor walked up to the table to glance at the audit reports. 'Oh, not an issue. All these have been done by Nirmal. He sits in the branch. Shall I call him?'

'Did you ask Nirmal to do these audits?'

'Actually, we need someone from outside collections to do these audits. This is essential to maintain independence of the process . . . to ensure that the person who has done this does not have a vested interest.'

'How does that explain Nirmal doing these audits?' Manish asked in a very irritated tone. He could tolerate preaching from Aditya, but not from someone levels below him in the hierarchy.

'Manish, as you know, we are always looking out for people to do these audits. Nirmal volunteered. Ever since, he is the one doing the audits for us. Suits us as he is from sales and hence no direct linkage into collections.'

'I understand that. Can you get him to come in quickly?' Manish's tone clearly spelt out irritation.

Nirmal walked in casually after lunch. He was the location manager for Hyderabad. The entire sales and customer service across all the twenty-two branches in Hyderabad reported to him. He was a senior player and had been in the NFS system for quite some time.

'You wanted to see me, Manish?' He was an old-timer there and hence addressed Manish by his first name. Manish didn't seem to mind.

'Hey Nirmal! How have you been?' Manish knew him. He used to be a branch manager in Mumbai. His closeness to Gowri and Sangeeta was not hidden from anybody. The same proximity was probably responsible for him getting a plum posting as location head of Hyderabad. Manish always thought that he was a dodo.

'I am fine Manish. Hope you are liking Singapore? Don't you feel like coming back?'

'The way you guys are going, looks like I have to.' This comment brought a frown on Nirmal's face. Manish didn't seem to mind. Okay, quickly tell me, how often do you do these audits?' Manish couldn't afford to waste time engaging in loose talk.

'Every month. Why?'

'Who does it?'

'I do it. Why?'

'How much time do you spend on these audits? Do you actually look at the receipt books when you audit?'

'Yes. Of course,' Nirmal gravely answered.

'Do you know that you have to physically check hundred percent of the receipts and not a sample?'

'Yes. I check hundred percent.'

'Hundred percent of the receipts for correctness of data, missing receipts, blank receipts and customer signatures?'

'Oh yes Manish.'

'Can't be Nirmal.'

'Come on Manish. I am telling you. Every one of the receipts are checked.' Nirmal had started fidgeting awkwardly by now.

'In the fifteen minutes that I sat with the receipt books Nirmal, I found out at least twenty-seven erroneous ones, twelve blank receipts and I have brushed through only about four hundred receipts. You have identified only twelve errors in your entire checking for November . . . out of about 2,500 receipts. Something has to be wrong somewhere. You couldn't have missed out so many mistakes.'

'Can't be,' Nirmal murmured.

'Look at this. Your October report. There is hardly any difference between your September report and October report in terms of qualitative evaluation. Someone seems to have taken the September report and just done a "Find and Replace" for September with October. Everything else is just the same.'

'Ha ha. Thank Bill Gates for that Manish. What would we have done without Microsoft Word? Ha ha!'

'I am not kidding Nirmal.' Manish was a no-nonsense guy and Nirmal's reply provoked his mind to start smouldering like Mount Vesuvius.

'Oh no Manish. I was just joking. That would probably have been a slip up. But, normally we check everything.'

'We? Who is "We"?' There was someone else who was also involved. Who was he?

'Myself and Raman Bhaskar.'

'Raman Bhaskar? Who is he? The same guy who was in Raipur?' The name rang a bell and arched his already elevated eyebrows to the zenith of his forehead.

'He is the collections head for Hyderabad now. Works for Victor. Yes, at some point in time he was in Raipur in collections. Moved out some years back. Went into sales as a branch manager for an upcountry branch. He is now back in collections. You know him?'

'Yes, of course. Wasn't he the guy who was about to be sacked in the Toyota car fraud case along with Vikas, when he was in Raipur? Gowri had saved him then and taken him into his own stream.'

'Same guy,' Nirmal nodded.

'Is he around? Get him. I want to meet him.'

'Sure. After our meeting, I will ask Victor to send him in.'

'OKAY. Coming back. He helps you in your audit for receipt books? This is supposed to be an audit of how his team adheres to process and the controls in his system . . . and HE helps you audit that?'

'Yes Manish,' Nirmal replied nonchalantly.

'Are you out of your mind Nirmal?' Manish was shocked. He was now blowing steam like an over-used and under-cleaned pressure cooker.

The receipt book audit that Nirmal was supposed to do was to check the performance of the Hyderabad team, i.e. to check Raman Bhaskar's team's compliance to laid out process. And here he was . . . taking help from Raman to do that. How ridiculous could it get? Manish was fuming.

'Not really. At times he only helps in providing manual support to the process. You know it becomes difficult for me to check all the receipts. He helps me with it.'

'You could have asked someone from your sales team to help you with it . . . rather than ask Raman Bhaskar to help you.'

'Sales targets are important. No . . . Manish. If we don't achieve them, how do we make our incentives? Pulling out sales guys to do this audit is not possible. No one will do it.' He was not too convincing.

'What the fuck is wrong with you Nirmal? This is complete bastardisation of the audit process. You could be in trouble if I report this.'

'Let me look into this Manish. I was only trying to help. You should be asking these questions to Victor.' Nirmal was surprisingly unapologetic. Manish realised that he was not there to change the system. He was there to find facts related to the Tulsiram case. He moved on. Nirmal could be dealt with later.

Manish probed further and asked a number of uncomfortable questions. The discussion with Nirmal lasted another forty-five minutes. It was planned to be a ten minute discussion. At the end of the heated conversation, Manish looked a shocked man. His facial expression, which till now had oozed confidence, had undergone a hundred and eighty degree change. Worried, he seemed to be torn between what was the right thing to do and what was the good thing to do. He couldn't believe what Nirmal had told him.

'OKAY. Thanks. You can go now. You will hear from me soon,' was his parting remark to Nirmal. He called Raman Bhaskar and was closeted in the room with him for over thirty minutes. Victor looked on from outside the glass walls of the conference room. There was an animated discussion going on inside. He couldn't figure out what the discussion was about.

By the time the discussion ended, it was already three in the afternoon.

'Do you need anything else Manish?' Victor asked him.

'No Victor. I am fine. In fact I am through with what I wanted to do. I am only expected at the airport by 6.45. I have some time to kill. What do you recommend I do?'

Victor just looked on blankly, waiting for some instructions from Manish.

'Tell me. Are you guys still in touch with Jacqueline?' Manish asked him.

'Once in a while. Not much after she left us.'

'Is she still in Hyderabad?'

'Yes.'

'Where is she these days?'

'Vodafone. She quit us and joined Vodafone.'

'Why?'

'You were not there Manish. There was no motivation for her to stay!' Victor winked at Manish and broke into a smile.

'Very funny.' Manish was not amused at this tongue in cheek remark from Victor. But the fact was that he had the hots for Jacqueline and it was known to almost everyone.

'Do you have her phone number?'

'Let me see.' He searched through the phone book on his cell phone. 'Found it. I am SMSing it to you.'

Jacqueline was the earlier collections head for Hyderabad for NFS. At one point in time she had worked with Manish, when he was in India, in his central team in Mumbai. Her marriage to a Hyderabad-based businessman had brought her to the city of pearls. A few months back she had quit NFS and moved on. Had Manish been in India at that time, he would have surely held her back. Unfortunately, he was miles away in Singapore. Now, since Manish had some time, he wanted to catch up with her. Wasn't she one of his favourites?

He left the office at four. More than the coffee, thoughts of Jacqueline had successfully stopped all his sleep cells from working. The excitement was showing on his face and in his mannerisms. Wasn't he glad that he was alone in the car? The meeting with Jacqueline had been fixed for 4.30 p.m. at her office. The Vodafone office, where Jacqueline worked as head of customer service, was only a ten-minute drive from NFS and Manish was standing before Jacqueline's office fifteen minutes ahead of schedule. Jacqueline was extremely pleased to meet him. The last time the two had met was over two years ago, and she was very nostalgic about it. When he was her supervisor, she had simply adored him.

The meeting was brief, lasted about fifteen–twenty minutes. There was a small interruption wherein Jacqueline had disappeared back to her workstation only to resurface within five minutes with a bunch of papers, which she handed to Manish. A quick cup of coffee, and he was on his way to the airport. His feelings were a mix of elation at having cracked the case and depression at having unearthed something sinister. He now had enough dope to keep Aditya occupied throughout the plane journey.

Aditya was already waiting inside the airport lounge when Manish joined him. As luck would have it, their flight was delayed by thirty minutes and they were stuck in the lounge. Manish looked tired and had a five O'clock shadow. He was patiently waiting for Aditya to ask him abut the details of his investigation. After an excruciating wait of ten minutes when Aditya didn't ask him anything, Manish couldn't resist.

'Do you want me to tell you all that I have found out?'

'Go. Get yourself a sandwich. Eat in peace. Let's get on to the flight. You will then have an hour and thirty minutes of uninterrupted time from me.' Manish didn't have a choice but wait till they boarded.

'How are you finding Singapore?' Time for some casual conversation as they had another forty-five minutes to go for boarding to be announced.

'It is okay Aditya.'

'You don't seem to be too excited.'

'India is India Aditya. No other country can be as good. Career is great, but I miss my family and friends. Seema is finding it difficult to adjust there.'

'I can understand. Natasha too found it very difficult to adjust in London when we went overseas for our first stint. She missed her parents, her friends, etc. She nagged me to death to come back to India.'

'Seema does the same.'

'So does this mean that you want to come back?'

'If there is an opportunity, then definitely yes.'

'Opportunities will come my friend. Soon. Have some patience and keep faith.' Aditya never drew a line without blurring it. Manish smiled. He understood bits and pieces of what Aditya was hinting at, but he could not be too blatant about his aspirations with Aditya. He kept his calm and poise. As long as Aditya understood his aspirations and desire to come back, it was fine with him. He knew Aditya would do something for him.

Aditya had asked his secretary to tele-checkin both of them and she had dutifully put them on seats next to each other. Finally, they boarded and the flight took off. They were both in business class so there was no chance of a third individual next to them overhearing their conversation.

'Shoot,' said Aditya the moment the flight had taken off. Manish was waiting for this moment. He turned towards Aditya and started speaking.

'Aditya, let me start from the beginning. I reached office this morning and met the key guys involved. I met Victor, who gave me all the documents for this case. He showed me the application form, the verification reports, the fraud check reports, the underwriting logic and also shared with me the details of the collection activity carried out in Tulsiram's case. I reviewed the receipt books, checked the receipt book audits and also met with the collection agent who was following up with Tulsiram. An agent called Sunder. I also met with Nirmal, the location head, who has done the recent receipt book audits.'

'Okay. What is the outcome?'

'Let me take you through my deductions of each individual activity. I don't know why, but I feel that you already know the outcome. Your hypothesis in the beginning is probably correct. But if you permit, I would still go step-by-step and walk you through what I found out.'

'OKAY. I am all ears. But make sure you finish this before we land in Mumbai . . . and please ensure I don't sleep off.'

'Ha ha! No Aditya. Coming back to the issue, the documents based on which the loans were given to Tulsiram, were all clean. No issues there. It fitted into our loan policy and the person who approved the loan was well within his rights and there was no mistake there. Anyone else would have done the same thing.'

'OKAY, so nothing wrong in that part of the story.'

'No Aditya.'

'Go ahead.'

I then asked for the receipt book audit reports, collection receipts for November and also the last three receipts of Tulsiram, since he had paid in cash.'

'Hmm . . .'

'This is where the problem started. There were lots of errors in the receipt books of November. However, the receipt book audit report stated that everything was in order. It did not pick up even five percent of the errors which were there – some of them were blatant errors, which had been ignored.'

'What kind of errors?'

'The receipts were incomplete, the amount details were not clear in many and in many cases the customer acknowledgement was missing. And the worrying bit is that in some cases, the receipts were blank. In some, the customer copy of the receipts were also in the receipt books, suggesting that maybe the customer was not even given a copy of the receipt. Forget that, it could even be that the customer never made the payment.'

'Any trends?'

'Almost thirty-five percent of the payments received in the last three days of the month did not have the customer signature. A number of payment receipts corresponding to the payment received in the last two days of the month were blank. This is what the sample check threw up. Not many of them reported in the receipt book audit.'

'What does this mean in your interpretation?' Aditya was like one of those people who would love to read the last few pages of a thrilling suspense even before reaching the middle of the book.

'I will come to that Aditya. Just give me a minute. Let me complete the story.'

'Okay. Go ahead.'

'November was the worst. A cursory check of the payment made file for November showed me that of the payments received on 30th November, four payments were made by cheque from the same bank account. An account which belonged to neither of the

four customers. Four different customers with different names, living
in four different corners of town cannot have the same bank account
number. Clearly someone is paying for these customers.'
    'And that someone is?'
    'Us.'
    'What? Are you sure?'
    'Yes Aditya. I am reasonably sure of this. All these cheques came
from the account of Vasudev Reddy.'
    'So! How can that be US?'
    'Vasudev Reddy is not a customer. He is the proprietor of Shobha
Debt Recovery Services, our collection agency in Hyderabad. Why
would a collection agency pay customers overdue instalments from
its own bank account?'
    'Understood.' This was meant to be more of an acknowledgement
of the fact that he was listening to.
    'I pulled out and reviewed the last three months' bills pertaining
to Shoba Debt Recovery Services. In every month there has been
a huge payment of approx Rs 40,000 made to this agency towards
"Professional Services rendered". This is over and above the regular
billing to this agency which is as per the approved collection agency
payout grid.'
    'The "Professional Services Rendered" is only a façade . . . to
camouflage the excess payment made to the agency.' Aditya's eyes
were closed, but he was listening.
    'You are bang on Aditya. My guess is that this money is being
used by the agency to pay the instalments of the customers who are
overdue. When I quizzed Raman Bhaskar about this, he had no clue.
He went all over the place without giving me a concrete answer on
what this amount pertained to.'
    'He is the one doing it . . . the bastard.' Aditya was fuming by
now.
    'Probably Aditya. Let me explain how this works. Raman Bhaskar
has a target to achieve. He is tasked with collecting the dues from

a certain percentage of customers who are delinquent. As long as he meets his targets, the delinquencies will be under control and no one questions anything. Everyone is happy.'

'I know.'

'The problem starts when he is not able to collect from delinquent customers. The reasons could be many. Customers may not be able to pay or maybe customers have taken the money and run away, something we call as "Skip" customers. This starts impacting the portfolio performance. We start writing off these loans and the losses mount. The first to get impacted is the collections manager on site. He misses his targets and hence his incentives tank. As the problem grows, it starts impacting the business guys as well. They are accountable for profitability of the portfolio. Lack of collections and higher delinquencies would even impact Gowri.'

'Stop lecturing Manish.'

'Sorry Aditya. I got carried away. You know how passionately I feel about these things. Anyway, the collections guys have found an innovative solution for this. Pay the collection agencies a little bit more than what they should be contractually paid. For instance in the case of Shobha, we needed to pay only Rs 1,32,000 as a payout for the work done by them in September. We paid them 1,72,000. Vasudev Reddy used the balance 40,000 to pay the instalments for customers who he could not collect from. Those customers go out of the delinquent list and hence the portfolio looks good and everyone from the collection agent to Gowri is safe. The problem gets camouflaged. And the targets for the collections guys are met and they make their incentives.'

Aditya was listening to Manish intently. He knew how this worked. However, for once he did not want to cut Manish's flow of thoughts.

'It works brilliantly Aditya. If a customer, who has a loan of Rs 1 Lakh for which he pays an instalment of Rs 2000, defaults on six instalments, NFS would write off the entire loan. Assuming in November a customer had six instalments overdue and doesn't pay before 30 November, then on 1 December NFS would write off the entire loan amount as a loss in their books, i.e. Rs 1 Lakh as a loss.

'Instead, if someone, in this case – the collection agency, pays one instalment before 30 November, then on 1 December, the customer will only have five instalments due. Hence the loan doesn't get written off. A loss of 1 lakh is saved. At what cost?'

'Only Rs 2000,' Aditya impulsively reacted.

'Right Aditya. The collections managers and the agency work hand-in-glove. The agency will normally not pay from their pocket and would bill NFS these monies . . . As Shoba Debt Recovery Services has done through the "Professional Services Rendered" bill. The collections managers clear these expenses, which are invariably multiple small bills and hence do not come under the scanner of anyone checking them. Our collections expenses go up but we save on write-offs. With 40,000 payout to Shobha Debt Collectors, they could have paid back instalments for over 20 lakh worth of customers. NFS incurred an illegitimate expense of 40,000 and in the process probably saved a write off of 20 lakh.'

'So what are we saying? Who is screwing us – our own staff or the collection agencies?'

'Both. Aditya, on a small scale this can be occasionally done by collection agencies on their own to meet higher performance benchmarks, but a large scale bastardisation of this cannot be done without the local management of NFS being involved. As you know, a higher credit loss gets noticed and hundreds of questions are asked by people at all levels, but a higher cost often gets ignored and is also easy to justify. This process which we call as funding in our collections world, cannot be going on without the explicit concurrence of the local management of NFS.

'How can you be so sure?'

'Aditya. I checked the bills of the collections agencies for the last three months. Normal bills are raised by collections executives and signed off by Raman Bhaskar. Only the bills for Shoba Debt Recovery Services have been raised by Raman Bhaskar and approved by Nirmal. Why? Raman Bhaskar has a signing authority of Rs 30,00,000. Why has he followed a different process for bills that are within his limit, but include the "Professional Services Rendered" line and got them approved by Nirmal? There can be only one explanation. He did not want many people to know about this arrangement. Between him and Nirmal they stuck a deal and executed the entire funding plan.'

'OKAY.'

'Our collections costs in Hyderabad also prove this Aditya. They are rising day-by-day. We are paying more for collecting the same amount of money from the customers. Even the telecalling that the central team has now done, throws up a large concentration of customers in Hyderabad, who have said that they haven't paid their dues, despite our systems reflecting their instalments having been received. If the customers didn't pay them, where did they come from? Who paid them? Clearly in most cases the agency paid for it and has billed us. Or the collections agent paid it under the faith that he will be able to collect it later from the customer. In the later instance, he makes his incentives and over the next thirty days keeps the pressure on the customer and collects the money from him.'

'Didn't our month-end audit catch this malpractice?'

'That's the screw up Aditya. I spoke with both Nirmal and Raman Bhaskar. Nirmal conducted the audits and Raman helped him with the audits. Have you met them Aditya?'

'I know Nirmal very well. Have I met Raman? The name does ring a bell.'

'Raman was a star branch manager. He even made it to your annual high performer convention.'

'What's he doing in collections?'

'That's the question I had too. Long back this guy used to be in collections in Raipur. We had detected an issue with repossessed cars.

At that time, we sacked the branch manager, but gave Raman the benefit of doubt, because he was too junior. Gowri had vehemently argued his case and agreed to take him into the NFS branch world. Raman owes his job today to Gowri. At various times since then, Gowri had been pushing for his move back to collections. When I was in India, I had resisted taking him in collections because I was not convinced of the guy's integrity. I had even spoken about this to Gowri. Looks like after I left and before Amit firmly took over, in the cusp period, they pushed him in. Amit would surely not have taken him. But by the time he came in, the deed was done.'

'He is Gowri's guy? In collections? How much better could it get?'

'Oh yes. Raman is Gowri's guy. As if you don't know Aditya! Gowri has a habit of ensuring that he has his guy in every team. This way he ensures that he gets to know what's going on and is able to act well in time. This also ensures that his political agendas are pushed through. Amit would not have hired him. I am sure. Specifically knowing that he was Gowri's guy?'

Aditya opened his right eye, looked at Manish and gave him a wry smile. 'I know. They hate each other, don't they?'

'Yes they do. However, coming back to Nirmal and Bhaskar, when confronted with this data, they have confessed that they were indulging in managing books through funding of delinquent accounts.'

'What the fuck? Why didn't you sack them immediately?' Aditya suddenly became agitated. Staff frauds were something he couldn't stand. Integrity issues had to be dealt with firmly.

'I will come to it. There is more to the story. In any case I have their signed confessions and they might put in their papers tomorrow. They know that they have been exposed.'

'You are scaring me now.'

'If I was you, I would be scared too. Before I elaborate, let me come to Sunder.'

'Who is Sunder? Haven't heard this name earlier.'

'Sunder is the collection agent, who was following up with Tulsiram for the payment. He claims that Tulsiram made his payment every month and that he promptly deposited the payment with NFS month after month. I checked the receipt book . . . and that's where the problem is. The receipts supposedly issued to Tulsiram for the payments collected in cash for the months of September, October and November, do not have his signature. Forget Tulsiram's signature . . . the receipts for November and October are blank . . . and even the customer's copy was in the receipt book itself. It was never given to Tulsiram.'

'OKAY, what does that prove? Don't go around in circles, come to the point.'

'Aditya, when I saw that none of the receipts had Tulsiram's signature and the receipts for November and October were blank, I dug deeper. I stumbled upon the fact that there is an ongoing contest for the collection agents, the tagline of which was – Money Lao Dollar Pao. The incentives paid out in this contest are in cash and are significant. A guy like Sunder, stands to make over 12,000 a month, just on achieving hundred percent of the stretch contest goals.'

Aditya nodded.

'Surprisingly, Sunder has exactly achieved hundred precent of his target in all the three months. In every month, he has achieved his target on the last day of the month and has exceeded his set target by one payment, i.e. he has collected one payment more from customers, than what his contest target was. Quite an eerie coincidence, isn't it?'

'Indeed,' Aditya agreed.

'On 30 September he got in four payments from customers. In the last days of October and November, he brought in four and three payments respectively – payments which helped him reach his target. Tulsiram is one of those guys whose payments came in on the last day of each of the preceding three months. I myself called the ones whose payments Sunder had brought in on the last day of November. Well, two of them, except Tulsiram. And both said that they did not pay any instalment to Sunder or any other agent of NFS. I did these calls myself and so I can speak with a fair bit of credibility.'

'What does this mean? These accounts are also being "funded".'

'The incentive Sunder has made in these three months adds up to Rs 36,000. He has been a very smart cookie. He waited till the last day to figure out the shortfall between his target and his actual performance. For example, on 30 September he realised that he was short of his targets by four customer payments. He decided to pay those from his own pocket. The four payments he has made on 30 September are the following.'

And he opened his laptop and brought up a spreadsheet on his screen. Aditya glanced at it. It had four names on the screen

Ramaji Reddy – Rs 2200

Gopal Kanji – Rs 1800

B.V. Sastri – Rs 2450

Tulsiram – Rs 1979

'The amounts are the instalment amounts for these customers. These four instalments add up to Rs 8,429. Sunder paid these instalments on his own. Well, who wouldn't? In return for this payment from his pocket, he hits the contest target and makes 12,000 in return. A straight gain of Rs 3,571.

'Now comes the challenging part. Out of the pool of customers allocated to him for collecting from, how does he select which customers account to pay into? Here Mr Smart Ass picks up on a customer who in his view is a low risk customer, a customer who would eventually on persistent follow up, pay up his dues. In any case Sunder has made his money. If he is able to recover money from these customers on whose behalf he has paid, that would be a double whammy. Tulsiram was one such customer, who features month after month, in Sunder's list – Sunder has in effect paid Tulsiram's instalment for all the three months.'

'Hmm . . . so that's the story,' Aditya was buying his view.

'Sunder didn't tell Tulsiram that he has paid on his behalf, and kept following up with him for his monies. Since Tulsiram never knew that his instalments had been paid by Sunder, whenever he would get a call from Sunder to pay up, he would presume that the call was from NFS, on account of the bounced instalment cheque.

'What did Tulsiram's suicide note say? The recovery agent from NFS demanded three instalments? Right? Tulsiram's story of NFS following up for three instalments was correct. That's what he thought. However, it was not us, but Sunder who was following up for his payment. Poor Tulsiram was not even aware that his instalments had been paid.'

'How sure are you?'

'I would not say so if I am not sure Aditya. Sherlock Holmes has always been my favourite detective series. For a change, I decided to play him in real life. Remember Jacqueline?'

'Oh ya! Isn't she that same chick who almost wrecked your home. The one for whom you nearly left Seema?'

'Ha ha Aditya. Well tried! I have a squeaky clean reputation as far as women are concerned. You can never nail me in these things. Okay I will go on. You obviously know who I am talking about. She has now moved to Vodafone as head of customer service. Thankfully, Sundar carries a Vodafone mobile. I met Jacqueline and she helped me in pulling out Sundar's call details. There have been calls and SMS's from his mobile to Tulsiram's mobile till as late as 16 December . . . and . . . and . . . Tulsiram died on the 15th. He has rigorously followed up with Tulsiram . . . at times he has even made as many as twelve calls a day.

'Aditya, Tulsiram's December cheque has cleared. We were lucky because his salary credit from Marriott got delayed and hence our cheque for his December instalment hit his account around the same time as his salary credit. He didn't have time to withdraw the money from his account. Given this, he is not a delinquent customer as per our records. His name was not even in the collections list for December. If you think about it . . . there can only be one reason why Sunder has been regularly calling him. Sunder was recovering his own money!'

'So you are saying Tulsiram was not aware that Sunder had paid his instalments to NFS and was following up for recovery of his payment . . . and that Sunder, in a way was accountable for Tulsiram's suicide.'

'In a way, yes.'

'So we are clean. No one can nail us, right?'

'No. No one can come back at us or hold us accountable for Tulsiram's death. We can publically state that Tulsiram is not delinquent with us and hence the question of following up to recover three instalments does not arise at all.'

'Good.'

'That was as far as Tulsiram was concerned. There is a bigger problem that we have to deal with in Hyderabad.'

'And that is . . .'

'The collections process here sucks. It has been completely manipulated by the collections officers. This is the last quarter of the year. The quarter when performance appraisals happen. Bonuses for staff get decided. Any screw up in the collections process in the last three months of the year influence the portfolio quality and directly the performance rating right up to the top. Hence in any company, the October–December collections performance is very very important.'

'Why are you telling me this? If I didn't know this I wouldn't be where I am?'

'I didn't mean it in that manner Aditya. That was not the intent. I got a bit suspicious when I saw the payment receipts for Tulsiram. They were blank. When I saw the receipt book audit process, I freaked. And when I came across the Shoba Debt Recovery Agency bills, it just blew my lid. I also picked a sample of customers whose payments have come in on the last day and telecalled on them. I mentioned this to you earlier.

'I checked with Nirmal, the guy who has audited the receipt books. It's clear that he had done it only for an academic purpose. He comes from branch network. Reports into Gowri's chain of command. The audit report was prepared by Raman Bhaskar and signed off by Nirmal. How can someone do this? What is the sanctity of the audit process?

'And this Raman Bhaskar . . . he comes with a background . . . with a not so good past. I told you about his relationship with Gowri earlier. When I confronted him with the various audits and the billing issues, he resisted for some time. Gave vague answers, but when I didn't let go, he agreed to have funded these accounts, through the collections agency. There are many more Shobha Debt Recovery Agencies in Hyderabad alone. This has become a menace in Hyderabad. If group audit gets wind of this, we will be terribly embarrassed. This is a collections malpractice, which is like a termite attack. If not fixed, it will eat up our entire system. This could have been identified and fixed, if only they had a robust audit process. That was not to be. Gowri managed to fix this process through his own guy.'

Aditya suddenly sat up at this comment from Manish. 'And why do you say that Gowri fixed this process through his own guy?'

'Gowri pushed Raman Bhaskar into collections in Hyderabad and had his performance on paper audited through Nirmal. Gowri was aware of everything that was going on in Hyderabad. Amit would not have even suspected this because as far as he was concerned an independent channel was auditing the collections performance. And the audit reports were fine. If I was him, given the equation with Gowri, I would have expected Gowri's man, Nirmal in this case, to go all out and critically examine my team's performance and try and pick holes in my delivery. If there was anything wrong in collections, then I would have expected Gowri's team to be the first ones to identify it and create a scene. I would not have backed Gowri to get entangled in this in such a manner.'

'What is your recommendation?'

'I think you should sack the guys in Hyderabad. Raman Bhaskar needs to go. Even though they will put in their papers, we should terminate them and not give them an option for an honourable exit. Nirmal compromised the audits and he needs to go too. You will have to quietly review collections processes across the country . . . and . . . and . . . you will have to take a call on Gowri.'

'Why Gowri?'

'Aditya, he was the one who legalised this practice in the branches. If I were to believe Raman, funding is happening in almost all branches and has executive sanction from Gowri. There had been times in the past, when Gowri had tried to influence me to get into this practice. I resisted and hence became unpopular with him. I am sure he would have tried to influence Amit too and would have failed. However, this time around he went a step ahead. He successfully manipulated this through the branch managers. He placed his own guys strategically to conduct the crime and policed it through the branch managers, who were also his own guys. He has systematically corrupted the entire place. I wouldn't have believed it till I saw it with my own eyes. As an evidence for his innocence, Raman Bhaskar showed me an SMS from Gowri, which said . . .' and he paused.

'Wait for a minute Aditya. I actually asked him to forward the same to me. Let me read it out to you. It says, "Raman go ahead and manage it as per our discussion. Do what you have to. Nirmal will help you clear the agency bills. Take his assistance if required to make the payout." This was a message he had sent among many others asking him to manage the funding of the portfolio. He has legalised this menace within NFS. As I said, if we do not curtail it, we will be in trouble.'

'Is it happening in other parts of the country?'

'I am sure it would be. Despite us separating collections from sales, I am sure they are hand-in-glove across the country. The relationship between Gowri and Amit is not helping either. They just don't speak to each other to resolve issues.'

The balance of the conversation was lost on Aditya. He was just stuck on three points. Gowri was involved in funding of accounts. He was the one who legalised the menace in the collections team of NFS. He still wielded significant authority over the branch credit and collections teams. With him around, things wouldn't improve. He had to have a conversation with him. Things were not going as per his plan. Aditya had to act before things blew up in his face. The suicide issue was staring at him. It was sure to have its repercussions.

The plane was flying over Mumbai. The air traffic congestion over Mumbai made sure that the plane was in the air for much longer. It gave time for him to dwell over the issue at hand.

'Amit too could have been at fault,' muttered Aditya as the lights got dimmed for the plane to land.

'Unlikely,' said Manish. Aditya was startled. He was just speaking aloud and had not expected Manish to hear and respond.

'I don't think so,' Manish continued. 'Given that the audit reports were all fixed and clean, there was no way he could figure out that something was wrong in Hyderabad. Had he known it, he would have fixed it. You can't blame him for something he didn't do.'

As the plane dropped in altitude and the landing announcements happened, Aditya sat up straight. He had made up his mind. Some decisions had to be taken in the interest of the organisation. Some decisions had to be taken in his own interest . . . to protect his own job. As if stung by the troubled decisions that Aditya had made, the plane landed with a huge thud and swayed for a couple of seconds before it steadied itself and taxied to the parking bay.

'In life, you are often confronted with situations when you become victims of incomplete information. You will, when put in such a position, have to back your gut and take decisions. Not taking a decision is the worst thing you can ever do,' mused Aditya, and made up his mind. The conversation with Manish was a telling one.

From the airport, Aditya went to meet Amit at the Bandra police station. Manish was too tired to go anywhere. He hadn't slept the previous night. Aditya's secretary had booked him into Hotel Sahara Star, right next to the domestic airport. He went to the hotel and hit the bed.

Aditya met Amit and Chanda at the police station and assured them that the weight of the entire organisation was behind him and that they would do everything physically possible to get him out. Ravi Subramanian, the bank lawyer, joined in the discussion and helped Aditya give solace to the two of them. After the lawyers left, Aditya also shared with Amit the crux of his discussion with Manish. Amit seemed shocked and devastated at what Aditya told him. 'Do not worry Aditya. Let me get out of here. I will fix everything. If the system needs a flush out, I will not hesitate,' he had said. Aditya smiled and left with a promise to meet him the next day, in court.

As expected when Amit was presented in court the next day, the Mumbai high court granted a stay on the warrant issued by the Hyderabad court. At around noon, Amit walked out of the police station, a free man, albeit temporarily.

That very evening, a mail was sent out from Aditya's office which had the following contents.

Dear colleagues,

As all of you are aware, we have over the past twenty-four months seen extraordinary progress and growth in NFS. From a little short of 150 branches in 2006, we have now grown our branch network to over 400 branches. We have achieved leadership status in personal loans and mortgages and we are also a large player in the durable finance business. All this has been accomplished under the able stewardship of Gowri Shankar. Gowri has been instrumental in taking NFS to higher than expected profit levels of USD 55 million in 2007 and this number is expected to be even higher in 2008.

After a successful stint as head of NFS, Gowri moves on to take over a more challenging assignment as head of a newly created asset management company for the group in India. He will be charged with building this company from scratch into a world class company, something which he successfully did at NFS. His distribution ability and skill at building scale in business will be leveraged by the asset management company.

Taking over from Gowri as managing director of NFS will be Amit Sharma, who has excelled in his role as head of credit and collections in India. He has been instrumental in developing a world class analytics and credit management platform and we look forward to his leadership and team building skills to grow the business in India and also lead our initiatives as we pass through a tough credit environment.

I have also requested the group to release the services of Manish Kakkar who will now be back in India to take over the credit and collections role for NFS that he had handed over to Amit. Manish is not a new face to NFS and I expect him to seamlessly take off from where he left and apply the skill sets that he learnt during his stint overseas. He will also be managing the overall credit strategy for NYB in India, in addition to his role at NFS.

Amit and Gowri's move is effective immediately. I will shortly announce Manish's date of release in consultation with the Singapore regional office.

Please join me in wishing Gowri, Amit and Manish, all the very best in their new role.

Regards,
Aditya

As a consequence of this, later in the day, the movement of Chanda to NYB as their customer service head was also announced. She couldn't have continued in any role in a company where her husband was the managing director. NYB internal regulations did not allow such an arrangement. She was not happy about it, but she didn't have any choice.

Amit moved in and took over the role from Gowri almost immediately. For Gowri, the clock stopped ticking at NFS, the moment he got a call from Aditya asking him to meet him. Aditya had called him and spoken to him on his way back from the police station, on that fateful night, when he had gone to see Amit. It was at Aditya's request that he met him at 8 a.m. the next morning.

When Gowri arrived at the Grand Hyatt at eight in the morning, Aditya was waiting for him at the reception. Over breakfast, Aditya presented the head of asset management company opportunity to him. He projected it as if it was the next biggest thing for NYB and that this initiative required the skills of a dynamic individual like Gowri.

Deep within, Aditya didn't want to lose Gowri. He knew that Gowri had great business building skills, business acumen and overall he was a great leader who had high levels of emotional quotient. His connect with his people was brilliant . . . though he had to temper down his aggression and desire to get to the end at any cost. Gowri was a potential retail bank head, and Aditya knew that.

'Can I think about it and get back? Say by tomorrow?' Gowri tried to buy some time. He did not want to react immediately.

Aditya initially told him that he was in a bit of a hurry to close this and make the change, but when Gowri did not agree and kept pushing him for time to think it over, Aditya dropped the bombshell. 'Look Gowri. I believe that this is a great opportunity for you. Unfortunately this is also the only opportunity that you can get within the group. You either take this and move to the asset management company or else you will have to move to some project role within the group. You cannot continue as managing director of the NBFC.'

Gowri was stunned. Was he being served the notice? Was the AMC only a honourable exit route that was being provided to him? Gowri, being Gowri was not the one to be easily cowed down.

'But why? What have I done?'

'Gowri, a number of issues at the branches have been traced back to your support. You have been running this place now as MD and even in the past as the network head on your whims and fancies – as your personal fiefdom. There have been several acts of indiscretion at your end.'

'Is it something to do with your and Manish's visit to Hyderabad yesterday?'

'So you have already heard about it. Well, partly Amit. Even in Hyderabad, many malpractices in collections have been linked to Raman Bhaskar. You knew that the guy's integrity was suspect. Yet you got him placed there whereas you should ideally have sacked him. Manish even cautioned you against him. Various practices in the branches are being followed at your behest. I don't think you want me to get into this.' Aditya cautiously stayed away from mentioning the collections funding issue.

Gowri didn't respond. He could not recollect which instruction he had given and when. What was Aditya referring to? Could be anything? He was scared to ask. It was true that he had been running the company as his own. A number of his decisions had been ad hoc and may not have complied with the group rules and regulations. He had given out of turn promotions, increments, doled out club memberships, expensive gifts to staff, etc. He had rewarded people aligned to him and the rewards were often not in line with NYB policy. He did not know what was being referred to here by Aditya. He had lived life on the edge. It was clear that his mom-and-pop style of running a large company had created monsters difficult to manage and control.

'If you do not want to take the AMC role, it's fine. The call is yours. However, I will be forced to approve a full-fledged investigation on you and if you are found guilty, you will have to go. If you are not, then you get to stay on in your current role. The choice is yours Gowri. I can only assure you that we will be discrete and not publicise this investigation. But you know our organisation. It is a very porous one. Word gets around. Also, you cannot remain as managing director till the investigation is complete. We will move you on to some project role. I will try and position it appropriately so that your social standing does not get impacted . . .' and with a pause added, 'on a best effort basis.'

Gowri was stunned into silence. His mind kick-started into thinking about all the repercussions. An investigation against him in NFS? What will people think of him? He had carefully built up a reputation over a period of time. What happens to that? It would lie on the floor of NFS, torn to tatters. And what if these guys are genuinely able to find something to nail him with? In a decade long career with NFS there could have been a few small mistakes that he had committed. Even if he comes out clean, an investigation against him would be enough for tongues to wag.

Aditya went on, 'The media, and the global head quarters too, will be looking at me for making management changes to take care of the negative publicity arising out of the Hyderabad issue. I want to take care of your interest too. I wish to protect your self-respect. But you will have to allow me to. I like you. At times I see myself in you. But you will have to give me the opportunity to help you. Please let me know by noon today if you are game for this or not.' He then got up and left Gowri alone on the breakfast table.

Gowri, one who was never known to cow down, signed on the dotted line. Aditya was a dark horse and Gowri hardly had any idea about how much Aditya knew and how much he didn't. The Pandora's Box was something he didn't want to open. Much before noon, he sent an SMS to Aditya which said, 'I am fine with what was being discussed. Look forward to my new role.' The same evening Aditya had announced the management structure change.

It was celebration time a few weeks later at the Sharma household when a special bench of the Hyderabad High Court acquitted Amit of any wrongdoing in the Tulsiram case and the warrant was revoked. In any case the court had earlier granted him permission to stay away from the proceedings and be represented by a lawyer.

Amit celebrated that night at home with a select set of friends. Manish too was invited. After a few drinks, they stepped out onto the balcony. It was just the two of them. There was a chill in the air. And their conversation was accompanied by the pleasant background score of sea waves lashing against the rocky Carter Road coastline.

'Thanks Amit. I didn't even imagine I would be back in India so soon. Seema was so relieved when she heard of my move.'

'Why thank me Manish? It was you who started this. Shouldn't I be the one thanking you?'

'Yes but . . .'

'Had you not called me that night after Aditya asked you to fly to Hyderabad, we would never have got to this stage?'

'Hmm . . . and to think of it, Aditya told me not to speak to anyone about my visit. He asked me to keep my visit a low profile one.'

'Thank God, you did not listen to him and called me instead.'

'And Amit, had you not told me how to position this to Aditya, we would not have achieved the ultimate goal.'

'Yes. That's what friends are for right? You called me for help, despite Aditya asking you not to call anyone, particularly me. How could I not help you? In the process, we helped each other.'

'Of course . . . of course . . . but tell me Amit, this is something I have been wanting to ask you for, quite some time. You told me about everything that was going on in Hyderabad. I didn't have to dig for anything else. You were bang on! If you knew all this, why didn't you tell Aditya yourself? You were there in Hyderabad the previous day.'

'Manish, these kind of practices, or should I say . . . malpractices, happen in every organisation. It happened when you were at the helm of collections in India, and it happens now too. The difference is in the scale of the malpractice. We had landed ourselves in a mess in Hyderabad. The question foremost in my mind was what could we do about it? Could we ensure that the organisation somehow views us as heroes? Else, how could we turn this into an opportunity?'

'And so you decided to fix Gowri?'

'Ha ha! We decided to . . . Manish. Not me alone. Remember we were together in it. Isn't our dislike for Gowri common?'

'Of course. Aditya fell for the story that we spun around Gowri's involvement in the systemic failure of process and controls. The killer impact was on reading out the SMS which Gowri was supposed to have sent to Raman. Aditya fell for it and really thought it was true.'

When Manish said this, Amit just gave a you-are-a-genuis smile. 'That was simply brilliant,' he drawled while sipping his drink.

'I knew he would fall for it. I also knew that it was important to make him believe that Gowri was central to the entire Hyderabad issue, knowing very well that he would never confront Gowri. Aditya is the one who made him the managing director. Sacking him for suspected malpractice would reflect poorly on Aditya's judgemental skills. Aditya would never have confronted Gowri without a proper investigation and hardcore evidence. I know that. In the past I have been a witness to Moses being sacked by Aditya. He helped him along and found him a job outside the bank. Aditya is too intelligent and knows that these things happen. He would not have been unduly unfair to Gowri despite the two of us rooting for his blood.' Amit gave a cheerful slap on Manish's shoulder and gave a half-hug. The camaraderie was very evident.

'It's just that when things blow up, organisations have to demonstrate that they are taking adequate action. I was sure Aditya's thought process was the same.' Amit paused and took another sip of his Glenfiddich. He closed his eyes for two seconds, enjoying every single drop of the fine single malt scotch whisky. It felt sinfully divine. He opened his eyes and then continued. 'And knowing Gowri, he has too much of pride in himself and in NFS, that he would not be willing to stand up to an investigation.'

Manish was passively listening as Amit replayed their discussion on that eventful night when Manish had made his way to Hyderabad.

'Also remember,' continued Amit, 'Gowri knows that he has run NFS like a mom and pop show. If his conduct is investigated, though nothing on the collections side would get thrown up, a number of other small instances of non-professional conduct would surely get highlighted . . . the people he promotes, the increments he gives to his coterie, the expensive gifts he showers on them, the money blown away on off sites and celebrations, manipulation of expense accounts, etc. All these would get highlighted and embarrass him no end. I was sure that even though he has not made a single pie for himself in a manner which lacks integrity, he would not agree to be investigated. As you just said, it would also be a blow to his self-esteem in an organisation where he had thus far, been worshipped like God. He wouldn't want to be seen as a devil there,' added Amit with a wicked smile and an arched eyebrow.

'Correct. But you could have told this to Aditya yourself. Why ask me to do the dirty job of lying to Aditya?'

'Look Manish, Aditya knows about my relationship with Gowri. Had I told this story to Aditya myself, despite the fact that he considers me one of his men, he wouldn't have fallen for it. He would have been convinced that I was trying to settle my personal scores with Gowri and trying to further my agenda. He would have thought that I was trying to divert attention from the suicide and collections related issue. Remember, he called you to investigate. He had to believe you and could not have possibly ignored what you told him. After all, he called you from Singapore with a few hour's notice to help him investigate. In this particular instance you brought in credibility which I could not have.

'And when you said so, Gowri was guilty even before Aditya gave him a chance to defend himself. The route we followed, my friend was definitely a safer one and one with a very high probability of success.'

'Smart,' said Manish and he smiled. 'I would have loved to see the look on Gowri's face when Aditya was having that conversation with him,' he added.

'Friend, let's forget the past and drink to our success. To a partnership which will take this organisation to a different level. And us individually to an ever higher level . . . ha ha ha!' and Amit burst out laughing.

'*Jai ho!*' screamed Manish as he raised his glass in a gesture of everlasting friendship.

Claang! Clang! As their glasses melodiously clanged against each other and a chorus of 'Cheers' rang the air, a quick-paced rhythmic jingle of a bell was heard. Both of them turned and looked towards the direction from where the sound came. Across the road was a temple where the priest was doing his last pooja for the day. He had rung the bell as a part of the normal ritual.

'Divine intervention. May your words come true,' said Manish even as he shifted his hand holding the glass of whisky behind his back, as if hiding it from God and bowed his head as a mark of respect.

'My friend, you are like that priest in the temple,' said Amit as he pointed to the temple down below. 'Every day hundreds of devotees gather in front of God and make thousands of offerings. Even God can't collect all the offerings that are thrown at him by all of them. Else the priests wouldn't be there . . . right? God only accepts offerings from the priest at anointed times during the day. Aditya, after all is human. You made him the offering at the right time and he accepted it. In return he granted our wishes. Ha ha ha!' Amit guffawed.

'Well said my friend. Well said. Gowri paid the price for something which was his own doing. He had grown too large for his boots. Let's not celebrate his downfall. Together we drink to our success . . . cheers!' and they gulped down the last dregs of the smooth malt and walked down to get another drink.

The Last Mile

The Tulsiram issue in Hyderabad blew into a full-fledged crisis for most of the banks in the country. Collection practices of banks were critically examined by the media and the regulators. NFS thankfully escaped with just a few bruises. However, a clampdown by the regulators and stricter debt management laws ensured that debt collection became difficult. This led to deterioration in the loan book quality of many organisations, some of which had to completely shut down their loans business.

NYB did make it to the front pages of *Wall Street Journal* – India, again after a decade. It was not viewed at kindly by the global management team and Aditya was shunted out. His plea of having brought in a management change in NFS, by moving out Gowri, the incumbent MD, was met with dismay and disdain. It didn't fly. He was moved out of the country within the next five months and replaced as CEO by Rahul Gupta. The latter came in from Singapore where he was the head of wealth management for the group. Aditya is now the Regional Head – Retail Banking, Middle East Cluster for the bank. He was lucky that his job was intact; probably the number of years that he had served at NYB came in handy.

Amit is now the managing director of NFS – a job that had become his through a complex manipulation of sorts, which in the final analysis seemed relatively easy. He had swung the deal without getting himself involved in the granularities. Smart that he was, he had ensured that had anything blown up, it would have blown up on Manish's face and not his. He is now dealing with the impact of the regulatory clampdown and an emerging credit crisis in the country. The chaos of the deteriorating credit environment is becoming too stressful for him to handle. NFS is today faced with problems of high delinquency and consequent high losses. This has lead to reduced and cautious growth, which has impacted his business and hence NFS's income streams. NFS has quickly turned into a loss making entity, as the company was unable to collect from hordes of delinquent customers who seem to have invaded their books. Amit realised that Gowri had milked the cow in its best years and had left him to hold the baby in a troubled environment. He is now contemplating quitting and moving on to a different vocation completely.

Chanda made the best of her move into the bank. NYB inherently paid more than NFS and hence the move meant higher pay, and of course a better designation. She has now become a vice president, and is away from the politics of Gowri and Amit. Away from bull and bear within NFS, life has become a lot more peaceful. With the interpersonal stress at work coming down by phenomenal levels, Chanda and Amit have rediscovered the spark in their lives. Their family is now complete with the entry of a cute little angel in their lives. Chanda has lots to look forward to, both at work and home, after the torrid time she had at NFS.

Manish moved back from Singapore into India in what was probably the worst period for a credit professional. High inflation, tumbling stock markets, crashing real estate and a rapidly deteriorating credit environment was what he had to deal with. 'It's good to manage the business when the economic cycle goes through a downturn,' he told many friends. 'I am learning to collect from defaulting customers in an environment where even God can't collect!' But does learning come without the associated pains?

Gowri moved to head the asset management company. Though he had not expected great kicks from the new role, he found out, on moving there, that the job was far more exciting than what he thought it would be. With the loans business going through a lean patch, every bank including NYB shifted its focus to investments and asset management business. Even the new CEO of NYB, Rahul, who replaced Aditya, was an ex-wealth management professional. It helped Gowri, because Rahul was extremely passionate about Gowri's business and wanted to see it grow. He got the investments required, the focus and the resources and managed to go about building a large and solid business. Gowri's stint at NFS was soon forgotten and he was talked about as the king of asset management . . . the rising star of the mutual fund industry.

Would Gowri, Amit, Manish and Aditya, the so-called kingpins of New York International Bank, ever change themselves and make NYB a better place to be in? Only time will tell. They were all humans and it was evident in the way they approached their challenges and relationships.

However, as a banker myself, I often wonder how different it would have been, if God was a banker? Would he have been any better or would God have joined these guys and just become another devil in pinstripes?

INDIAN BOOK SHELF
55, Warren St., London W1T 5NW
Ph. : (020) 7380 0622
E-mail : indbooks@aol.com